An Excerpt fr
Diva (Ironclad Bodyguards 2)

She rubbed her temples and sat back against the tub, and pulled the white hotel shower curtain around her. There. No more guy in a red tie, asking her irritating questions.

He yanked the curtain back and crouched in front of her, and held out a bottle of water. She took off the lid and drank. It tasted weird.

"What is this?" she asked.

"Electrolyte water. Do you remember passing out?"

His curt question triggered delayed memories, backstage bustle and distant music, a suit jacket. An ID badge. This guy wasn't a gigolo or groupie. Greg had told her he was a bodyguard.

But why was he here in her room, peppering her with questions? She didn't need a bodyguard, even if he was handsome as fuck. The festivals were huge and she was surrounded by tons of strangers all the time, but they were ravers, not criminals. The only thing they were violent about was dancing. The man had a ridiculous set of muscles under his pristine white button-down. Huh. Overkill, those muscles, cause no one was after her.

He nodded at the bottle. "Drink some more water. You need to rehydrate."

She took a sip and grimaced, feeling trapped between the tub and the man's large frame. Why wouldn't he leave? Why was he looming over her and staring at her that way?

And what the fuck had he been doing in her hotel room while she was sleeping? She felt violated. Or pissed off. She didn't actually know how she felt. At least the room had stopped spinning. She drank more water and sat up straighter.

"Ready to get up?" he asked.

She glared at him. "I like sitting on bathroom floors."

He took her arm and dragged her to her feet…

Copyright 2016 Annabel Joseph/Molly Joseph/Scarlet Rose Press

Cover art by Bad Star Media
BadStarMedia.com

* * * * *

This book is a work of fiction. Names, characters, places, and incidents are products of the author's imagination or are used fictitiously. Any resemblance to actual events, locales, or persons living or dead, is entirely coincidental.

All characters depicted in this work of fiction are 18 years of age or older.

DIVA

Ironclad Bodyguards #2

Molly Joseph

Other Books by Molly Joseph
The Edge of the Earth
Pawn (Ironclad Bodyguards)

Books by Annabel Joseph
Mercy
Cait and the Devil
Firebird
Owning Wednesday
Lily Mine
Disciplining the Duchess

Fortune Series:
Deep in the Woods
Fortune

Comfort Series:
Comfort Object
Caressa's Knees
Odalisque
Command Performance

Cirque Masters Series:
Cirque de Minuit
Bound in Blue
Master's Flame

Mephisto Series:
Club Mephisto
Molly's Lips: Club Mephisto Retold
Burn For You

BDSM Ballet Series:
Waking Kiss
Fever Dream

Rough Love Series:
Torment Me
Taunt Me
Trust Me

1. PARADISE

Ransom followed the back of Greg's bald head as the two wove through bobbing, jumping ravers at the edge of the festival grounds. A twenty-something man screamed at them and waggled his tongue. Rhinestones lined his eyelids—and his tongue. The woman beside him wore a bedraggled fur hat and little else. Beads of perspiration made her glow blue in the pulsating lights.

There were so many freaks here, and it was fucking claustrophobic, a bodyguard's worst nightmare. The gyrating spectators steamed with sweat even though Belgium was chilly in March. The festival crowd packed together in one huge mass, the heat of their bodies billowing upward in a stifling, drug-scented fog exacerbated by the twenty smoke machines lined up along the edge of the stage. The ground shook under his feet in time to the beats.

"How many people are here?" he shouted at Greg, his client's tour manager.

"What?" He made the universal sign for *I can't hear you*, shrugging and gesturing toward his ears. Ransom leaned closer and tried again, now that the woman beside them had stopped shrieking on every downbeat.

"How many people are here?"

"Here on this field? Or here at the festival?"

When the wiry, beak-nosed man shouted "festival," droplets of spit spewed through the air and landed on Ransom's face. He turned his head to the side, then shied away from a raver with electric blue hair. The dude was his height—over six feet—but unlike him, the guy looked thin and lanky enough to collapse as he writhed in time to the music.

Greg pulled Ransom forward as they worked their way closer to the stage. "I'd say there's fifty or sixty thousand kids here on this field, now, because Lola's the main event. The whole festival? Maybe a hundred thousand? Brussels isn't a huge venue. The German and French festivals bring one-fifty, one-eighty, easily."

"One hundred and eighty thousand *people?*"

Greg nodded and dragged him deeper into the center of the crowd. One hundred and eighty thousand people in attendance? How was that organizationally possible? How was that safe?

He should have done his research before he took this assignment. He would have done his research if Ironclad hadn't yanked him off a detail in Dallas and diverted him to Belgium with barely enough time to pack his shit. The big boss, Liam Wilder, said this Lola person "needed his skill set." That meant she needed more than a bodyguard. She needed someone to keep her in line.

From what he could gather, his twenty-year-old client suffered from a combination of insta-fame, immaturity, craziness, and a newfound interest in recreational drug use. Tons of performers and celebrities used drugs and alcohol, but not all of them were headlining a multi-million dollar tour across Europe. Ransom's job, above and beyond protecting her, would be keeping her safe from her young, crazy self.

A cluster of blonde, topless girls rubbed against him as he eased past. One of them grabbed his ass with a throaty coo. "Jesus," he muttered, not that anyone could hear him over the blaring music. Kids these days. How old were those girls? He was only thirty-seven, but he felt way, way older, and it wasn't just because of the suit he wore, or the badge on his hip.

They were halfway to the front now, in the middle of an undulating, glowing sea of wacked-out Belgians. The music was so loud it rattled his teeth, and the stage rigging swam with what must have been a million lights. The bulbs flashed in time to the throbbing rave beats, running in patterns so disorienting that it took him a moment to locate the performer at the sound console, the DJ who was making this crowd lose their ever-loving shit in the crisp night air.

Her legal name was Lola Mae Reynolds. Her stage name was Lady Paradise, and at a mere twenty years old, she'd risen to megastar status in the EDM universe. EDM was short for Electronic Dance Music, which Ransom hadn't known until Lola's manager told him half an hour ago. The EDM scene apparently involved a lot of repetitive music, rhinestones, iridescent bracelets, and spirit hoods.

Greg demanded his attention and pointed to the stage, to the petite, Memphis-born woman who'd become too difficult for the tour brass to control. *Lady Paradise.* He'd read her file on the flight over the ocean.

Lola Mae Reynolds was the daughter of blues legend Mo Reynolds. She'd grown up in a musical family, enjoying an "unconventional" childhood, whatever that meant. According to her file, she had tons of energy, tons of personality, but not much self-control. Of course, what twenty year old had self-control?

He studied his new client as she mixed music at the sound console. She looked small but strong, with blazing pink hair and a massive pair of headphones half on, half off her ears. Were those dreadlocks on a white girl? Ransom shook his head. He preferred music created by people playing actual instruments. All she seemed to be doing was pushing buttons, adjusting knobs, and occasionally pumping her fists while screaming into a hand-held microphone.

But he wasn't here to critique her eardrum-assaulting version of music. He was here to protect her from overzealous admirers, and to make sure she stayed sane enough to finish out the last twelve stops on this tour. He'd built a reputation as a celebrity wrangler over his ten-year career, and had used those skills to reach the top echelon of Ironclad's pay scale. His latest performance review was full of words like *solid*, *dependable*, *trustworthy*, and *unflappable*. In the end, it all boiled down to not taking any shit.

The pink-haired girl onstage would doubtless give him shit in the beginning, but he could handle it. She'd learn soon enough that he wouldn't put up with her craziness the way other people around her did.

He watched her work the crowd, riling the ravers into a bouncing mass of adrenaline. One moment her spiky head was lowered over the sound console, and the next, she was waving her arms and jumping up and down with the same abandoned energy as her audience. She looked minuscule on the massive stage amidst the obnoxious lights, but anyone would look tiny up there. Well, except for him. He was six and a half feet of hard-eyed, muscular Latino male; he often depended on his size to gain cooperation from his clients.

He could deal with this pink-dreadlocked pixie any day. She wore the skimpiest of bikini tops and a pair of skintight gold lamé booty shorts. So slutty.

But slutty didn't matter. Safety mattered. He maintained his focus even as he shouldered through a maze of sweaty, blissed out ravers. This crush and noise would become his world for the next two months, until the end of Lola's tour. The lights made his brain throb and the volume seemed to work itself into his chest, causing his heart to pound twice as hard as usual. Ear plugs. He'd have to invest in some quality ear plugs for this assignment, and maybe a defibrillator for the irregular heartbeats. Shit.

Greg nudged him and spray-shouted another volley of words in his face. Ransom didn't have the first clue what the manager was trying to say, but it was pointless to attempt speech this close to the massive bank of speakers. At this point, they were near enough for him to make out Lola's features. She was pretty, yes. Animated. She was a kinetic sculpture in a bikini. He'd bet his life she was high as shit.

The beats tumbled over each other, louder and louder, faster than seemed possible. The ravers around him were going crazy, out of their minds. His bodyguard radar pinged *Danger Danger Danger*. There were too many uncontrolled bodies, and too little space to move if something went wrong. Up on the platform, Lola leaped on top of the console and turned her back to the audience, and started to twerk wildly along with the building beat. The melody, such as it was, climbed in time with the mania of the audience, and Lola...

Well, she clearly wasn't wearing panties under those gold booty shorts. They were pretty much painted on her round, taut ass.

He was a man. He had to stare just for a moment. He had to admit to himself that her ass was magnificent, and that it would probably feel like paradise to bend her over and jam his cock between those cheeks.

He narrowed his eyes, mentally berating himself. Looking at his client was okay, but fantasizing about having filthy, twerking butt sex with her wasn't. He stopped ogling her and glanced over at Greg instead. He was staring at her ass too. It was hard not to when she flaunted it so recklessly, so confidently in front of thousands of pairs of eyes. She crouched down to push some more buttons and twist some switches on the sound board. The beat intensified and slithered into something even harder and sexier. As Greg whooped beside him, the crowd chanted "Drop, drop, drop!"

Lola straightened and reached toward the sky, and shook her short pink dreads, then turned and opened her arms to her audience as the music barreled to a fever pitch.

Jesus fucking insanity. He couldn't look away. She seemed to focus the crowd's ratcheting energy as she held her majestic pose. Screams assailed his ears, and then the drop arrived in a thumping spill of audio. The deep bass explosion vibrated his testicles. Sixty thousand people went euphoric.

And Lola soared into the audience, arms and legs flung wide.

Ransom shouted and surged toward her without thinking, shoving kids aside as the bass boomed over and over like a cluster bomb attack. "Get out of the way," he yelled. He had to help her, rescue her and check her for injury. She was lost in the convulsing mass, wearing only a bikini and a pair of skintight shorts. Greg grabbed him from behind and shouted something he couldn't understand. Ransom turned away, fighting to get to Lola, but the manager grabbed him again. This time Ransom made out the words.

"Stage dive, yeah? She's okay."

As Greg said it, he pointed to the front of the crowd, where Lola surfaced on the audience's upraised hands. Ransom quivered on the balls of his feet, still poised for rescue. She wore a beatific expression, her arms spread to each side, her scrap of a bikini top still somehow in place. *Not safe, Lola.* Holy fuck, so not safe, but wow. She looked wild and fearless, a goddess carried on the up thrust palms of her worshipers.

"What the fuck?" he shouted to Greg. "That's fucking dangerous."

"She's not supposed to stage dive." He shrugged. "But that's Lola. She loves a good drop."

Ransom followed her progress with impatience until the security guys at the front hauled her back onstage. She grabbed the mic from the console and exhorted the crowd to "fucking dance, motherfuckers." He wondered how many of those motherfuckers had groped her through her booty shorts. He wondered why he cared. Greg grinned at his flabbergasted expression.

"I know, right?" The screams had tapered off to the point Ransom could just about hear him. "She's crazy. Stage diving is risky, and the tour company doesn't like risks."

No, a tour company investing millions of dollars in an entertainer generally didn't like risks. Now that he was here, Lola wasn't going to stage dive anymore, or perform while she was high, or let dozens of people molest her through her golden shorts. Fuck no. He threw his shoulders back, trying to shake off the shock of seeing his client dive headlong into a roiling mass of strangers who were most likely as high as she was.

Fuck. This one was going to be more trouble than he'd anticipated.

"Her set's winding down," said Greg. "Let's head backstage."

* * * * *

Lola shoved her hair out of her eyes and grabbed the water bottle Greg handed her. Thirsty. So thirsty. She tugged her bikini straps into place as she tipped back her head and chugged. The set was amazing and she was still buzzing hard. It wasn't a huge crowd, but they had a great vibe, and the small white pills Marty had given her only made it better.

As she guzzled the water, Greg waved his hands for her attention. His lips moved as he gestured to a giant, dark-haired guy behind him. Nice suit, but man, she was fucked up. She couldn't hear a word. Her manager frowned and pointed at his ears. Huh?

Oh, her ear plugs. She took them out and tried to shove them in her pocket, but she was wearing shorts with no pockets, so she held them instead and stared at both men, trying to focus. She was on some new designer drug, something Marty had described as "related to ecstasy." She felt like she was swimming through warm glue. It was loud behind the stage, almost as loud as out front.

"What?" she asked, squinting at Greg.

"This is Ransom. Ransom Gutierrez." He pointed again at the man in the suit. That's when she noticed the badge clipped to his waistband. Holy shit. A cop. Was he one of those DEA undercover guys? Why had Greg brought him here? She thought in a panic of all the drugs stowed in the tour bus.

Oh.

No.

No, the stash wasn't there anymore. Marty had decided it was safer to buy small amounts on the way, rather than drive around holding a bunch of stuff the way they had during the U.S. tour. There were always pharmaceutical pipelines at these festivals, not that it was all about the drugs.

It didn't used to be all about the drugs.

Lola had always been a "Just Say No" type until she'd taken her first dose of ecstasy midway through her last tour. She'd done it so she could better understand what her audience was feeling and hearing when she played her sets, and she'd decided she really enjoyed the high. Now Marty, her assistant, acquired pills to keep her energy up, to keep the party rolling while she was onstage. He took care of everything, kept her from taking too much, kept her from sleeping too much, kept her safe when she went flying too high.

Where the fuck was Marty? She was flying pretty high right now on whatever he'd given her. He must be cleaning the drugs out of the bus.

She eyeballed the suit guy. Did they have DEA agents in Europe? Fuck. She reminded herself again that there were no drugs on the bus. But maybe he had other evidence of her drug use. Maybe she was about to be arrested. Maybe Marty was already in jail. Fuck, why were the cops here? And why pick on her when ninety percent of the people at this festival were wasted off their faces?

"I'm totally clean," she said. She reached to turn out her pockets but she didn't have pockets, so she ended up pulling at the crotch of her too-tight shorts. "I'm clean, officer."

Greg rolled his eyes and took her elbow, and led her through the chaotic backstage area to the much quieter bus paddock. The tall man in the suit followed behind them. Fuck.

"There are no drugs on the bus," she whispered to Greg.

"You and your fucking drugs."

"At least, I don't think there are." Her voice trembled with anxiety. "But maybe there are. You'll have to distract the cop while I take a look."

"He's not a cop," Greg said in an exasperated tone. "He's a bodyguard."

A bodyguard? Lola sometimes used bodyguards in L.A., but she didn't need one now. Marty provided all the security she needed for this tour. She opened her mouth to say that, but then she thought she better not lose her shit in front of this fucking cop.

No, *bodyguard*.

They climbed onto the bus and she backed away from the two men. The bodyguard looked even taller here, where everything was scaled down to create more space. She'd let Greg handle this. That's what tour managers were for. She headed toward the back, to the private compartment that served as her bedroom.

"Lola!"

She only stopped and turned because Greg sounded so angsty. "What?"

When she said "What?" it slurred out into a long, distorted sound that confused her. Shit, shit, shit, she was coming down too fast, considering what she'd paid for these "designer" pills. The dark-eyed giant stood with his arms at his side, assessing her with a frown. She didn't like his scary looking badge or his menacing shadow of stubble.

"Sit down," Greg said, pointing at the sofa. "We need to talk."

She sat where he indicated and stared at both of them. In the distance she could make out the faint disco beat of the next set. She'd had a good set though. Yeah.

"This is *Ran-som Gu-ti-er-rez*," Greg said, speaking to her as if she was three years old. He pointed to the giant, who folded his outsize frame into the seat next to her manager. "He's the bodyguard from Ironclad Solutions. The one the tour producers hired for you."

Ransom? she thought. Like, the thing people demand for kidnap victims? What kind of name was that for a bodyguard? Wait, was he a cop or a bodyguard? Was he here about a kidnapping? Her brain wasn't working so great.

"What?" she asked. "Who is this again?"

"The tour producers hired a bodyguard to look after you. He's going to stay with us until the final venue." As Greg's features wavered in and out of focus, he turned to the kidnapper and frowned. "This might not be the best time for this conversation."

Oh. Lola knew how to make conversation. She could be a great talker when she wanted to be. "It's nice to meet you," she said, because...politeness. She meant to offer her hand but it wouldn't move. Fuck, she was winding too far down.

"It's nice to meet you too," he replied. His voice sounded low and growly. Greg said something else but she didn't hear it, because the bodyguard's deep, thick voice was still traveling through her brain like syrup. The edges of her vision started to flame.

"I'm so high," she said, and then wished she hadn't, because there was a cop on the bus. She was going to pass out, she could feel it.

Ugh.

2.
THE BODYGUARD

When Lola woke, the faraway beats had stopped. It was quiet and dark, and she wasn't on the bus anymore. She was in a bed in a hotel room, in some unknown European city. A sliver of light shone through a gap in the curtain and bisected the wall across the room.

Scary that she didn't remember how she'd gotten here. What the hell kind of shit had Marty given her last night? They must have driven here and checked in while she was dead to the world. That wasn't good. Too much lost time she couldn't account for. At some point, she must have put a tee shirt over her bikini and gold shorts. Her eyes felt crusty with makeup, and a dull pain throbbed in the middle of her skull.

"Fuck." She sat up and passed a hand over her face. "Fuckity fuck."

She had to stop with the party pills. She said that every time she woke up feeling like this. Her empty stomach rolled over, and then *she* rolled over, grasping the sheets. As she stared into the darkness, two eyes stared back at her. There was a man in a chair by the window, and he was too big to be Greg or Marty.

She didn't know whether she should scream for help. Maybe she'd invited him to her room the night before. She tried to call up a memory, a name, but her stomach revolted before she could find it. She pushed back the sheets and stumbled in the dark for the bathroom. When she found it, she hunched over the toilet, hacking up dry coughs and cloudy spit.

Gross. She hated throwing up. She hated that the bathroom spun like a planet off its axis. She wanted everything to be still. She closed her eyes tight, pressing her fingers to her lids, trying to calm the nausea. Her head pounded with unbearable pressure. She'd need to have a talk with Marty about the shit pills he'd given her, because "related to ecstasy" felt more like "related to brain damage." The high had felt incredible while it lasted, but now...

She cringed and coughed, heaved again, and realized the man from her room was standing behind her.

"Tell Marty I need him," she said over her shoulder. "Get Marty for me."

"Marty's gone."

"Gone? Where...gone? Who the fuck...?" Questions sputtered out, none of them complete. "What?"

She wanted to ask who this dude was and why he was here, but she couldn't seem to string together a coherent sentence. He looked too old to be a groupie, and too grim to be a gigolo, but she'd been with enough of both to know they came in all shapes and sizes.

Had she picked him up backstage last night? Or in some bar? Blackouts terrified her. She might have done anything while she was out. She peered at the guy from between her fingers. Tall, muscular, dark, just the type of guy she'd pick up for drug-fueled sex. Had she fucked him?

Two-day stubble. Strong jaw. Those hands. If she'd fucked him, she'd probably enjoyed it. She was sad she couldn't remember.

"Did we fuck?" she asked, because she was tired of feeling confused.

"Excuse me?"

Great. Now he was offended. Whatever. He looked so uptight, he'd probably never fucked anyone. He wore a dark red tie and a starched white shirt, like he'd gotten lost on the way to Wall Street. Maybe he was a preacher or drug counselor. Maybe he was trying to stage some kind of intervention.

"Go away," she said. "Close the door. Can't you see I'm sick?"

"What can I do to help you?"

Through the blackout haze, she remembered the sound of his voice from yesterday, the low, liquid growl.

"You can help me by going the fuck away. Where's Marty? Go get Marty."

"Marty's gone," he said in a patient, fuck-you voice, and that's how she remembered he'd told her that already.

Why was Marty gone? Where the fuck was he? He was her paid assistant. He was supposed to help her. "Greg, then," she groaned. "Tell Greg I'm sick and I'm not going to be able to perform tonight unless..." *Unless Marty comes back here with some new, different pills to make me feel better.*

"Your next show isn't until tomorrow, and your manager knows you're sick. We were both with you last night when you passed out. And you're not really sick. You're fucked up from whatever drug you ingested. What were you on last night?"

"Some ecstasy thing." She rubbed her temples and sat back against the tub, and pulled the white hotel shower curtain around her. There. No more guy in a red tie, asking her irritating questions.

He yanked the curtain back and crouched in front of her, and held out a bottle of water. She took off the lid and drank. It tasted weird.

"What is this?" she asked.

"Electrolyte water. Do you remember passing out?"

His curt question triggered delayed memories, backstage bustle and distant music, a suit jacket. An ID badge. This guy wasn't a gigolo or groupie. Greg had told her he was a bodyguard.

But why was he here in her room, peppering her with questions? She didn't need a bodyguard, even if he was handsome as fuck. The festivals were huge and she was surrounded by tons of strangers all the time, but they were ravers, not criminals. The only thing they were violent about was dancing. The man had a ridiculous set of muscles under his pristine white button-down. Huh. Overkill, those muscles, cause no one was after her.

He nodded at the bottle. "Drink some more water. You need to rehydrate."

She took a sip and grimaced, feeling trapped between the tub and the man's large frame. Why wouldn't he leave? Why was he looming over her and staring at her that way?

And what the fuck had he been doing in her hotel room while she was sleeping? She felt violated. Or pissed off. She didn't actually know how she felt. At least the room had stopped spinning. She drank more water and sat up straighter.

"Ready to get up?" he asked.

She glared at him. "I like sitting on bathroom floors."

He took her arm and dragged her to her feet. "Keep drinking the water. I'll order us something to eat."

Order us something to eat? That sounded awfully cozy. Maybe she *had* slept with him. No, she'd remember if she'd gone to bed with this monster. He was built like a fort.

He dropped her off at the chair by the window and drew open the drapes, causing her to shy away like a vampire. He frowned and drew them half closed again. There was still too much sunlight. How long had she slept? What city were they in? Marty usually answered all those questions, but her assistant wasn't here. What had the guy said? Gone. Marty was gone. Gone where?

The bodyguard stood in front of the window and ordered breakfast in slow, patient, neutral-American English. She took the opportunity to study his face, now that he wasn't looking at her. The sun illuminated his dark brows and strong cheekbones, and his prominent, masculine nose. His lips were sexy, full and expressive even when he wasn't speaking.

"Yes, I know it's after two o'clock," he said, turning away. "Could you please make an exception?" In the end he got his way, because he said thank you in both English and some Euro language. Show off.

But wow, he had a marvelous ass for an older guy. He had a really, really great, firm, sculpted ass beneath those Wall Street pants.

He turned back and caught her staring at his ten-out-of-ten posterior. She quickly dropped her gaze. Now that the ache in her head had subsided, reasoned thoughts emerged. It wasn't polite to stare, and she was suddenly, painfully conscious of her skimpy bikini and skintight shorts. She wondered if *he* was the one who'd put a shirt on her after she passed out last night.

"I'm sorry," she said, looking back up at him. "I forgot your name."

"Ransom Gutierrez."

Oh yeah, the whole kidnapping thing. "Look, Mr. Gutierrez—"

"You can call me Ransom. We're going to become very good friends."

She hated the way he said that. "I don't need a bodyguard." She downed the last of the electrolyte-enhanced water. "Greg keeps the crazies away, and I have another assistant who helps m—"

"If you mean Marty, he's been fired."

"What?"

Shit, shit, shit. Fired? Marty was her lifeline. He helped her dress and eat and sleep, procured her drugs, and even fucked her sometimes when she couldn't find anyone else.

"Why was he fired?" she asked. "He was my employee."

"I think you know why he was fired, and I think you understand why I'm here. Your illustrious tour sponsors are concerned about you becoming a liability."

"A liability?" She threw up her arms. "Those assholes. I'm the entire fucking reason for this tour. If I'm not here, no one shows up."

"Exactly. They lose a lot of money if your lifestyle renders you unable to perform."

"My *lifestyle*?" Her stomach started churning all over again. "What lifestyle?"

"The alcohol. The drugs. The shady friends. The all-night parties and marginal nightclubs."

But... But... "I didn't go out last night."

"Because you blacked out after your show." He sat on the bed across from her chair, so they were eye to eye, and regarded her with his hands braced on his knees. "Rule number one, Miss Reynolds: No more drugs, not on this tour."

She couldn't stand the imperious way he talked to her, like he was the master of the universe and she was some peon. She was Lady Paradise, and she'd sold twenty-five million singles last year. "I don't use that many drugs," she said.

He gave her an arch look. "You're talking to the person who carried your limp, boneless corpse through the hotel lobby and up to this room last night at four in the morning."

"They were bad pills, or I took too many or something. Lesson learned."

"Have you really learned a lesson?" His nostrils flared like he smelled something unpleasant. She didn't know why she noticed that. She didn't know why everything had turned so scary and serious. "MadDance, Inc. thinks you're getting worse, not better," he said.

"Who's MadDance Ink?"

"MadDance Incorporated. They're paying for your tour expenses and manager, in exchange for your fitness to perform. You understand how all this works? You signed a contract, Miss Reynolds."

She remembered signing a contract. She didn't need some towering, muscle-bound bodyguard throwing it in her face. What the fuck kind of name was Ransom anyway? "My name's Lola," she snapped. "You calling me *Miss Reynolds* in that fucking tone doesn't make you a polite guy."

"I'm not here to be polite. I'm here to keep you alive and healthy for the next two months."

Ugh. Jerk. Smartass. He was going to throw attitude at her all fucking day and all fucking night. She stared out the window at the sunlight and wondered what city she was in. She didn't want to ask because she didn't want to admit how out of touch she'd become with the day-to-day schedule. She didn't want to admit how dependent she'd become on Marty during this tour.

"Why don't you get out of here so I can sleep?" She left the chair and went back to her rumpled bed, burrowing under the sheets. Had he slept in the other bed? She couldn't tell. It was neatly made up.

"You should take a shower before the food gets here," he suggested. "Or are you just going to wear that same outfit on through to tomorrow night?"

"That's none of your fucking business." But yeah, she was gross. Her clothes were wrinkled and slept in. She needed to take off her stale makeup. Her haphazard braids looked like rats had been gnawing on them. "I want to take a shower, but not with you in the room."

"Sorry, I can't leave. I'm on supervisory detail."

Ugh. She'd known he wouldn't leave.

"If you stay here, you're probably going to see me naked," she said, in some pathetic attempt to rattle him.

"I pretty much saw you naked during your set last night."

No, not rattled at all. He raked a gaze over her body, and even with the shirt on over her skimpy costume, she felt exposed.

"Listen, kid," he said when his dark eyes finally meandered back to her face. "I've seen plenty of bare skin in my line of work. It doesn't matter to me. I have a job to do, and that job is getting you to each venue of this tour on time and in shape to perform. You can parade around naked if you like, or you can wrap up in a towel. You can sing in the shower. You can pick your nose or scratch your ass. You can pretend I don't exist, but I'm going to be within ten feet of you for the next couple months, so if I were you, I'd just take that shower."

She went to her luggage in a huff, dragging it with her toward the bathroom door. She thought she might still have some ecstasy tablets stashed in the front pocket of her cosmetics bag.

"Oh, and just so you aren't disappointed, I've already been through your things and confiscated the items you're not allowed to have."

She froze mid-step. "What do you mean, you've *been through my things*?"

"I mean that I looked through all your belongings and confiscated items you're not allowed to—"

"What the fuck! You pawed through my personal shit?"

She had private journals and lingerie with her. Condoms and lube and sex toys. She could see from the glint in his eyes that he'd found all those things and more during his illegal luggage search.

"Just doing my job," he said.

"You're an asshole. I never agreed to this. I'll quit this fucking tour and they'll be sorry." She put her hands on her hips and let him have it, even though he was so much bigger than her. "I don't need the money from these festivals, you fucking prick. Do you know how much I made last year? Enough that I don't have to put up with this kind of bullshit."

He didn't say anything. He didn't have to. They both knew she couldn't quit, because she'd signed a contract, and somewhere in that contract it probably said they reserved the right to hire asshole bodyguards to interfere in her life.

She went into the bathroom and slammed the door, then leaned on the sink, taking deep breaths. She felt like she might vomit again, but there was nothing to bring up but a bunch of shitty electrolyte water. Fuck this shit, fuck him and his judgey frowns, and his illegal searches and confiscations. He wanted her to stop partying and going to nightclubs? Fat fucking chance. She was Lady Paradise and she had an image to uphold.

MadDance, Inc.? Fuck em. At the end of the day, they needed to dance to her tune, because this tour was nothing without her.

* * * * *

Ransom sighed and sat by the window to wait for the food to arrive. Fuck. That hadn't gone well.

Not that he'd expected it to. He'd assumed he'd get some blowback for ousting her assistant/drug mule, and informing her he was going to be living inside her ass for the rest of the tour. Rich, successful artist types rarely enjoyed hearing news like that.

But everything would be okay. From what he could see, his client wasn't a hardened junkie, just a dumb kid who wanted to party. He didn't know what was worse, that she'd asked him if they'd slept together, or that she actually believed he would have slept with her while she was blacked out. Had that happened to her in the past?

Dumbass kid. She didn't have the body weight for the chemicals she was ingesting. Last night, when he'd picked her up and carried her off the bus, she'd felt so light she might fly away.

If she was a true junkie, she would have flipped out to find her small stash gone. He'd thrown away ecstasy and pot, amateur shit, although she'd been wired on something harder last night. He wasn't sure what she'd taken, only knew he'd arrived here just in time.

Fucking Marty. He could tell in the course of one conversation with her "assistant" that he was a horrible influence, a hanger-on taking advantage of a rich, gullible young woman. Money led to drugs, drugs led to partying, partying led to questions like *Did we fuck?* It led to exploiters and users, and danger.

But Ransom was here to keep the danger away. The hard partying was over, at least for the rest of the tour, and if she had a problem with that, she could try to fight him. He was pretty sure he'd win.

Room service arrived just as she turned off the shower. By the time she opened the door, he'd set out the German idea of late breakfast: bread and cheese, fruit, yogurt, and miniature glazed doughnuts sprinkled with cinnamon. He wanted to stuff about twelve of them in his mouth. Wrangling hungover, immature brats made him hungry.

She came out of the bathroom with a thump of her luggage and a muffled curse. He looked up and paused mid-doughnut.

Lola Mae.

Those were the first two words that came to his mind, because he wasn't looking at Lady Paradise the mega-millionaire DJ anymore. Without the slut makeup, without the riotous braids, without the bikini and booty shorts she looked...

She looked like a lost, befuddled kid named Lola Mae.

He felt a puzzling rush of attraction, a reaction to her rumpled, vulnerable freshness, and quickly turned away. It wasn't his business to find his clients beautiful or attractive, especially when they were half his age. He hadn't fallen for a client once in his career, and he wasn't going to start now, not with this one. Her hair was pink, for fuck's sake. It was darker pink now that it was wet. She wore a pale gray tee that made her blue eyes pop, and some worn jeans that fit obscenely well.

Okay. So she was sexy. She was fucking beautiful. Maybe he should have fucked her last night, if he could have pried off her skintight shorts. She wouldn't have remembered it today.

He mentally shook himself and shoved the rest of the doughnut in his mouth. These inappropriate feelings wouldn't last. He wasn't the type of guy who panted over dwarf-sized, pink-haired twenty year olds. His last girlfriend had been a high-powered lawyer in New York, a statuesque prosecutor who was strong enough to challenge him both physically and intellectually. Those were the type of women he sought when the job gave him time to pursue a social life.

Not...this.

Lola tripped over her luggage and let loose a string of epithets in her Memphis drawl. *Fucking motherfucker goddamn cocksucker piece of shit.* Was she talking about the luggage, or him?

"Come eat something," he said.

She gave him a dirty look and righted the luggage. "I'm not hungry."

"Why'd you haul your whole suitcase into the bathroom?"

Her dirty look grew even dirtier. "What, I'm supposed to leave it out here so you can paw through it again?"

"I'm done pawing through it. I already got rid of the stuff you can't have."

Instead of coming to the table, she collapsed face down on the bed and closed her eyes. Her hair was a tousled, wavy mess now that it wasn't tamed into those silly dreadlocks. The sun fell across the bed, slanting over the sinfully round ass showcased by the world's sexiest jeans.

I want to be slanting over that ass. I want to be inside it.

Fuck. Ransom, really. That's enough.

"When did you eat last?" he asked aloud.

She didn't open her eyes. "I don't know. I had something before last night's set."

"Come have something to eat, then."

"I want to sleep. Leave me alone."

Ransom usually tried to give women what they wanted, but in this case, he couldn't.

"Here's how this is going to go," he said in a firm, direct voice. "I have a job to do here. So when I tell you to eat, you're going to eat, whether you feel hungry or not. When I tell you to sleep, you're going to sleep."

"Are you going to tell me when to blink and breathe too?" she murmured, stretching and arching her back.

Was she trying to seduce him? Or was she just naturally, horribly provocative? He pretended to be unaffected. "Get up and eat something. Don't make me shove it down your throat. You only have a day or so to get yourself straightened out for the next set."

She turned on her back and regarded him from beneath her lashes. "Would you really shove it down my throat?"

Jesus. *Don't think about shoving anything down her throat, cowboy. Focus.*

"Get up and eat," he said. "When you're done, we'll head out for a walk."

Her lips twisted in disdain. "A walk?"

"A walk. I doubt you'd survive a run, but we could try it if you'd like. Either one."

She glared at him like she wanted to argue, but in the end, she got up and came to the table. Sometimes you just had to remind someone they were hungry. She bent a slice of bread around some cheese and stuck it in her mouth as Ransom poured her a glass of water.

"A walk," she muttered. "I don't even know where we are."

"Hamburg, Germany. You have a show tomorrow night. Don't worry, I'll get you there."

He pushed the plate of fruit and leftover doughnuts toward her, and checked his phone while she put away a decent amount of breakfast. *Feed her. Walk her. Keep her on the leash, even if she tugs a little. Or a lot.*

"How are you feeling now?" he asked when she was done.

"Shitty."

He put down his phone and regarded her. "Why do you think you feel so bad, Lola?"

"Because you won't let me sleep. I'm tired. My performances take a lot of energy."

He couldn't muffle the snort that escaped. "What? Pushing buttons exhausts you that much? Those dials must be hell to twist."

"Playing rave sets is more than pushing buttons and twisting dials, you idiot. It's way more difficult than that. You have to engage the crowd. You have to help them escape to this otherworld so they feel the magic. You have to create satisfying run-ups and drops. It looks fun and careless, but it's very complicated."

There. There was a spark of real emotion beneath her bitchy veneer. "Tell me about it," he said, trying to draw her out more.

She bit her lip and looked away. "You wouldn't understand. You don't understand anything about what I do."

"I saw the final part of your set last night. I saw you have some kind of epileptic fit."

"That was dancing, asshole."

"I saw you fling yourself into the crowd." He pointed at her, serious as sin. "Don't ever do that again, by the way. No stage diving. It's forbidden in your contract."

"So what?"

"Would you like to be paralyzed by a spinal injury, or trampled by the crowd?"

"They don't drop you, dude. That's the point. They catch you."

He rolled his eyes and gave up the argument. For now.

"Ready for that walk?" he asked, pushing back his chair.

"I don't want to walk."

"I don't care."

She remained planted in her chair. "You can't make me walk if I don't want to walk."

"Going to throw a tantrum? How old are you?" he asked, although he knew exactly how old she was. Old enough to know better. Like him. There was a damn good reason he needed to get her out of this hotel room, not that he cared to think about it too deeply.

She polished off the last doughnut and glared at him. "So this is all about you making me fit and healthy? Are you my new trainer?"

Oh, he'd like to train her, but not the type of training she thought. He'd like to train her to show some fucking respect to people who were trying to help her. "I'm your bodyguard," he said, "as I've explained several times. And if you ever dive off a stage again during this festival, we're running five miles nonstop. That's a promise." He cut her off as soon as she opened her mouth. "Don't ask how I'll make you. You don't want to know."

He would make her if it came to that, ride her and browbeat her until she ran a full five miles. He didn't make empty threats. "Are you ready to walk?" he asked again.

"Walk where? We're in fucking Hamburg. I don't know anything about this place. I can't just walk around. It's not safe."

He nodded toward her bags. "Go put on some shoes you can walk in. No six-inch platforms. Regular shoes."

"I don't have regular shoes."

"I went through everything. I know what you have."

She groaned and pushed back from the table. Ransom watched her flounce across the room. Jesus, those jeans were criminal. They were a sex offense. He turned away before she bent over, because he wasn't made of steel. Well, one part of him was made of steel.

He looked back at his phone until she was ready. "It's chilly," he said. "Put on a jacket."

"If something happens to me on this godforsaken walk, it's on your head."

"Nothing's going to happen. You ready?"

Her tousled pink hair was almost dry. It stuck out from her head every which way, and she didn't give a fuck. She was adorable. And still bitching about safety, like going for a walk was the most terrifying thing she'd done all year. He finally stuck out a finger and pressed it to her lips.

"Listen to me, kid, and try to understand. I'm your bodyguard. I'm here to protect you. As long as you're with me, you're going to be safe."

3.
CRAZY

Lola walked beside him through the scenic streets of Hamburg, and yes, she felt safe, even if her legs hurt and she didn't want to be hanging out in the crowds and the sun.

"It's a beautiful day," he said. "Anything you want to see?"

"My bed in the hotel room. I'm tired."

"Yeah? You have a busy day ahead of you. Greg said you're scheduled for a radio interview this afternoon, and dinner at some famous Hamburg restaurant. I might let you hit a few nightclubs afterward if you behave yourself. You can sleep after that. You notice I said *sleep*, not *black out*."

"What's the difference?"

He was silent a moment before he answered. "I think you remember the difference, Lola Mae."

Yeah, maybe she did, but every time he called her *Lola Mae* she wanted to punch him. Even Lola threw her off, because for the past two years everyone had called her Lady Paradise, and she'd come to think of it not just as her stage name, but her persona. Lady Paradise was the deity who stood behind the sound console and reigned over the worshipping masses.

Lola was the real her, the awkward, emo geek who'd lost her mother at five and her father at fifteen, which was the worst possible age to lose the bedrock of your life. After his heart attack, she'd moved to L.A. to live with a rich aunt and uncle and attend a rich-kid high school. Her pop had never emphasized school in Memphis, so she was far behind her classmates. They'd called her *stupid, redneck, slow.*

To cope, she'd remade herself into the school's crazy party girl, the rave head, the slut, so the boys at least would like her. When they made fun of her Memphis twang, she stopped talking and made beats instead. Those beats eventually won her a recording contract, but Lola would always be the sad, desperate outcast masquerading as a goddess.

And Lola Mae...

Lola Mae was that girl with the twang, her pop's special girl, and this bodyguard wasn't her pop. He wasn't even her friend.

"What are you thinking about?" he asked, an abrupt poke into painful memories.

"Nothing."

Fuck him. She wasn't letting this guy into her thoughts, not telling him about anything going on inside her. The last guy she'd let in was Marty. Now he was gone and she thought maybe, *maybe* Ransom was right, that Marty had done bad things for her. To her. Maybe Marty had been using her for her money, but she'd allowed it. He'd kept her too drug-happy to care.

Drug-happy? Or drug-sad?

Oh, she was going to need more pharmaceuticals. A few pre-show happy tablets quieted her neuroses and gave her confidence and energy. They helped the beats flow. The bodyguard would never understand that, because he had no flow. He was unrelentingly businesslike. He walked too fast, and he got way more attention from passersby than she did. Men and women both slowed to look him over. One woman almost walked into him, she was mentally undressing him so hard. So he was tall and big, and dark, and disgustingly masculine and handsome. So what? What a cliché.

She didn't care how sexy he looked. He did nothing for her, because she liked interesting men. Complicated men. Ransom was so boring and wholesome. For fuck's sake, he was still wearing that fucking red tie.

The only break she got from her bodyguard over the next twenty-four hours was the radio interview Greg had arranged, which was awkward and stressful. By the time they returned to the hotel, Ransom had showered and changed—into another suit and tie.

It freaked her out that she had to share a hotel room with the man. She complained to Greg but he said he couldn't do anything. "You chose this consequence," he told her. "You started partying too hard."

Now she was standing in the shower before dinner, looking at a stranger's soap and shampoo. A male stranger's. He'd been respectful so far, even waiting to take a shower until she was out with Greg, but still...she didn't know him. How was she supposed to live like this?

She needed something to help her cope. She'd have settled for a bottle of wine at this point, even though she hated the taste of it, even though it gave her worse headaches than the drugs. But she had no wine, and no drugs either, thanks to Ransom. She could probably subsist on some hot, monkey sex...

A therapist had warned her once that she had sex for unhealthy reasons. Nope. She had sex because it was fun and passed the time. Tonight, at the clubs, she'd find a good, strong candidate and invite him back to the hotel room. Maybe more than one guy. Maybe a whole slew of hot, horny guys to work her over and make the tension go away.

Ransom could stay and watch if he wanted to be protective, but he wasn't telling her no. She needed some fucking release, and sex was an all-natural indulgence. German guys were beautiful, athletic, and enthusiastic, and she still had plenty of condoms in her luggage. Unlike the drugs, Ransom hadn't thrown those away, which counted as permission to be as slutty as she wanted.

Well, she was choosing to interpret it that way.

* * * * *

As soon as the nightclub's management learned that Lady Paradise had arrived, they swept her into the DJ booth. Ransom watched for signs of irritation, but she didn't seem to mind. She spun an hour-long set as the massive club filled with more and more bodies. Word had gotten around Hamburg's party scene that the megastar was in their midst.

But everything was okay. The club had an adequate number of emergency exits and an impressive amount of security staff. He monitored these metrics for his client's protection. They wouldn't have stayed here otherwise.

And with Lola in the booth, he could supervise her much more easily than when she was twerking and slithering on the dance floor. Honestly, the way she moved her body... It should have been illegal. It probably would be, if more women were capable of it.

Ransom sat by the booth's entrance and tried not to ogle her too much, but it was difficult. She was wearing a mesh crop top with a barely-there bralette, and sequined leggings that left nothing to the imagination. Instead of scattered braids, her hair was tamed into a dozen or so mini-buns that rose from her head like proliferating antennae.

And damn her, she was still beautiful. It wasn't right.

He forced his eyes from her body to her fingers, flitting nimbly across the bank of audio equipment. He couldn't seem to match up the sound coming out of the speakers with anything she was doing, but then he realized she was working on a delay. That was why she took the headphones on and off as she played with the buttons. Her head never stopped bobbing.

Her ass never stopped shaking.

Fuck. He had to pull himself together. She was too young, too wild, too pink, and he was too professional to think about what it might feel like to press her back on that mixing console, tear off her clothes and yank apart her thighs, and—

"Hey, bodyguard!" She turned to him, waving her arms in the air. "How come you never dance?"

"I'm here to work, not dance."

"Do you even know how to dance?"

He slid a glance over her bare torso and undulating hips. "Not like you."

She laughed and turned away. Headphones on, headphones off, lights flashing, a frenetic buildup of beats he'd already come to recognize. Next would come the thing she called the "drop," the testicle-rumbling bass explosion that made everyone go wild. The entire club screamed in the throes of aural orgasm. The other DJ in the booth grabbed Lola and kissed her on the mouth.

Ransom stiffened, every muscle going tense. The man's arms snaked around her waist but she did nothing to pull away. They only kissed for a few seconds, but it was too long, because the man was some random Hamburg DJ she didn't even know.

She turned away, laughed again, and adjusted a few levers. Headphones on, her shoulders scrunched up, her features taut with concentration as her fingers lingered on the dials. Headphones off, more laughter, and the beats rolled on and on and on. He still didn't have those ear plugs.

She finally gave the spotlight back to the regular DJ and exited the booth. People applauded as she reappeared on the dance floor and sketched an exaggerated bow. Ransom took her arm and leaned to speak in her ear.

"How long are we staying? This place is really crowded."

"I know. Isn't it wonderful?"

She surged into the energetic mass, insinuating herself between pockets of humping, bumping dancers, which was easy enough to do when you were tiny. He had to nudge people aside to follow her. No way was he letting her roam freely around this place. People were drunk and high and really handsy.

His last client had been an alcoholic actor. There had been no nightclubs, no sequined hot pants, nothing but making sure the client didn't drink too heavily before he learned his lines for the next day.

Ransom would have given anything to be running lines with a half-drunk actor right now.

He called Lola's name when she got too far away from him. Somehow she heard it, even in the deafening clamor of the club. She turned to him and held out her arms. "Dance with me."

He shook his head and leaned against a nearby pillar, close enough to watch her, but not so close that she could grind against him with those hips. She found someone else to grind on, a sweaty, muscled Teutonic Adonis with spiky blond hair. The man leered down at her like a creep, and she encouraged him, drawing his arms around her.

Ransom rolled his eyes and let out a sigh, even if no one in this godforsaken club could hear him. He was the only person in the vicinity who wasn't jerking to the skull-shattering music.

A few minutes later, Lola was gyrating in the middle of a Hans and Franz sandwich. Hans, the original creep, had been joined by a creepy friend and all of them were basically having sex without taking off their clothes. Bodies pressed in around them, party people who wanted to brush up against the actual, real Lady Paradise. People took pictures, poking her, prodding her to get her attention, but she kept dancing, and Hans and Franz kept most of the interlopers away.

Finally, Ransom got too disgusted to deal with it anymore. It was almost two in the morning. Time to go. He wove through the group surrounding Lola and got her attention, and pointed at his watch.

She laughed and shook her head. He pushed past Franz, holding up a hand when the man released a string of irritated German.

"We need to go," he said to Lola. "Say goodbye to your friends."

Instead she gripped Hans and Franz's hands and dragged them along with her as they made their way to the quieter lobby of the club.

"Come on, Ransom," she whined. "It's so early."

"It's the opposite of early, and you have to perform tomorrow. I mean, today." He scowled down at his watch, then grabbed one of the security guys and asked him to hail a cab.

Lola huddled with her German studs, her eyes bright and flirtatious. They stroked and fondled her, spellbound. Ransom had to resist the urge to swat their hands away. At last the manager gestured from the door.

Ransom tapped Lola on the shoulder. "Come on. Ride's here."

She popped up along with her fondlers, and brought them with her toward the exit. Toward the taxi. Ransom stepped in front of the car door before they could slide in.

"Whoa, whoa, whoa. No extra passengers."

"It's okay, Ransom," Lola called from inside. "You can sit in front. We'll sit in the back."

"They're not getting in the car. We're leaving."

She looked out at him like he was an idiot. "They're coming with me. They're coming back to the hotel."

"Like hell they are. No."

The taxi driver watched without comment, his dark eyes bugging behind black-framed glasses. Lola pouted and reached for the men. "They're coming back with us," she insisted.

"They're not coming back with us," Ransom replied in a calm, patient, and very firm voice. "They're going back inside the club, and you're returning to the hotel to go to bed."

Hans and Franz exchanged tragic glances. Ransom jerked his head toward the nightclub's door. "Leave. Go back inside. Not tonight, fellas."

Lola grabbed their hands and spoke to him through clenched teeth. "I don't think you understand. They're not leaving. They're coming back to the hotel to have some fun with me. I have needs, you know. You can wait out in the hall if you like."

He could *wait out in the hall?* Disbelief transformed to something more like fury. She thought he'd wait in the hall while she cavorted with these two complete strangers in his hotel room? "I don't think *you* understand," he said, aware that a dozen or more people were watching this sordid exchange. "No one is coming back to the hotel with you." He said it slowly, with dire emphasis. "No one. Tell your boys goodbye."

She must have seen something in his eyes that finally convinced her she wasn't going to win this battle.

"Fine," she yelled. "Fuck you." She turned to the Teutonic wonders. "Good fucking night. It was nice meeting you."

She ducked back into the cab and slid across the seat as he entered behind her. "Fairmont, *bitte*," he said to the driver, giving him the name of the hotel.

The cab eased into traffic as Lola seethed beside him. "You're such an asshole," she said. "You're so joyless and horrible. I hate you. I fucking despise you."

"I'm sorry you feel that way."

She turned to him, ready to attack. He grabbed her hands before she could hit him. "Don't. Ever," he said, and he meant it. "Calm the fuck down."

"I can't calm down. I don't want to calm down. You're going to deny me sex when you've already taken away my drugs? How am I supposed to have fun?"

"You seemed to have plenty of fun tonight without the drugs. Now it's time to get some sleep."

"I won't be able to sleep, you stupid ass bodyguard. I'm fucking horny as shit and you just double cock blocked me."

He glanced at the cabbie, who was pretending not to listen to the drama in his backseat. "Keep it down, okay? You're going to be embarrassed about this in the morning. Show some self-respect."

"Self-respect?" She looked like she was about to combust. "I wanted to fuck those guys. They were fucking hung."

"How do you know?"

"Because they were rubbing their erections on me for the last half hour."

"Oh, that's classy, Lola." She flabbergasted him. He didn't know what to say. "You seriously thought I'd allow you to bring those two guys, who you've never met before, back to the hotel room?"

"You could have waited outside!"

"Forget the whole waiting outside thing. It's never going to happen. I'm your *bodyguard*. Strange, foreign men alone with you in a hotel room? Not a fucking chance."

"What am I supposed to do for sex?"

He had to hand it to the cabbie for keeping a straight face. "Use those toys I saw in your luggage," Ransom said. "They're safer."

"Fuck you." She turned away from him, blinking at the back of the seat. "Are you seriously telling me I can't have sex the entire rest of the tour?"

"I'm saying you can't pick up strangers in nightclubs and bring them to our hotel room."

"Who else am I going to have sex with?" She turned back to him, her cheeks flushed with vitriol. "Maybe you should fuck me, Mr. Bodyguard, since you just dismissed my perfect chance at two big, fat, delicious co—"

He held up a hand to silence her. "No. That's enough. You're not allowed to talk to me that way."

"Who's going to stop me?"

"You're going to stop yourself, because you're screaming at me like a jonesing crack whore, and it's uncomfortable for everyone in this car. Enough."

She subsided. He expected her to, because he'd used his mean bodyguard voice, and it was no-nonsense.

She turned instead to the window, her fingers tapping against her knees. After ten blessed seconds of silence, she started up again, only quieter this time. "Any woman who enjoys sex must be a whore, right?"

"I didn't say you were a whore. I said you were screaming like a crack whore, which is the truth."

"Those guys were hot."

"They were strangers. It's not safe." He put a finger under her chin so she'd have to stop fuming and look at him. "And for the record, I don't ever want you to talk to me about other guys' cocks again, especially about how fat and delicious you imagine them to be. Do you understand? Have some respect."

"I don't respect you. I'll never respect you."

"I'm talking about respect for yourself."

That shut her up all the way back to the hotel, although he began to think her ranting and raving was better, since it distracted him from inconvenient thoughts. *Who else am I going to have sex with?* she'd asked. *Maybe you should fuck me, Mr. Bodyguard.*

If he wasn't her bodyguard, and she wasn't his nutso client, he would have been happy to assuage her rampant horniness. But that wasn't possible. Aside from the fact that he'd probably break her if he fucked her the way he wanted to, there would be the messy emotional aftermath. He knew with a sixth masculine sense that her aftermath would be crazy. Batshit, atomic crazy. He'd dealt with enough craziness in his career.

He didn't need or want it in his personal life.

* * * * *

Once again, Lola found herself standing in the shower, staring at a stranger's fucking toiletries. A cock-blocking stranger who'd lectured her like he was her dad, although her dad had never lectured her like that. Where did Ransom get off?

Ugh. She needed to get off.

And it wasn't happening tonight.

She'd tried. She'd attempted to rub one out in the shower, but his dumbass shampoo was staring her in the face, making her go cold.

She couldn't go on like this. At the very least, they needed to move to a suite, so she could escape into the privacy of her own space, and not just the privacy of a long, hot shower. Greg would have to help her convince the tour producers. If he wouldn't, or couldn't, she'd have to beg them herself.

She finally gave up on trying to find release in the shower, and shut off the water with a string of oaths, the nastiest ones she could think of. Because he was out in the room, she had to dress in the steamy, humid bathroom. Either that, or parade naked in front of him. She considered doing it, just to make him as blue-balled as he'd made her, but in the end, she couldn't scrape up the courage.

She pulled on her pajamas and the long fleece robe she was glad she'd packed, even if it took up a lot of room in her suitcase. She'd brought it because hotel rooms were sometimes cold.

And sometimes infiltrated by asshole strangers.

When she opened the door, she found Ransom stretched out on top of his bed in a worn tee and dark gray sweatpants. It was the first time she'd seen him without the suit and tie. He looked more like a regular man, which was unsettling. She wondered if he was married, even though he didn't wear a ring. Jesus, she'd screamed at him about fat, delicious cocks. She'd screamed that he had to fuck her.

No, not exactly. She hadn't exactly said *that*, but she'd been thinking it.

She was still kind of thinking it now, but that was just because of frustration and horniness. Ugh.

She put on some hand cream and went to her bed. Ransom ignored her, flipping through the local TV channels, and she was grateful for it. She slipped off the robe and got under the covers, pulling the sheets up as far as she could without smothering herself.

"Going to sleep?" he asked.

"Yes." *God, yes, I don't want to stay up and spend time with you, you cock-blocking asshole.*

He turned off the TV and got out his laptop. "Just so you know," he said as he opened it up, "there's an alarm on the door. If you touch it, or try to disable it, it'll go off."

"Afraid I'll sneak out?"

"No one's been able to manage it yet, so I wouldn't recommend trying. It'll also keep anyone unwelcome from sneaking in."

She turned away from him and closed her eyes, and tried to think how she felt about a door alarm. All of this was crazy. She lay very still so he wouldn't look at her, but she found she couldn't drift off. It'd been a long time since she'd gone to sleep on her own, without the help of downers or black outs, or minibar booze, or sex, especially after she'd been out partying. She felt wound up, with too many thoughts. She couldn't sleep.

After a while, she heard him get up. In the silence she could make out his progress across the room. He went into the bathroom, peed, and brushed his teeth. She heard all of it. It was both fascinating and disgusting. She covered her eyes in dismay. God, this was so messed up, but Greg was right. She'd brought this on herself. She'd been too wild, too careless, too much of a party girl.

Ransom came back out when he finished brushing his teeth. The darkness behind Lola's lids got darker, and she knew he'd turned out all the lights. She could hear the bed sigh under his weight, and the whisper of the sheets as he pulled them up over his body. Without drugs to dull her senses, she was hyper aware of every sound of his existence. She could even hear his breathing, in, out, slow, calm. *This must be the quietest hotel ever*, she thought, *to hear him so clearly.*

In the end, it was his slow, steady breathing that finally delivered her into sleep.

4.
UNSETTLED

She was grateful he let her sleep until afternoon, but when she woke, there was another healthy breakfast, another forced walk through the busy streets of Hamburg. This time they walked around the lake beside the hotel, through the touristy area. A couple of people recognized her and stopped to ask for photos and autographs, which made her feel better even if she felt like shit.

Ransom said nothing about her meltdown the night before. She'd been stone cold sober enough to remember everything, which sucked. He hardly spoke at all on their walk, aside from telling her which way to go when they came to a corner, and coaching her through intersections like she needed help crossing the street.

Whatever. She was coming to accept this as her life for now, but it was only a few more weeks before the tour ended and she could return to her regular activities in L.A. She had a great house there, and lots of friends to party with. She'd also accumulated a sizeable stable of fuckbuddies. Tons of men wanted her, so she could take her pick and demand whatever she wanted from them. Now that she had money and fame, she could pretty much get whatever she wanted from anyone.

Except one person.

She slid a look to the side, to the tall, suited bodyguard who shadowed her. What kind of freak exercised in a jacket and tie? She wore a sweater and jeans, which made more sense for a walk, but whatever.

Nothing about him made sense. Walks were stupid. He wouldn't let her listen to music when they walked either. He said it wasn't safe for her to wear earbuds, that she needed to be able to hear who was around her, and listen to his directions if something happened.

But what the fuck was going to happen? This walk was a waste, and she had work to catch up on back at the hotel. She had samples to preview and songs to listen to, beats that people sent her from all over the world. Even big artists sent her music, asking her to use excerpts in her tracks or live sets. Her whole life revolved around music now. Walking aimlessly? Not so much.

"When do we go back?" she asked.

He pointed to the hotel in the distance. "We're walking around the lake. We'll be back when we're back, unless you want to swim across."

He was always saying snarky shit like that, although it didn't exactly sound snarky because of his deep, formal voice. He looked Hispanic, and his last name was Hispanic, but he didn't have any noticeable accent.

She looked across the lake. Ugh. Walking was so boring. That was the only reason she decided to talk to him, to kill time. "So, where are you from?" she asked.

He shoved his hands in his pockets before he answered her. "Los Angeles. Eastside. Lived there all my life."

"Oh. You're not from, like, El Salvador or something?" She said *El Salvador* with an obnoxious Spanish accent. She thought it was funny, but he gave her an irritated look.

"Do you realize that's offensive?"

"What?" She blinked at him. "Are you racist against *El Salvadorans*?" She used the accent again. His frown deepened.

"I'm an American, Lola. I was born in L.A. My grandparents lived in Ohio and Pennsylvania before that. I'm not racist against anyone, except maybe people with pink hair."

He never smiled when he said anything, but that made it funnier. She grinned at him. "I'm just giving you a hard time because I don't like you very much."

"Unfortunately, the feeling is mutual."

They walked another moment or two in silence. Then she asked, "Do you hate all your clients?"

He gave a big, dramatic sigh. "No. Not always. But nine times out of ten, my protectees and I don't get along."

Ooh, *protectees*. How official and bodyguard-y. "If you don't get along with most of your protectees, why do you do this job?"

It took him longer to answer this time. "The money's good," he finally said, "and the opportunity came along at the right time." She could tell by his expression that wasn't the whole story, just what he was willing to tell her.

"I suppose you earn that money, working with pains in the ass like me. How long have you been doing this? Bodyguarding and stuff?"

"A while now. Almost eleven years."

"You're married, huh?"

He turned to her, his brows drawn together. "Why do you think I'm married?"

"I don't know. Because you're old, and you always wear a suit."

"First of all, I'm not old. I just turned thirty-seven." He straightened his tie. "And I wear a suit because I'm a professional, not because I'm married."

"So you're not married?"

"Not yet. But I've got a pretty big extended family. Parents, stepparents, four sisters, three brothers, and all of them have been churning out kids."

"Do you like to hang with your nieces and nephews?"

His frown deepened. "When I get back to the old neighborhood, yeah. It's tough to make time in this business. I work a lot."

"Building up a nest egg for when you get married and have kids?"

"What's with you and the marriage and kids?" He turned the question on her. "Do you want to get married and have kids?"

She gave him a flirty smile. "Thanks for the invitation, but no. You're way too old for me."

She was hilarious, but he didn't appreciate her sense of humor. He only rolled his eyes. She crossed her arms over her chest, sighed, and stepped up the death march toward the hotel.

"Are you cold?" he asked.

"I'm bored." She didn't want to look at him and his judgey expressions and eye rolling. She kept her gaze forward. "I want to get back. I've got shit to do."

"What kind of shit?"

"Work shit. I do work, you know. I've got to spend time mucking around and putting beats and melodies together. Those festival sets don't just materialize out of my ass." Defensiveness crept into her voice, although she usually tried to maintain a flippant, carefree vibe. People found that more attractive than the stressed-out reality. "I have to listen to a lot of music in order to create music. I have to plan dance sets. I have to come up with new mixes or people get bored."

"People get bored, or you get bored?"

She shrugged. "What's the difference? The point is, I have to stay on my game, even when someone's trying to fuck things up."

"If you're talking about me—"

"Who else would I be talking about?" She turned to him, not being flippant or carefree at all. Oh well. He saw through her cool girl act by now. "You're the one who's living in my space and rooting through my shit, and taking away my stash so I can't relax. You're the one cock blocking me when I had two big-ass, gorgeous German guys on the hook—"

"Sometimes you act like a pig, you know that? It's not attractive."

"I'm not trying to attract you," she shot back. "And it's obnoxious to call a woman a pig."

"I call it like I see it. You would have just used Hans and Franz and sent them home?"

"Why not? Guys do that kind of thing all the time."

"Some guys," he said under his breath.

"What?"

"Not all guys do that," he said in a louder voice. "Not all guys objectify women and use them as throwaway objects for sex."

Lola huffed out an irritated noise. She was done with this conversation. What the fuck did he care, anyway?

"It's none of your fucking business," she muttered.

"Your safety and well-being is my business, at least until the end of this tour."

They stepped out of the way to let some young kids run by. "You keep saying that," she said, "but you're making me miserable."

He didn't answer. She thought if he had, he would have said *The feeling is mutual* again, so she was glad he kept his mouth shut. They returned to the hotel in stony silence. Lola retreated into her solitary, aural world for the rest of the afternoon, blocking him out with headphones. She made notes for that evening's set, and saved a few ideas for future mixes. She categorized each song in her library by beats per minute, whether it was her work or someone else's. The cardinal law of EDM mixing: know your beats.

Later, backstage at the festival, Ransom followed her like a fucking bloodhound. She'd hoped to score some pills before her set, but in the end, she had to take the stage sober. It was still fun to rile up the crowd and make music. Just not as fun. Now and again she looked to the side, and there he was at the top of the stairs from backstage, standing with his arms crossed over his chest. He never danced, just watched. He made her feel imprisoned a little, and smothered.

But in some way, he also made her feel safe.

* * * * *

Ransom banged out a second set of push-ups, tensing his muscles as the purple-carpeted floorboards vibrated beneath his palms. As soon as they boarded the Lady Paradise tour bus, Greg and Lola had disappeared into their rooms, leaving Ransom to cool his heels in the central living area.

They were on their way to Amsterdam, on a drive that was almost, but not quite, long enough to say *Fuck it, let's take a flight.* When you factored in airport and security nonsense, it just made more sense to drive. Tour buses were part of the musician mystique, he supposed. This one had dark velvet covered benches, gleaming chrome walls, and royal purple shag carpet that didn't quite stifle the noise of the road.

Or the other noises.

Ransom completed his set, sat back on his heels, and listened. She was still at it. At first, he'd thought she was masturbating. Lord knew she was a horny little monster. She'd almost taken his head off when he'd refused to let her enjoy her Hamburg threesome.

But no, she wasn't masturbating. She was crying, and trying to be quiet about it. Ransom had pretty good ears, and those ears were attuned first and foremost to his client. She was making pitiful sounds, muffled sobs and gasps, and occasional squeaks that could only be described as injured-baby-animal grief.

He didn't think her set was that bad. Maybe she wasn't crying over that. Maybe she was crying because of Hans and Franz.

No. Women didn't make injured baby animal sounds over men they'd picked up in a nightclub. Those types of guys doubtless offered themselves to Lady Paradise in every city.

He lowered himself to hands and toes and did another set of push-ups with his tie tucked between the buttons of his shirt. When he was finished, he stood and stretched, and did some squats along the abbreviated length of the common area before coming to rest beside the kitchenette. He took out a water bottle and drained it. He could still smell the smoke machine chemicals in his clothes. That shit had to be toxic. Lord knew how much of it Lola inhaled in a typical week, but that might explain her erratic behavior and crazy ass moods.

He walked back over to her bedroom door and stood outside, listening. They were on the highway, so there were no stops or starts, just smooth, uninterrupted cruising. He didn't hear any more crying. He thought she might be sleeping, but then he heard a soft, melodic strum. A guitar?

He sat at the end of the velvet-cushioned bench nearest her room and listened to her aimless noodling. He didn't play guitar himself, but he recognized capability. Interesting. Lady Paradise could do more than push buttons and move levers. Why hadn't she told him so when he'd mocked her?

He decided he'd better check on her since she'd been crying. It was his job to supervise her, to make sure she was safe. He wasn't one to coddle and comfort a sobbing client, but now that she seemed to have her shit together, he ought to poke his head in and see if she needed anything.

Oh, you want to poke your head in, all right.

He ignored his all too savvy conscience and went to the kitchenette to grab more water and some kind of healthy snack. Finding nothing on the bus that qualified as "healthy," he grabbed a box of crackers instead, and headed back to her room. She was still messing around on the guitar, plucking out a hesitant melody that sounded both wistful and sweet.

He knocked when the meandering notes came to a stop. Her abrasive "What?" was in direct opposition to her soulful playing.

"It's me," he said.

"Go away."

"I have food and water. Are you dressed?"

She slid open the narrow pocket door without getting up, and glared out at him from her bedroom, which was really just a compartment built around a queen sized bed. The sheets were rumpled, and the back of the platform was piled with pink pillows that matched her pink plaid pajamas and pink hair. Her eyes were still red.

He held up the water and crackers, and she reached for them. "Give me. Then go away."

"Are you playing the guitar?"

She still had it cradled in her lap. She gave him a withering look. "What, are you listening at my door?"

"I can hear it from out there." He flicked a thumb over his shoulder. "It sounds nice." He paused. "Is everything okay?"

"Everything's fine," she said too quickly. "I was just winding down."

"Must be hard to wind down after those sets. They're pretty loud and intense."

"Yeah."

He leaned against the narrow doorway, thinking of topics that might engage her. If he could bond with her, even a little, the next few weeks might be easier for both of them. She gave her light wood guitar an accidental strum as she opened the box of crackers.

"You going to eat those in bed?" he asked. "Cracker crumbs in your sheets will make it even harder to sleep."

"I never sleep on the bus." She pulled out a sleeve of crackers, tore it open, and started popping them in her mouth. "I mean, I try buh I'ff nefer—"

He held up a hand as she spewed cracker crumbs. "Swallow first. Then talk."

She finished what was in her mouth and twisted open the water bottle. "I try, but I've never been able to drift off without..." She grimaced. "Pharmaceutical help."

He shook his head when she offered him some crackers, and tried to tune his anti-drug message to her wavelength. "Pharmaceuticals can help in the moment," he said, "but long term, they can really mess you up."

"I know, Mr. Life Coach. Do you think I don't know that?"

He nodded at her guitar before she could work herself into another sass attack. "What came first?" he asked. "The sound console or the guitar?"

She studied him as she pounded a couple more crackers, then scooted sideways and gestured to the bed. "If we're going to talk and shit, it would be more comfortable if you weren't towering over me."

"We can sit in the other room."

"I never sit in there. The couches suck."

He agreed that the couches sucked, but it would be unprofessional to lounge on her bed with her. Then again, he didn't want to rebuff her when she was finally acting friendly.

When she scooted over a little more, he gave in and sat next to her, keeping his feet on the floor. That way he wasn't officially in bed with her, right? *Even though you'd love to be in bed with her.*

Damn. He was still waiting for familiarity to blunt the attraction he felt for this pink-haired slice of trouble. One night with a real woman and he'd be over Lola's allure, but he wasn't dating anyone, and even if he was, he was in the middle of a European bus tour. He rubbed his eyes. It was late, but his body felt wide awake.

"Want me to play something for you?" she asked through a mouthful of crackers.

"Don't choke on those."

She grinned and took a sip of water. "What kind of music do you like, Ransom?"

"Classic rock. Grunge. Anything with a good melody."

Her grin turned into a laugh. "Grunge has good melodies?"

He gave her the bodyguard glower. "You're going to judge what I like? The only melody in that music you make is *loud* or *louder*. *Fast* or *faster*. Louder and faster is pretty much the apex of what you do."

If she wasn't in a teasing mood, he wouldn't have poked her. But seriously, judging his musical tastes when she made electronic noise for a living?

"I can play melodies," she said. She handed him the sleeve of crackers, which she'd mostly demolished, and brushed her fingers against her pajama pants. Such a child. Such a mess. She curled around the guitar like she was hugging it rather than playing it, and began to strum some aimless chords.

Ransom listened. His first impulse was always to scoff at her, to belittle her because she was such a brat, but the music she played was...beautiful. It wasn't a song he knew, but it was intricate and soothing, a simple melody constructed in a plaintive key. Now and again, she hummed along, or sang words he couldn't decipher. When she finished and looked at him, he had no choice but to compliment her.

"That was cool. Did you write that?"

Even as he asked, he knew she had. She played it like someone would play their own song, with that attentive kind of love.

"I write a lot of songs," she said. She started on another, a more upbeat number, but stopped halfway through. "My father was a musician in Memphis. A blues guitarist. He couldn't read a note of music but he could play anything." She laughed softly to herself. "He made me take music lessons, but the joke was that I never got as good as him." She sobered. "He died of a heart attack when I was fifteen. It majorly sucked."

Ransom noted the tender emotion flitting across her features. "I'm sorry. I imagine that was hard."

"It was, because my mom was already gone and my father was..." She got a little choked up. "He was my whole world, you know? Beale Street and his clubs and music, and his friends. His laughter. He had a huge laugh. You could hear it over everything, even the music. He really lived life. My mom had died, you know, from cancer. I hardly remember her, I was just a little kid."

You're still a little kid, he thought. Maybe this was why she acted so crazy sometimes. It had to be tough to lose both parents by the age of fifteen. He'd read all this in her background file, but to hear her tell it in her sad, self-conscious way ripped at his heart. "I'm sorry," he said again. "There should be a rule that parents can't die until you're grown."

"Are your parents alive?"

"Yes." And he didn't appreciate them, because they drove him crazy. His mom smothered him with selfless love, while his father obsessed about *family*, *legacy*, and *honor*. Every time he visited, they asked when he would come back to church and marry a nice girl, and give them some grandkids. Jesus, like they didn't already have enough. He sighed. "My parents and I haven't always seen eye to eye. There were a lot of years I wasn't a model son."

"Were they high pressure parents? You could never be good enough?" She eyed him. "That would explain a lot."

This pink-haired hot mess was going to play therapist? "It's not that they were high pressure," he said. "I just didn't live up to their ideals. I took some wrong turns in my twenties."

"What kind of wrong turns?"

"The kind of wrong turns that twenty year olds make. I listened to the wrong people and made some destructive choices." He arched a brow. "Kind of like someone else I know."

She ignored that dig and started playing a song that was so pretty and complex he lost the thread of their conversation. He was content to listen as her fingers danced over the strings. "My dad could jam like this forever," she said when she finished. "He came up with songs all day long. Not just the blues. Any melody that sounded interesting. I wish I had half his talent."

"I don't know. You're pretty good. Probably almost as good as him."

She gave a laugh that wasn't quite a laugh. "I'm good at selling myself. Playing a role. I'm good at making people dance, but he was a better musician than I'll ever be. He really felt the music."

"You feel the music." Ransom waved his arms in a reenactment of that evening's performance. "I've seen you dance during your sets. You're feeling something."

"I mean, I feel it. It's hard not to feel it when it's beating you over the head, like rave music does. But there's really only one emotion in EDM, you know?" She plucked a lonely note. "There's only happy. I mean, that's what it's all about. Get happy, get high, lose your mind like everyone else is doing. You never see sad people at raves. If there was someone crying in the audience, what would everyone think?"

She looked past him, at nothing, still plucking random notes on her guitar. *You were crying*, he wanted to say. *You're sad. What would everyone think?*

"Do you know how to play?" she asked.

"No, I don't play anything. I didn't have the patience for music as a kid, although I killed on the soccer field."

She laughed again. She had the brightest, easiest laugh for someone with so much secret pain. "Soccer, huh?"

"I wanted to be an international superstar, but it turned out you had to be pretty good for that. I got too big, too gangly."

"Poor Ransom. So you went into security instead, and now here you are, looking after a crazy EDM artist."

There'd been another life between soccer and security, but he wasn't going into that. "I still dream about getting the call one day. You know, European leagues or something."

She smiled, and her gaze slid over his shoulders and chest. He supposed she was imagining him as an athlete, perhaps admiring his muscles. He didn't go out of his way to flaunt his physique, but it pleased him that she noticed.

He should have done more push-ups. He should have stayed out in the other room. This was too close, and she was too sleepy and sexy and complicated and talented.

"Do you want to try?" she asked.

Try what? Try sex? Try putting my cock in your pussy? Yes. No. Help me, God. He realized she was talking about the guitar, holding it out to him.

"Um. No. Probably not. I don't know anything about music."

"It's not hard."

Next thing he knew, she was on her knees next to him, smiling and shoving the guitar into his lap. She lifted his left hand, showing him how to press his fingers against the strings.

"If you learn a few chords, you can play almost anything. All those classic rock songs people love? They're made up of, like, three or four chords. Anyone can play them."

"I don't—"

"No, look. This is E minor. Two fingers, and they use it in tons of songs. Try it."

She was kneeling against his back, her arms around his, forcing him to play even though he could think of nothing besides the warmth and feel of her body.

"No, these fingers," she said, snaking an arm around him to correct his fingering. "Okay, now strum."

She put her hand over his and guided his fingers across the strings. It made a nice, full sound. He knew nothing about guitars, but this one seemed very similar to its owner: glossy and curvy, and full of life. Maybe it just felt that way because her fingers were on his, little twenty-year-old fingers over his big, rough, older-bodyguard fingers. He wanted to take those fingers and twist them behind her back, and bend her over, and...

No. He couldn't let his mind go there. He was so unsettled by his flagging self-control that he allowed her to teach him another chord.

"See?" she said, like he was already mastering them. He'd forget them by tomorrow. The shock of her body against his? He'd remember that his entire life. "Okay, now put them together and you're making music."

She was so enthusiastic he had to laugh, even though none of this was funny. He let her coach him through the progressions. "E minor, C, C, E minor. Strum! Now, guess what, you can play *Eleanor Rigby* with only those two chords."

"Bullshit."

He turned his head when she laughed, saw pink hair and pink pajamas and everything that could ruin him if he wasn't careful.

"I'll show you how to do it," she said. "It's possible for real."

With her fingers guiding his, they played an iffy, halting rendition of the Beatles' *Eleanor Rigby*. He thought it was pretty amazing. He thought it was probably the most fun anyone could have in a tiny bedroom on a tour bus in Europe in the middle of the night.

Well, almost the most fun.

"You did great," she said when they finished. "You're a quick learner."

He acknowledged her compliment with a nod as she finally slid away from him. "All part of the job. I have to think fast." He handed over her guitar and stood. As enjoyable as this interlude was, it was his responsibility to bring it to a close. "It's getting late, kid. You might as well sleep the rest of the way to Amsterdam. We can check into the hotel when we get there."

She turned away from him, laying the guitar in a worn black case. "I told you, I never sleep on the bus, not without drugs or..." She paused as she closed the lid and flicked the latches shut. "Well. Marty used to hold me. Sometimes when he held me, with the road noise and the vibration, I was able to drift off."

Ransom was already shaking his head. No. Slope. Slippery. Full of prickly bushes and pointy rocks. "I can't lie in bed and hold you," he said, because that was the plain truth. "It's not part of my job."

Two bright dots of color bloomed on her cheeks. "Yeah, I know."

"Not that I don't want to help you. It's just—"

"I know."

"Not professional."

"Can we let it drop?" Her blush deepened. "I was just telling you that Marty used to do it, and it used to work for me. But he's gone now, so..."

Ransom waited for the rest of it, some flailing stab at seducing him, or some vitriol about his part in firing Marty, but nothing else came. *Time for you to leave, sport. This awkward silence? That's your cue.*

"Well, good night," he said. "Even if you don't sleep."

"Good night."

He went sideways through the door and heard it close behind him with a thump. Catastrophe averted. In some horrible way, it was tempting to curl up next to her, but in some other, more rational way, he knew that would lead to all kinds of fucked up shit. She was a client and he was a professional. He was old enough to know better.

He just needed one night with a real woman. That would put all this inappropriate attraction to rest.

5.
BREATHE

They had four days in Amsterdam before the festival, and by the end of the second day, Lola was losing her shit.

No sex. No partying. No wandering around and getting into trouble with the local club folk. Nothing. No fun.

Oh, he'd take her wherever she wanted to go, but once she was there, he was on her tail like a fucking deer tick, and nothing could pull him away. She'd been sure she could score some ecstasy from the team of EDM producers she met with on Thursday, but no. An entire day in the studio, and he was at her elbow the whole time. The producers loved his suit and red tie, and thought he was cool because he never talked. They dubbed him Random Ransom, and needled him to give opinions on the tracks they laid down.

She wanted to scream at him to go away.

As long as she agreed to walk with him during the day—ugh, those walks—he let her go out to the clubs at night, but by the third night she gave up and stayed in, because nothing fun could permeate his iron barricade of control.

It was hard to hit on potential sex partners when a man in a suit was standing beside you scowling at them. And of course, he did everything he could to look like a fucking DEA agent in his fucking business suits, so no one carrying drugs would even look her way.

She was in Amsterdam, where they had the best party scene, the loosest laws, the strongest drugs, and she was helpless to take advantage of it. Her mojo was fucked up from lack of sex and she was PMSing hard, and everything in life sucked, and it was his fault. This tour was supposed to be the time of her life. Fame could be fleeting, and youth was definitely fleeting. When she explained this to him, he gave her that judgey look that made her want to punch his handsome face.

"You need to stay healthy," he'd say. "Don't party so hard. You have a long life ahead of you."

Just a few more weeks and she'd be rid of him, and then, fuck, she'd party like crazy. She'd reunite with her L.A. posse and make up for all this lost time, and he wouldn't have any authority over her anymore because the tour would be done. When she told him that, he joked that he was going to keep coming to her for guitar lessons.

But she hadn't given him any more lessons because it was too hard to be that close to him when she was starved for sex. Just touching him made her wet. No, just looking at him made her wet.

Which really sucked, because she hated him with the fire of a million suns.

If she couldn't have sex, she at least needed some happy pills before the Amsterdam show. The whole crowd would be high and she wanted to be high too. She was sure she could get something at the venue. She only needed to slip away from Ransom for five minutes to find a provider and make a deal. She'd watched Marty do it plenty of times. She had a wad of cash in her pocket, and room to store the ecstasy tablets in that same pocket once she bought them. If she could buy a few extra, she'd have some for the next show too.

An hour before her set, Lola was ready to rock Amsterdam—and get high. Her hair was done up in fun pins and twists, her makeup was applied, her bikini top was double knotted, and her shorts had deep pockets that zipped. Once they got backstage, Greg gave her the out she needed, taking her to the restricted area to introduce her to the head sound guy, a pierced, tattooed gargoyle who reeked of pot. She pitched into a discussion with him about the songs on her set list until Greg got bored and wandered away. As soon as he was gone, she asked the guy if there was anyone backstage who could sell her some ecstasy.

His chubby cheeks spread in a smile. "You want Rave Dave."

"Hell, yeah, I want Rave Dave. I need Rave Dave. Show me where he is. Quickly, please." She looked over her shoulder, but Ransom wasn't allowed back here and Greg was chatting up a dude in the VIP area.

Five minutes later, Lola had made the acquaintance of Rave Dave and scored a bonus quantity of the best ecstasy available. It took all her money, but he assured her the tablets were epically pure. "Don't take too much," he warned after she popped the first pill. "You're small. Start with one."

"I always take two." She waved her bottle of electrolyte water. "I'm super hydrated. It'll be fine." She took the second one and zipped the rest of the tablets into her shorts pocket just as Greg came meandering back.

"All set?" he asked.

"All set."

They returned to Ransom, who stood by the stage entrance looking out at the audience. "You ready for this?" he asked, turning back to her. "Biggest crowd yet."

She detected a note of admiration in his voice. It made her feel good that he respected her work, but it also made her feel guilty. He was trying to psyche her up to do a sober show when she'd just pounded two doses of ecstasy.

She didn't want to deceive him. It was just that he didn't get it. He didn't understand how the rave thing worked. She had to feel the music in a more heightened way, especially in a huge venue like this. She had to escape into it. She had to let go in order to let her music go.

The act before hers was winding down, and she still wasn't feeling much effect from the ecstasy. While the techs set up for her time slot, she broke one of the extra tablets in half and washed it down with lots of electrolyte water. The water didn't taste so bad once you got used to it, and the electrolyte boost helped before a show. She stuck in her ear plugs and hopped up and down on her toes. A familiar floating feeling suffused her as the ecstasy began to take effect.

God, very nice. Nice shit. Rave Dave had come through for her, and it wasn't too strong at all. Since she had two entire hours to party, she took the other half of the tablet when Ransom's back was turned.

There, three pills was the perfect amount for a big gig like this. Now she was ready. Hell yeah. The festival field was packed. There were thousands of ravers swarming in front of the stage like ants on an anthill.

Balls bounced in the air. Glow sticks waved and lights flashed in psychedelic patterns that made her heart sing. These were her people and this was her life, and she was going to surround them in sick beats until they were off their heads.

She looked to the side and saw Ransom standing at the top of the stage stairs. Not leaning, or sitting on the edge of the platform the way the techs sometimes did. He always stood straight and tall, and watched her just like a bodyguard would. She didn't know why that made her feel so tingly and pleased. Maybe it was the ecstasy. She noticed him putting in his ear plugs, and thought she'd better put hers in too.

Oh, yeah. She had them in already. Ha.

At last they announced her. Gibberish, gibberish, gibberish, LADYYYY PARADIIIISE. The crowd went crazy and Lola felt warm and magical and radiant with love. She was Lady Paradise, and the Paradise groove was magnificent. She kicked in the first set of beats, watching the electronic tones dance in the air like fairies. One rhythm led to another, and to another, woven together with melodies she'd dreamed of her whole life. *I love you, I love you, I love you.* This was the acceptance she craved, the feeling of fitting in. All of this was love, and she incited her people to dance harder as strobe lights raked the crowd.

She felt so free when she was playing a set. All the notes she needed were programmed into her computers, and all the songs were at her fingertips. Sometimes she sampled other songs she liked, wound them into her own melodies until they twisted into new delights. No set was the same, and no song was the same, except the recorded versions her label distributed. She created the live music from her heart, so even the people who followed her across Europe from festival to festival heard new things at every show. *You're welcome. I fucking love you.*

A photographer flitted around her as she played. She flashed him a smile and a peace sign. She couldn't stop grinning. The thing about ecstasy was that it could make you feel all powerful, like the God of your own world. She tried to remember she wasn't all powerful, but it was hard when the music was jamming and the lights were flashing in perfect rhythm. Energy surged through her veins until she wanted to jump out of her skin. She wanted to dive into the crowd, but then the pills might fall out of her pocket, and besides, Ransom had told her not to. What had he said? He'd make her run five miles.

Right now she felt like she could run twenty-five miles. Two hundred and twenty-five miles. She looked over at him. He frowned back at her. What was wrong with him, seriously? Out of the jillion bazillion people on this field in Amsterdam, he was the only one who wasn't shaking his ass. Too bad, because he had a great ass. She hadn't gotten laid in forever. How many days since Marty left? And Marty sucked in bed. She preferred the professionals, the gigolos, but she couldn't always find them, and now...

Too bad Ransom was so uptight in the fun department. He'd make a great gigolo if the bodyguard thing didn't work out. She imagined dragging him onto the stage and making him feel the music. If only she could make him *feel*, they'd both be so much happier. She'd take off his clothes and dance naked with him on top of the sound console, then throw him down and fuck him in the middle of the stage, with the lights and fog machines, and the ravers dancing, and the beautiful beats rattling their souls as they found ecstasy.

Ecstasy. Ha. She started laughing as the music built to a hammering crescendo. She wasn't laughing because anything was funny. She was laughing because life was amazing, and people were amazing, and her bodyguard was gorgeous even if he didn't dance. Maybe she'd ask him to fuck her when the set was over. He'd probably say yes. Men always said yes to her.

"That's the plan, that's the plan," she sang, even though no one could hear her over the music. The photographer snapped another photo as she pressed a button, killed the buildup and initiated the drop. The stage rattled so hard from the bass, it felt like it was falling apart. The crowd went apeshit and Lola jumped in manic bliss. She could have jumped forever, for five miles, easily. She felt like she was jumping ten feet in the air.

The crowd was a blur, but the beats went on, and her mind raced to keep up with the beautiful world. The stage manager swung by, holding up two hands. Wow, ten minutes to go? What had happened to the time? She'd been playing for almost two hours, but she could have played four more hours. Forty more hours. She laughed again. Yeah, as long as the pills held out. She started building toward another massive drop, the final drop. She'd make it a masterpiece.

She wove the beats in a new way, driven by the glittering images in her head. *This beat goes here. This beat goes there. These melodies play together nice. Oh, so nice, like E minor and C.* She swayed, waving her hands in the air. The crowd was an undulating mass, illuminated by a blinding light show. *Yes, yes, yes, jump, jump, jump, me, me, me, me, me, you, you, you, you, yooouuu...*

When the drop came, it was crazy hot. She almost did a stage dive. She almost ran to the edge of the platform and threw herself into the beautiful sea of people, but her chest felt aflame with all her happiness, and she worried she might set the crowd on fire.

Instead, she danced until the end of the song and took a bow. The crowd's love rolled toward her like a neon tide. She basked in it as the ravers screamed her name. *PARADISE! PARADISE! PARADIIIIIISE!*

She loved these people. She adored them. She blew a few final kisses and ducked behind the sound console to get her water. She felt so wonderful, so happy and high. Rave Dave had the best fucking shit on the planet, the most phenomenal shit of all time. She decided to sneak another half pill before she was back in Ransom's clutches, just to celebrate, just because she'd fucking killed that set.

"Great show, Lady," someone shouted.

She swallowed and turned, and saw the chubby cheeked sound tech from backstage. They shared a fist bump. The photographer gave her a thumbs up. The crowd still roared her name, but she had to go. She waved and headed toward the stairs. Greg met her at the edge of the stage.

"Amazing set, babe. Crowd went out of their minds!"

She couldn't stop smiling. "Thank you."

"What can I get you? Need more water?"

She ignored Greg and danced over to Ransom, pulling out her ear plugs. "Did you love the set? Did you totally love it?"

He didn't smile. He didn't look like he'd loved the set. "Are you ready to go?" he asked.

He was so beautiful. His voice was so deep and rich and *beautiful*. "You're beautiful," she said, wrapping her arms around his waist.

"Right." He gripped her elbows and tried to dislodge her. "I think we need to get you back to the hotel."

The photographer returned, documenting her deep love for her bodyguard. She smiled and waved at the man, then turned and licked

Ransom's face for the camera, because his stubble felt amazing on her tongue. Greg laughed. Ransom held her waist hard. Wow, he was strong! She flung her arms around his neck and his warmth was her warmth. She wanted him inside her. He was so strong and beautiful, a perfect specimen of manhood.

"I want your manhood," she said, wrapping her legs around his waist. Greg wouldn't stop laughing. The backstage was crazy with people, but all she could think about was how great it felt to be in Ransom's arms, with her body pressed to his. He started walking, turning his face away when she tried to kiss him.

"I love you," she said in his ear, then nibbled his earlobe. "I want to fuck you so bad. I want to fuck you and fuck you and fuck you. I love you so much I could fucking eat you."

He didn't say anything, but she was pretty sure he felt the same.

* * * * *

Ransom carried his writhing client onto the bus to the sounds of Greg's maniacal laughter.

"What the fuck?" He spun on him. "Are you high too? Seriously? What the fuck is going on here? What did she take?"

Greg worked to compose himself, then held up his hands. "Nothing. I gave her nothing."

"She's—" He ducked away as she licked his jaw again. "She's off her face, man."

"She wants you."

Ransom tried to pry Lola away, but as soon as he removed her, she was on him again like a spider monkey.

"I love you," she said for the fortieth time. "You're *so strong*."

"Jesus." They didn't pay him enough for this. He grabbed her shoulders and tried to catch her gaze but she was flying in the ethersphere, and Greg was a giggling mess.

"It's Amsterdam," her manager said, waving his hands like there were still beats. "Everyone's high here. She played the set of the century. Didn't you see?"

Oh, yeah, Ransom had seen it. She'd been pure joy, pure genius. Pure ecstasy. He'd thought she was sober. He'd been so fucking impressed with her performance until he realized she was chemically altered.

He'd fallen in love with her a little as she reigned over that massive crowd and spun a seamless set of pounding melodies. He hated this electronic shit, but even he had to admit the set was inspired. She'd inspired him, and then she'd devastated him because after all his efforts to reform her, his client was high again. He had to figure out how, and why, and keep it from happening again. He'd only left her alone for the sound check, entrusting her to Greg's supervision.

He scowled at her tripping manager. Lesson learned.

Now she was clinging to him, a quivering bundle of sexualized nerve endings riding a chemical high. She reached down again to fondle him. The worst thing was, his body responded to her. It responded to her energy and boldness. It responded to Lady Paradise, who'd stood on that stage and made the world a million different sounds and colors.

"Stop that," he said, pushing her hand away from his thickening cock.

"I love you. I want you to fuck me."

"I know you want me to fuck you, but I didn't give you permission to touch me that way."

She didn't seem to care. He patted her down at the same time she groped his body. He found what he was searching for in her left zippered pocket. He removed the bag of ecstasy tablets and held it out of her reach when she started grabbing for it. She climbed him like a junkie and he let her fall when she lost her grip on him. Greg laughed while Lola wailed, and then she laughed too. "Oh, fuck," she giggled, clutching her chest. "My heart. Jesus." Her features tensed, then she burst into laughter again.

Ransom stood over her, watching her. "What do you mean, your heart?"

"I love you," she said. "I love you, bodyguard."

He knelt beside her and tried to take her pulse, but she squirmed and reached for him again. "Stay down," he ordered, in a voice harsh enough to subdue her even though she was high.

She lay back and watched him, winding her fingers through her wrecked hair. Her pulse rate was alarmingly high. He put a hand over her chest, over her skimpy bikini top, and felt her heart pumping faster than any of the beats she'd played.

"How do you feel?" he asked.

She gazed up at him through dilated eyes. "I love you."

"Besides loving me, how do you feel? Lola, this is serious. Answer me."

She put her hand on top of his. "My chest hurts. It burns."

"Stay there, okay? Don't move." He turned to Greg. "Help me out, man. Keep her still."

Greg got down on the floor beside her, his eyes as dark and dilated as Lola's. Ransom muttered a curse and dug an ecstasy test kit out of the first aid bag. The tests were as ubiquitous as the drugs at these festivals. They helped identify if the tablets exchanging hands were pure and safe, or adulterated with hazardous shit like meth, BZP, or fentanyl. While Lola and Greg stared at each other and made fucked up conversation, Ransom crushed one of the tablets and added the reagents.

Shit, shit, shit. The test lit up hard for mCPP and amphetamines. He looked over at his client. Greg was still talking but Lola had gone silent.

"You okay?" he asked. She looked so fragile. She reached out to him with trembling fingers.

He knelt next to her and propped her against his side. Greg was still talking to himself, soft, gentle babbling as he caressed his own face.

"How's your breathing?" Ransom asked.

She tried to lick him again. "You're beautiful."

"Fuck. Come down. Come the fuck down. How much did you fucking take?" He tapped her face as she zoned out. "How many tablets did you take, Lola?"

Her eyes darted around, seeing nothing. She wasn't there anymore. She was somewhere else, probably thanks to the mCPP, which caused hallucinatory trips. The meth was wreaking havoc with her heart rate, and she was too small to metabolize it the way an adult male might.

"Lola Mae," he said, shaking her. "Stay here. Come back to me."

"Don't." She trembled in his grip. "I'm tired. It burns."

He put a finger on her neck and started counting. 180 beats per minute. 200. 220. She was too small. The veins stood out in her neck as she sucked in air.

"Greg." He kicked her useless tour manager. "Greg, go get the medics."

He giggled and turned over. Useless.

"Greg. Fucker. Wake the fuck up." He kicked him harder. Nothing. He picked up Lola and carried her to the door. The bus driver stood outside, smoking a cigarette.

"Are you high?" he asked.

He was an older man. He had a kind face. "I'm not high," he said, flicking down his cigarette. He glanced at Lola. "Need something?"

"I need medical help, as quickly as possible."

"The medical station's right over there," he said, gesturing to a tent about five hundred yards away.

"Help me get there. Please. Help me make my way through this crowd. It's an emergency."

The man nodded and set off with him toward the tent, nudging a path through the sparkling, flashing festival goers who pointed and squealed as Lady Paradise went by. *Hurry, hurry, hurry.*

Ransom pressed Lola to his chest to make sure she was still breathing. "It's going to be okay," he told her. "You have bad stuff in your system, but it's only temporary."

"I can't... I can't..."

"Don't panic. Slow breaths."

She rested her head on his shoulder, shuddering, panting against his neck. She was probably on a scary trip above and beyond the physical suffering. Part of him thought, *well, she deserves it*. Part of him thought, *don't die*. He pulled her closer, rubbing her back as they neared the red and white tent.

"Breathe with me, Lola Mae." He moved his hand up and down her spine like that might stop her heart's dangerous acceleration. "Take deep breaths, in and out."

"I can't," she gasped, a broken whisper. "I can't feel my brain. I took— I took three."

"When?"

"And a half."

"Jesus Christ. When?"

"Just— Before— Help."

He closed his eyes and rested his head against her soft pink hair, and prayed. Three and a half shitty, amphetamine-laced pills. She was a brat, but he didn't want her to die. He knew CPR. He could keep her alive if her heart stopped, but what if they couldn't start it again?

When he jostled her to keep her awake, she started babbling about drowning, flailing at the slack mouthed ravers they passed. He tried to keep her from hurting anyone. Whatever she'd ingested had sent her into chemical, mental breakdown.

"Breathe," he said. "Breathe with me. You're gonna be okay."

The medics looked up as they barged into the tent. The bus driver explained the situation as Ransom soothed Lola through another flailing panic. They waved him through the back, to a waiting ambulance with open doors.

"I can't breathe," she sobbed as the medics climbed in behind them. "Can't... Drowning... Scared... Stay..."

"I'm here."

They had to strap her down on the gurney, and even then she kept trying to reach for him.

"H-help m-me."

I'm trying. I'm trying to help but you fucked up this time. He told the EMTs what he knew about the drugs, and when she'd taken them. In the back of his mind, he kept thinking, *I threw away the tablets Marty got her.* Marty was an asshole, but he would have known enough to test the drugs he bought for her. Lola, on the other hand, must have bought from the first dealer she could find, and taken the shit without testing it first. His fault for letting her out of his sight. His fault for underestimating her craziness.

His fault for taking away her safe pills.

"Deep breaths," he said as they struggled to start an IV in her jerking arm. He kept repeating it, like he could fix what was wrong with her. "Deep breaths, kid. Come on. Please."

"Can't..."

"You have to. Stay calm. Breathe in, breathe out."

"Just wanted...fun..."

She went limp and passed out, panting even in unconsciousness. The medics said something to each other in Dutch, and Ransom didn't ask for a translation. You could tell, in just about any language, when something wasn't good.

6.
THE MONEY

"Illegal drugs," said Mr. Fuckhead, CEO of MadDance Fucking Incorporated. "This is exactly what we were afraid of."

Ransom bit his tongue rather than point out that their entire rave business was built on the backs of illegal drugs.

The MadDance contingent consisted of Mr. Fuckhead and Mr. Asshole, both of them gray-haired businessmen who cared more about money than the human being they discussed. It made Ransom furious.

His boss at Ironclad, Liam Wilder, leaned forward to address Fuckhead and Asshole in a polite but firm voice.

"I'd like to reiterate that it was *your* tour manager who enabled Miss Reynolds this time. My agent left her under Greg Plume's supervision, and that was when she procured the adulterated drugs."

Liam was in a suit like them, but he didn't have gray hair, and he wasn't an asshole. Unlike the other suits, he'd actually visited Lola's hospital bed and gazed down at her sleeping figure with true concern in his eyes.

As for Greg, he was gone. The manager's firing had been the first order of business. The rest of the "team" was huddled in a lounge down the hall from Lola's hospital room.

The taller man, Fuckhead, frowned down at the paperwork in front of him. "You must understand our concern. We hired Mr. Gutierrez because you said he was the best. We hired him to keep our performer sober."

"You also hired Greg Plume," countered Liam. "If not for Mr. Gutierrez's presence—and his sobriety—Lola might have died last night."

Ransom suppressed a shudder. It had been so close. He'd seen death in her heaving chest and pained features. Her pulse had raced into the mid 200s. If she'd gone into cardiac arrest, he wasn't sure they would have been able to bring her back.

He'd paced outside her room for the last twelve hours, unable to sleep, unable to regroup. The MadDance jerkoffs had filed a complaint with Ironclad, and the CEO had flown in from London to assist him with the situation. Ransom was both horrified and relieved when Liam showed up. He was horrified because Liam Wilder was the big fucking boss, and he was here to clean up Ransom's mess. He was relieved because he couldn't have dealt with these assholes himself.

"Do you deny that my agent saved Lola's life last night?" asked Liam.

Fuckhead and Asshole exchanged a look. "He may have saved her life, but we're not impressed with his ability to keep her sober."

"I left her with the manager," Ransom said. That was his mistake, one that would haunt him.

"Mr. Gutierrez is one of the top agents in the world for this type of protection," Liam said to the gray-hairs. "I'd consider long and hard before I replaced him with someone else. I don't have anyone better."

And Ironclad was the best security company on the planet. The math added up, but Ransom had failed. Why? Because Lola was a reckless, brainless brat? Or because he'd been distracted by an unprofessional fascination with his client? That was the root of his mental anguish. From the moment he'd seen her twerking on top of that sound console in Brussels, he'd entertained inappropriate thoughts.

He'd fantasized about what it might be like to grasp that ass in his hands and fuck her. He wanted to throw Lola Reynolds down and go feral on her body, client or not. He never got emotional or physical with clients, but he'd gotten flustered—and hard—when she climbed all over him yesterday, and not noticed her medical crisis until it was almost too late.

He looked up at the expectant pause in the conversation. They'd asked him something. His mind was a million miles away, or just down the hall, where Lola slept. "I'm sorry. It's been a long night. Can you repeat what you just said?"

"How confident are you in your ability to keep our client safe from this point forward?" asked Liam.

"With a sober tour manager? Very confident." He cracked his knuckles under the table. "From now on, I won't let her out of my sight."

Mr. Asshole piped up. "You must understand how essential it is for Lady Paradise to complete the entire tour."

"I get it," said Ransom. "She's the money. Her name is Lola, by the way."

Mr. Asshole scowled. "Do you have any idea how much we've invested in her?"

"Probably way less than you've made."

Liam nudged his leg under the table. Ransom mashed his lips shut.

"At the end of the day, this is business," said Mr. Fuckhead, being fuck-all honest about their mercenary interests. "There's no one popular enough to replace Lady Paradise if she can't perform. Without her, the monetary loss would trickle down not just to us but to all the other artists in this festival. Her absence would disappoint attendees and create bad feelings in the EDM community toward our future promotions."

With every word, Ransom clenched his fists tighter. They didn't give a writhing fuck about Lola, who'd almost died last night. They cared about profits and future attendance. He wanted to take the contracts spread out in front of them, set them on fire, and shove them down the men's throats.

But that wouldn't accomplish anything but his firing, not just from this job, but from Ironclad altogether.

"Can we have a moment, gentlemen?" asked Liam.

Thank God. He had to get out of this room. Liam gestured for Ransom to precede him into the hall. Without thinking, he turned in the direction of Lola's room. His boss walked beside him, his tall frame almost as large as Ransom's. Female agents swooned over Liam's handsome features and shoulder length hair, but Ransom respected him for being a thoughtful person. Another boss would have fired him by now. Maybe Liam still would.

"I'm sorry," Ransom said. "I just can't stand the way they talk about her, like she's a...a commodity."

"They think about the money. We think about the person. What happened last night? Your people don't usually end up in the hospital. Is she salvageable? Are we in over our heads?"

"No, she's not a junkie. She's not seeking out the harder stuff. She takes party drugs for fun, like ninety percent of these raver kids. She just happened to buy a batch of ecstasy with stupid levels of meth and mCPP. She hasn't been using long enough to understand about testing for adulterants."

"Then you'd better educate her. That's the thing about these infant superstars. People assume they're smart because they have money and power, but they're really just..."

"Kids. She's a struggling kid, and nobody cares. Those assholes back there don't care."

"You care."

His boss accompanied those blunt words with an assessing gaze. Ransom shrugged, feeling heat rise in his cheeks. "Of course I care. She's a client. I care about my job, and Ironclad's reputation—"

"You care about her. You're torn up about this."

The stare deepened. Ransom felt the flush spread to his neck. "It was scary last night. I've never had a client code on me. I thought she was going to die in front of my eyes, and it would have been..."

Would have been so senseless. So horrific. So soul-destroying.

"It would have been a huge waste of a talent," he finished, because every other answer seemed to skirt dangerous ground.

They stopped outside her room. The curtains were drawn, but he knew what she looked like in there. Small and defenseless. Innocent, even though she wasn't innocent. Pathetic, for all her vaunted fame. "On stage, Liam, she's incredible."

"Yeah, I gather she's good at what she does."

More words burst out, rough with regret. "I hate that I fucked up on the job. I left her alone for ten minutes. I thought she was with the manager."

"They're hiring a new manager." Liam paused. "Shall I have them hire a new bodyguard? There's nothing wrong with saying a situation isn't working for you."

"No." He didn't even stop to think about it. "No, I want to finish the job."

"Are you mentally up to finishing the job? I've never seen you rattled like this. You look like hell."

Another quality Ransom admired in the Ironclad CEO—his directness.

"Not only that," his boss continued, "but you're not presenting yourself to the clients with your usual air of capability. It's natural to hate those fuckers, hell, I abhor them and everything they stand for, but they're paying for your services and you need to behave professionally. They need to be reassured that you're competent. If you want to finish this job, you've got to pull yourself together. You made a mistake, and both of you survived it. I'm assuming a mistake like that won't happen again."

"It won't."

Liam watched him for a moment, leaning back against the wall. "How's everything else? How are the two of you getting along?"

Ransom gave a short, bitter laugh. "She doesn't like me that much when she's sober."

When she was high...well. When she was high, she licked him and begged for sex. But that had no place in this conversation. "We get along well enough for a minder and client."

"Does she need rehab? Perhaps after the tour?"

"She needs better people around her. She needs to rest and eat well, and regain her equilibrium. Her life is crazy. She's achieved so much, so fast." Ransom frowned. "But I don't think she's happy."

Liam looked surprised. "She sold out thirty-five shows in the U.S. last year, and slayed all of them. Twenty more shows in Europe and Asia. Why wouldn't she be happy?"

"Fifty-five shows in a year, man. That's a lot for someone her age."

"She's what? Twenty-two?"

"Twenty."

Liam gave a low whistle. "And you're right, she's had too many assholes around her. With that said, I have other bodyguards I'd trust to take her on."

"No." He wasn't ready to give up on her yet. She needed help, and he believed he could help her, even if she was crazy and rebellious, and had pink hair. In some way, he understood her.

In some way, he saw his twenty-year-old self in her, which was the scariest thing of all.

"She doesn't have a lick of fucking sense," Ransom said, "but I want to see this through."

"You're sure?"

"I'm sure."

Liam patted his arm and nodded at Lola's room. "My assistant is in there. Mem can look after her for the next few hours while I smooth things over with these producer jerks. Go back to the hotel, shower, take a nap, and get yourself back up to speed. When she wakes up, she's going to need the fucking talk. She needs to understand that choices have repercussions."

"I know."

Liam Wilder was aware of Ransom's history—the darkest parts of his history. He knew that Ransom knew.

* * * * *

Lola heard voices, deep, low voices from far away. Her arm felt sore and her head ached. She couldn't see anything. She thought, *I've gone blind.* She heard a keening sound and realized she was the one making it. A cool hand touched her cheek.

"Shh. It's okay." Ransom's voice.

"I can't see," she whispered.

"Open your eyes."

Oh. She fluttered her lids, and then closed them again. Even the dim light was too much. "Ransom?"

"Yes?"

She cracked her lids. Everything looked white and sterile. A monitor beeped beside her bed. She felt overwhelming relief that he was there with her, that she wasn't alone. "Where am I?"

"A hospital in Amsterdam. You had a life-threatening drug reaction last night."

She opened her eyes and stared into his. He stared back, his masculine features stern and sober. Memories flashed through her disordered mind. Ransom standing by the stage stairs, the roar of the festival crowd, Rave Dave and a bag of yellow pills. Hot burning in her chest, thunder in her ears. Ransom holding her, ordering her to breathe.

He'd rubbed his hand against her back as she'd struggled to draw air. *Help me. Help me.* She'd been sure she was going to die.

"How do you feel?" he asked. "Are you awake enough to talk?"

She wanted to stay awake so he wouldn't leave her, but her eyes started to drift closed.

"Lola." His voice pried them open again. "Try to stay awake until the nurse gets here."

She didn't remember anything after that. She woke to muted sunlight and a woman taking her blood pressure. She looked around the room and saw Ransom in a chair by the window. His eyes were closed. He was asleep.

"What time is it?" she asked the nurse in a hushed voice.

"Time for you to sit up and eat something," she replied in a heavily accented whisper. "It's four o'clock in the afternoon."

The nurse seemed pleased with the blood pressure numbers and undid the Velcro cuff with a *rrrip*. The noise woke Ransom and he sat up, his shoulders taut. His intense gaze fixed immediately on her.

She stared back at him, and darker memories assailed her. The worry in his voice, the humid night air, his harsh breaths against her ear.

"You're awake," he said, as the nurse bustled out.

She didn't reply. There were words she knew she should say, but she couldn't get them out. *I'm sorry. Thank you. Are you pissed at me? Will they fire you for this?*

Why are you still wearing a tie?

When she didn't speak, he stood and walked to the side of her bed. She saw a lot of emotions in his face. Reproach, frustration, relief. He sat on the edge of the thin hospital mattress, nudging the IV tubing out of his way. She felt crowded and a little scared as he peered down at her.

"You look better," he said.

"I feel awful."

"You deserve to feel awful." A muscle ticked in his sculptured jaw, just visible through a few days' worth of stubble.

"Where's Greg?" she asked.

"Gone. Fired. There's a new guy named Iain. As far as I can tell, he's a raging prick."

She digested this news. "I'm getting everyone fired, aren't I?"

"Almost everyone." He crossed his arms over his chest. "The tour guys flew out here, and so did my boss. I wasn't fired, but they weren't happy. There was a long, uncomfortable discussion about what happens next, about how to keep this from happening again. Your overdose and hospitalization is all over the news, although some people are being kind and calling it an episode of 'exhaustion.'"

"I feel exhausted."

"I do, too." He brought his hands to his face and rubbed his forehead with unnerving ferocity. "Listen, kid. This can't happen again, because next time it might not be a hospital. It might be a coroner, and I'm being paid to keep you alive."

"Will they take that money back if I die?"

"This isn't funny. Look at me."

She did, even though she felt ashamed and sick and frightened. His voice was low, vibrating with an iron warning.

"No more drugs," he said. "Swear to me. You don't take a single fucking Advil without notifying me first."

"I won't. I don't want to." That was the honest truth. She'd thought taking ecstasy was a harmless habit, a way to let off steam and have fun. She didn't think that anymore.

"Promise me." His dark brown eyes hardened to fearsome black. "A promise is your fucking word, for what it's worth."

"I promise."

He stood from the bed and walked to the window, then turned to look at her with his hands jammed in his pockets. "The thing is, I don't believe you. I don't trust you. I was starting to trust you, but now..."

Lola closed her eyes. She wanted to scream at him to stop staring with that disappointed, accusing gaze, but she felt too weak to scream.

God, she felt *so weak*.

"I don't care if you trust me," she said. "None of it matters anyway." Tears squeezed from under her eyelids. Her face felt out of control, like her emotions. She opened her eyes and then covered them again. "Stop staring at me. Please."

She didn't know if she was crying because she was such a mess, or because *he* knew she was a mess. It was getting too hard to maintain the party girl persona everyone cheered for, the Lady Paradise character that wasn't really her. She missed being Lola Mae and getting hugs from her father. She missed her laid-back circle of friends in Memphis. That was a whole other world, a whole other life that she'd lost.

She blinked, peeking out from between her fingers. He was still watching her, his lips curved into a concerned frown. The more she tried to stifle her sobs, the more gasps and sniffles escaped.

"What can I do?" he asked. "Tell me how to help you."

"You can't help me. Just go away."

Instead of going away, he came closer. He placed a big, strong hand over her hand, over the taped IV tubing. It felt gentle and comforting, but it was *his* hand, and she was confused how she felt about him. Part of her hated him. Part of her wanted to curl up in his arms until this emotional maelstrom calmed.

But he was her bodyguard, not her boyfriend. She couldn't have boyfriends anymore, because she traveled too much and worked too much, and partied for the sake of partying, and slept with too many guys. She stared at his fingers and felt miserable and needy and stupid.

"My job is to help you," he said, and then repeated, "What can I do?"

"There's nothing you can do. I chose this life. I chose this tour."

"Do you want to quit?"

Yes, sometimes she wanted to quit, but that was spoiled and weak. She turned her face into the covers. "I can't."

"You'd lose a lot of money, but you could quit if you wanted to, if the pressure's too much. We could call the producers today."

She peered out at him through a haze of tears. He was serious. He would help her quit if she wanted it. She'd seen enough of his fucking face to understand that his expressions never lied. Did she want to quit the tour?

No, not really.

She just wanted to get better at living this life.

"I don't want to quit. I just don't know...how to handle it." Her words whispered out between sobs. "I want all of...this...but sometimes I think...I can't...handle it."

"That's common. That's normal, Lola."

Something in his steady tone calmed her down, at least enough to listen to his words.

"Fame's an adjustment for anyone," he went on, "and you're so young. But if you don't figure out how to handle it, you'll be dead by twenty-five, and no one wants that." He paused until she met his gaze. "I can help you learn to handle it, if you'll let me. We can work together. That's what I'm here to do. That's my job."

His hand still rested over hers. *That's my job.* He wasn't her boyfriend, as much as she wanted to curl up in his arms. He was her bodyguard. She hadn't really admitted until now that he was mainly guarding her from her own immature lack of control. She was drawn to his strength and sincerity, while he saw her as a total fuck up. Ugh.

She pulled her hand from beneath his, feeling the sickly twinge of the IV in her vein, or maybe just the tape pulling her skin. "I need help," she admitted. "But I don't know if you can help me. I'm pretty fucked up."

"I'll try." He touched her cheek, a soft, fleeting touch. "We'll work on life strategies and coping skills. You'll figure things out."

His kindness filled her with self-loathing. Confusion. Shame. It was so difficult to admit she needed help. Rather than taunt her for her weakness, he was offering his strength, even after she'd almost gotten him fired. He wasn't an asshole at all. He was a good guy, a hero.

If she wasn't careful, she'd fall in love with him. She buried her head in her hands.

"You okay?"

She nodded so he wouldn't touch her face again in that tender way, or come any closer. "I'll be okay. When's the next show?"

"Five days away. Saturday, in France, if you're well enough to perform."

"Paris?"

"Lyon."

She massaged her temples. "Do you think I'll be able to do it?"

"I think you'll bounce back stronger than ever, if you stop medicating yourself and get your shit in order. I don't think you want to live like this."

Her eyes leaked a few residual tears. "I don't. But I think I perform better when I'm...medicating."

"You only think you perform better. The pills make you think you're doing better sets, but you were sober in Hamburg and you were amazing. You don't need the drugs."

"Yeah, but..." She bit her lip.

"But what?"

"If I don't use drugs, then maybe I won't be..." She blinked her eyes against a new flood. Damn.

"You won't be what?" he asked.

"You know. Fun enough. Crazy enough. People expect this person..."

"What person? They expect you."

"No, they expect Lady Paradise!" She said it too loud, with too much freaked out anger. Where was the nurse? Why was she stuck here with him, melting down, tethered by machines and IVs? "You don't understand how hard it is to be this famous, exciting person all the time."

"Don't be, then." He sighed, brushing away her tears. "Rest sometimes. Be human. You're an amazing human, believe me." He wiped away more tears, then pushed her bangs back from her eyes. "I keep meaning to ask...are you naturally pink? Or do you dye this?"

A choked laugh escaped her. It kind of hurt her chest. "It's not natural," she admitted. "I'm a blonde."

He gave her a look that pretty much substituted for a blonde joke. He wasn't an asshole, but he wasn't always nice either. "I like your pink hair," he said. "And I'm looking forward to more sober performances. I think they're better. I think you're more real when you're not wacked out on chemicals. What do you think?"

"Maybe." That was all she was going to give him for now. Maybe she mixed better when she was sober. It was hard to know. "The Lyon festival's not that big," she said. "There's a bigger one the week after, outside Paris."

"I know. You have a few days to get up to speed."

A few days? She was scared. She didn't know when she'd become such a coward. She thought maybe it was the first time she'd taken the drugs Marty offered her. *It'll make things easier*, he'd said. So not true.

The nurse returned with a tray of food that looked surprisingly appetizing. "I ordered one for you, too," she said to Ransom, "even though you aren't a patient here. You will be," she scolded in a thicker accent, "if you do not get some rest."

The woman looked between the two of them. Lola wondered if she knew their story, that she was a performer, and that this was her bodyguard, who was sometimes a jerk but also sometimes a rock for her to cling to. Maybe he could help her. He was pretty damn strong.

Ransom thanked the nurse as another woman entered with a tray. Both of them stared at him far longer than necessary before filing out. Lola thought she heard them giggling in the hall.

She couldn't blame them. Ransom was hot, which was fucking hard to live with since she wasn't getting any sex. She tried not to dwell on that as she took inventory of her tray. Chicken, gravy, roll, some kind of white substance that might be mashed potatoes or cauliflower. Apple slices and a pink soufflé thing for dessert. *I like your pink hair.* That meant a lot, coming from a guy so straitlaced he hardly ever took off his tie.

He sat back in the chair where he'd slept, and balanced his tray on his lap while she ate in her hospital bed. She wondered how much they were paying him to work with her. This was combat duty for sure, sleeping in a chair in a hospital room, and eating bland hospital food.

"I don't want to be in any more hospitals," she said.

He looked up at her, mid-bite. She could tell by the way he ate that he'd been really hungry, but he hadn't left her to go get some food. He'd stayed with her instead so she wouldn't wake up alone. He was her bodyguard, her protector. Maybe, a little bit, her friend. Crap, she was dissolving in tears again.

"It's okay." His firm, steady voice really made things seem okay. "No more hospitals. We'll figure things out."

7.
Lightning

Ransom opened the ecstasy test kit and lined up the reagent bottles beside the white ceramic plate he'd borrowed from the hotel kitchen. They were lingering in Lyon, taking a couple days off before Paris. Lola was mostly better, but her brush with death still haunted him. He had nightmares about running with her to the medical tent, and woke in a cold sweat, gasping for breath.

They'd spent the last week or so getting her stronger, taking walks, eating healthier, getting more sleep. She was mostly cooperative. Her overdose had gone a long way to scaring her straight. But you never knew when someone might relapse, especially if they were stressed. Lola butted heads with the new manager daily. Belligerent, pushy Iain was the opposite of laid-back Greg, and Ransom suspected MadDance had hired the prickly manager to put the screws to Lola.

Ransom tried to stay out of their spats, but it fell to him to calm her down afterward—and she couldn't always be calmed. If she decided to buy drugs again in some rebellious fit, he wanted her to know how to test them for adulterants. He opened the ecstasy kit's chemical indicator chart, a meticulously laid out rainbow of danger and death.

Lola glanced at the ladder of colored rectangles and crossed her eyes. He ignored that vote of non-confidence and pulled on a pair of latex gloves, and made her do the same. Then he used a knife to scrape some powder from the ecstasy tablet onto different quadrants of the plate.

"We don't have to do this," she said.

"Yes, we do. If you take ecstasy, you need to know how to test it."

"I'm not going to take it anymore."

"Anymore is a very long time, and I can't be your watchdog forever," he said, brushing the powder into separate sections.

"But—"

"Lola, please. I just want to know that you know how to do this."

She relented, pressed her lips shut, and turned her attention back to the kit. He put the first reagent bottle in her hand.

"Okay, take off the cap and squeeze a single drop onto the first bit of powder. Don't get any in your eyes, or on your skin."

She wrinkled her nose at the sharp smell. "Jesus, what's in this shit?"

Your safety, he thought. Aloud, he said, "Caustic compounds. Sulfuric acid and other dangerous chemicals. Just be careful."

He hovered over her as she dripped the various chemicals on the tiny hills of powder he'd created. There were six tests, because there were so many things they were adding to tablets these days. *Just be careful.*

He needed her to stop being reckless and start being careful, because something had happened in the past few days. He'd stopped thinking of her as an irritating work duty and started thinking of her as more of a friend. He'd come to recognize not just her bad behaviors, but her internal struggles with the unrelenting pressure of fame.

As she fought to turn her life around in this three ring circus of a rave tour, he'd become more and more aware of her resilience and strength.

"Okay," he said. "Show me how to read the test. Look at the colors of the powder. What do you see as far as adulterants?"

She sighed, glancing at the chart. "I told you, this is pointless. I'm not going to take drugs anymore. I'm done."

"Show me," he insisted.

Done, my ass. He trusted her about as far as he could throw her, which wasn't very far, even with the positive strides she'd taken. A month and a half from now she'd be back in L.A. with her party posse, and he expected her to go crazy and do a bunch of stupid shit.

"This pill has caffeine mixed into it," she finally said, poring over the indicator chart.

He nodded. "Most of them do. It's a cheap stimulant, often mixed with amphetamines—and you remember what amphetamines do."

She wouldn't look at him. He wondered if she remembered that night as clearly as he did, if she remembered how fast her heart had hammered in her chest. "What else?" he asked.

She looked back at the chart. "Looks like there's...pa-ra-cee... How the fuck do you pronounce this?"

"Paracetamol. It's a painkiller."

"They sure do put a lot of random shit in these pills."

"Some of it more benign than others. A tablet mixed with PMA can kill you. Bath salts, ketamine, heroin, they've all been found in ecstasy tablets. One bad batch full of fentanyl, and dozens of people die. The truth is, you don't know what you're getting unless you do one of these tests." He sounded like a cop giving the Just Say No talk to a bunch of sixth graders. Whatever. She needed it. "So, having done the tests, we understand that this pill's not too bad. You could take this and not have too many problems."

He looked at her and waited. She blinked at him.

"No, Ransom. I would never, ever consider taking that. Sooo unsafe, even if it's relatively pure. Where'd you get it?"

"None of your business."

He'd bummed it from someone in the groupie crowd outside the bus last night. Two guys and one girl had offered ecstasy to him in hopes their favorite DJ would get high off it. Ransom had accepted all three tablets even though he only needed one. Did he think taking three measly pills out of circulation would do anything about EDM's rampant drug culture?

Sadly, no.

He capped the test reagents, then went to the bathroom to wash the tablet and powder down the drain. By the time he returned, Lola was curled up in a pile of pillows, strumming through a series of chords. She hadn't offered him any more lessons since the bus ride to Amsterdam, but he'd come to enjoy her impromptu concerts. As it turned out, she'd written a lot of songs, some of which she played for him, quietly, like secrets.

He understood why she kept them a secret. If her sweet, folksy emo songs ever got out, they would mortally wound her dance cred. Her guitar tunes had no beats, no rolls, no drops, nor were they very much like the heavy blues her father played.

Ransom had searched *Mo Reynolds* online and watched a few videos of concert footage from crowded Memphis clubs. In one of them, he'd seen little Lola Mae sitting off to one side, knobby knees resting against the side of a speaker. She'd been about seven years old in the video, nodding her head to the thumping cadences of southern blues. He hadn't been sure it was her until the little blonde smiled. That impish grin had barely changed in the ensuing years.

No, her music was nothing like her dad's, even if she'd watched him play back then with worshipful eyes. A couple minutes in, Ransom had closed out the video, feeling like a stalker. He'd only searched "Mo Reynolds blues" because of his fascination with Lola, and that was inappropriate because she was a client, and almost two decades younger than him.

He took off his tie and sat back on the bed to rest his mind before they headed out to dinner. *Grandpa needs a nap.* Between the two of them, he was more fit, but she had boundless energy and amazing creativity. She never did her hair the same twice. She wore outfits that both puzzled and attracted him. Then there were the wistful tunes she played on her guitar.

"Are you going to sleep?" she asked, switching to a lullaby.

"No."

"Your eyes are closed."

He sighed. "I'm not going to sleep." He never slept unless she slept, and she only slept at night. He didn't trust her to be awake and on her own, even trapped in the room with the door alarm.

He cracked an eye open as she began to sing in a soft, sweet voice. *"Lullaby, and good night, go to sleep Mr. Ransom. Lullaby, and good night, time for bodyguards to sleep."*

"I'm not sleeping," he muttered.

She ignored him, continuing her made-up song. *"I won't take off your clothes. Or at least I'll try not to. I'll protect you from harm..."* She thought a moment. *"As I stare at your arms.* Hmm, that's kind of tame. Oh, I know!" She started the phrase over. *"I'll protect you from shock, as I stare at your co—"*

"Lola." His sharp voice brought a high-pitched spate of giggles. He wanted to be irritated by those giggles, but the sound of her laughter aroused him just like everything else. *No, man. No. Get over it.*

He knew he wouldn't feel so drawn to her if she wasn't always flirting with him. She had no clue about couth and professional relationships, or maybe she just didn't care. He wished he didn't have to care. He wished he could act out the fantasies churning in his brain, but he knew he'd end up hurting her. For all her sexual bravado, she was an emotionally fragile, frequently tearful twenty year old who probably had no idea what a real man could do in bed.

Not that it was his job to teach her.

Sometimes being the older, more responsible one sucked.

He braced as she started a new verse. *"Lullaby, my sweet knight, with your five o'clock shadow. Such a handsome face to lick, how I'd love to suck your—"*

"Seriously, stop it. That's crass. Why are you singing lullabies anyway? It's light outside. We're going to dinner soon."

She grinned. The more he tried to be the distant, professional bodyguard, the more she poked at his growing frustration. "I like lullabies, Ransom. And you like to listen to me sing. You said my voice was pretty."

"It is pretty, when you're not singing profane lyrics." He turned to her with his head on his hand. "You shouldn't come onto me. Don't you understand how inappropriate it is?"

"Inappropriate?" She rolled her eyes. "You sound like a freaking dad." One second. Two blessed seconds of silence, then: "Can I call you daddy when we finally hit it? *Ooh, daddy, harder, faster!*"

"Lola, enough." His seriousness finally seemed to get through to her, or maybe it was his tone. He'd beg her to leave him alone if he had to. His self-control could only hold so far. "What you're doing here constitutes sexual harassment. I'm your bodyguard, not your boy toy."

Emotions cycled across her face. Shame, embarrassment, humor, and that frightening feminine voodoo that undid him every time. She knew she had power over him. She knew she was making him suffer, and protest, and want.

"You want me," she taunted in a soft voice. "Why can't you just admit it?"

He turned his head away like a coward, then turned back to face her, because he needed to deal with this head on. "I'm your bodyguard. I'm here to do a job."

"So am I. I'm on tour. I do interviews and dream up new mixes, and sweat through sets in front of thousands of people. That doesn't mean I can't have fun. I can play the guitar. I can go out to clubs. I can fuck my bodyguard."

"No, you can't."

"Why not?"

Yes, why not, Ransom? She didn't understand about professional distance, personal space, and self-protection. She was a reckless, pink-haired kid, and he wanted to fuck her every hour of every day, and he was coming to hate himself for it.

"I'm waiting for your answer," she poked.

"You're not getting an answer, because we're not going to have this conversation. Nothing is happening between us, ever."

"I'll pay you."

He held up a hand. "Don't even go there."

She pushed her guitar aside and flung herself onto her stomach. "I'm good in bed. You'd like it. I'd suck your cock for days, whenever you wanted. I'd let you do anal. I fucking *love* anal."

"You know what I love?" Ransom asked, wishing he could unhear everything he'd just heard. "Clients who don't sing lullabies about my genitalia."

"Oh, come on!"

"I'm sorry, but you and I are not happening. I'm not like you. I prefer not to have casual sex."

"What does that mean?" She laid on her side, gazing over at him, the very picture of outraged disappointment and lust. She loved anal. He wished he didn't know that.

"It means that I prefer to sleep with women I love, who are in a relationship with me," he said. "I need to feel emotionally connected to my partner."

She threw back her head and laughed. "That's bullshit. You wouldn't look the way you look if you didn't want to hit it all the time. I see women drooling all over you everywhere we go."

"How many have I slept with? You may not share my views, but that's how I feel. I don't like empty sex. I need it to mean something."

She gave him that flirty smile, that smile that *knew*, that saw through all his lies and protests. "We've been together for weeks now, Ransom." She jumped up off her bed and climbed onto his, flinging herself against his chest. "I almost died in your arms, remember? I don't mean something to you?"

He moved away from her, even as his body responded to her closeness. He was going to say something that would hurt her. It was necessary, even if it was a lie. "A paycheck, kid. You mean a paycheck to me, every two weeks."

Her lips went tight. No answer for once, no grinning comeback. She turned away from him and got off the bed, and went into the bathroom. Crying? Maybe. Probably. Yes.

He wasn't lying when he said he didn't do empty sex. He wouldn't only hurt *her* if they started some shallow, hookup relationship. She would hurt *him* too, and he'd endured enough sexual desolation in his life.

He closed his eyes again. Maybe he should have taken Liam up on his offer to leave this assignment. Maybe he should have removed himself from this fucked up situation, for both their sakes. But what might happen to her? He didn't want to lose ground when they'd made so much progress. She was way more than a paycheck to him, and he was a liar, and all of this made his head hurt, and *was she crying?*

She came out of the bathroom and flopped back on the bed. If she'd been crying, she'd composed herself. Now she just looked mad.

"I'm sorry for what I said," he began.

She held up a hand. "No. Forget it. You're a sexless virgin prude or something, so whatever. Your problem, not mine. But I have needs, and you aren't helping me meet them. I haven't had sex in ages and you won't let me pick up anyone in the clubs."

"Because they could be creeps. They might be carrying drugs. They might hurt you, and I'm your bodyguard. I'm supposed to keep you from getting hurt."

"All you're keeping me from is getting laid, and it's totally unfair, so here's the deal: when we get to Paris, I'm hiring a gigolo."

"Lola—"

"I've done it before. I promise I'll go through a legit agency. Hell, you can pick out the fucking guy if you want, but I'm having sex, do you understand? I'm getting laid in Paris."

Her voice had risen to a yell, while he thought, *I'll pick you a gigolo over my dead body.*

"Can't you call someone?" he asked. "Isn't there someone back in L.A. you know and trust, who can fly to Paris to entertain you for a night or two?"

"Hell, no, I'm not flying anyone out here for a night or two. All the dudes in L.A. are fame whores, and they all suck in bed. Gigolos are better. They're skilled labor, and when you're done with them, they go away."

Ransom didn't know how to handle this. Maybe a gigolo was a reasonable request. Why did it bother him so badly that she wanted sex? Most twenty year olds had rampant libidos, and he was all for women getting it as good as men. Why couldn't he just let her pick up some manwhore and fuck him, and get it out of her system?

Because he couldn't bear to know she was doing it with anyone other than him.

But he wasn't willing to put out for her, and he couldn't force her to live like a nun for another six weeks, not without suffering these constant meltdowns, and being barraged with lullabies about his cock.

"You can't just wait until you get home to L.A.?" he asked in exasperation. "You have your whole life to have sex."

"I might die tomorrow," she shot back. "I can't wait."

* * * * *

Ransom paced the hotel hallway, berating himself for letting this happen. The goddamn gigolo was five minutes late, which seemed like the perfect excuse to cancel everything.

He'd interviewed the agency manager himself after Lola made the appointment, to reassure himself this was legitimate, that this manwhore would be safe and trustworthy. Monsieur Vivant had promised complete discretion and satisfaction from the most exclusive escort agency in Paris.

Fuck. Ransom wasn't okay with this "satisfaction."

Lola, on the other hand, was fresh off a successful Paris appearance, showered and primped, dressed in a miniskirt and a mesh top that pretty much revealed everything. He wanted to take off his suit jacket and wrap it around her every time she stuck her head out the door to ask "Is he here yet?"

"He's going to be ugly," Ransom said. "And he's late."

"The traffic's horrible in the city. He'll be here."

Ransom stared toward the elevators because he couldn't bear to look at her. He'd told her she was the most reckless, stupid, self-indulgent client he'd ever had to wrangle, but that hadn't made her reconsider her plans.

She went back into the room and slammed the door. He rubbed his eyes. He'd have to get a different hotel room tonight. He wouldn't be able to bear the smell of Lola's scent mingled with someone else's, couldn't sleep with even a hint of sex in the air.

He opened his eyes, and then blinked in disbelief at the man sauntering down the hall. Black vest, black vinyl pants, every cheesy tattoo imaginable, and more piercings than he'd ever seen in someone's face. His hair was a black, glossy mop that ended just below his ears. He carried a duffel bag with a screen print of a snake on it. *Hell no.* This was what passed for "exclusive" in Paris?

The man stopped when he got to the room. Ransom would have laughed in his face, but none of this was funny.

He studied Ransom for a moment, then shrugged. "*Ménage à trois?* Okay."

"No. *Non.*" Ransom stared at him, flabbergasted. "You're from Vivant? You're the..." He couldn't say it.

"Why else would I be here?" the man answered in a thick French accent. He dropped his bag and ran his palms down his skintight vinyl pants.

Ransom suppressed a shudder. "I'm the bodyguard. I'll need to look through your bag before I let you in."

The lip piercings gave way to a lurid grin, as he raked his eyes down Ransom's body. "Go ahead. Maybe you like what you find."

Ransom rolled his eyes and leaned over the duffel, unzipping it. The first thing he saw was a cheaply made flogger. Handcuffs, blindfold, rope, ball gag, all of questionable quality. He looked up at the escort in consternation.

The man shrugged. "The ladies, they love the *Fifty Shades of Gris, non?* I come prepared."

His grin turned Ransom's stomach, and it wasn't just the alarming number of piercings that stretched apart whenever he smiled. He was just...ugh. Not attractive. Possibly high. Lola opened the door and stuck her head out, then did a double take at the gigolo's numerous piercings. Ransom glared at her.

"*This* is the guy you picked out?"

She looked down into the bag as Ransom drew her attention to the tacky fetish gear. "I said I wanted someone hardcore."

That note of uncertainty in her voice ended everything, at least for tonight. "We'll try again," he said under his breath. He took her wrist, squeezed a little too hard. "Another night, okay? Someone else."

She pulled away. "No. Tonight. I need cock, dude. Go down to the bar for an hour. Go away."

"I'm not going away." There was zero chance he was going anywhere and leaving her alone with this creep. "Is this seriously what you wanted?" he hissed in her ear. "Does this guy do it for you?"

Lola gave the gigolo a dubious look, but Ransom knew she'd sleep with him just to prove a point, just to irritate him and have her way.

He wasn't going to allow it. No. She wasn't getting it hardcore from some stranger who looked like Prince Valiant crossed with Marilyn Manson. He was the bodyguard, so he made the judgment, one he knew she wouldn't like. He shoved the guy's accoutrements back into his bag and started going through the smaller pockets. It took him about thirty seconds to find what he needed to end the date: three fat joints and some ecstasy. He scowled at her. "You asked him to bring drugs?"

"No. I didn't!" He could tell from her expression she was telling the truth. "I don't have any control over what he brings in his fucking bag."

The gigolo grabbed his drugs, in fact, snatched his entire rig from Ransom's grasp. "Never mind. I go."

"I don't want you to go," said Lola. She pushed Ransom in the chest. "Get lost, okay? This is none of your fucking business. You said I could have sex in Paris."

"Are you really going to yell that down the hall?" he snapped back at her.

"This is not my scene," said the gigolo, holding up his hands. He glared at Lola. "Why you call Vivant anyway, when you have a perfectly good porn star right here?"

"What?" Lola blinked at him. "Porn star? I thought you were an escort."

"No, not me. Him. Rico Rockhard." He pointed toward Ransom.

Ransom stared back at him. *Fuck, fuck, fuck.*

Lola's brow wrinkled in confusion. "He's not a porn star. He's my bodyguard." Her laughter died when she noticed Ransom's face. He tried to fix his oh-fuck expression, but it was too late.

The man shook his head at Lola, and pointed again at Ransom. "You don't know he's Rico Rockhard? He made *sooo* many films."

"Shut the fuck up," Ransom snapped.

The man ignored him, trying to make his point to Lola. "He has a, how do you say, *éclair* tattoo on his prick." The man pronounced it *preek* and gestured to his crotch. "He's famous. They call him *Le Grand Eclair*."

"What?" Lola turned to Ransom, aghast. "You have a doughnut tattooed on your cock?"

"Lightning," he corrected, equally aghast. "A lightning bolt. *Eclair* is the French word for—"

For lightning. And also for being fucked, because he might have pretended mistaken identity before. There was no way to do it now. But for fuck's sake, he didn't have a doughnut tattooed on his cock, and no one had ever called him *Le Grand Eclair* outside of France.

"So it's true?" Lola gawked at him. She hadn't even noticed the gigolo escaping down the hall. "Is this fucking accurate? You're a porn star?"

"Can we go in the room, please?"

"No!" She shoved him back against the wall. "Answer my question. Are you, or are you not, a porn actor named Rico Rockhard with a lightning bolt tattooed on your penis?"

"I *was* a porn actor, okay?" Ransom held up his hands to stop himself from pressing them over her mouth. "Was. Past tense. Look, it's a long story. It's also ancient history, so I'd appreciate if you'd never mention it again."

He reached around her to key open the door and push her inside. She sputtered and turned on him, her eyes alight with fury. Why should *she* be angry? He was the one who'd just been outed by a buffoon of a French gigolo. He should have just let the two of them fuck. He should have shut his mouth and waited down in the lobby.

"I. Cannot. Believe. This." She said each word like a condemnation, a curse. "I can't fucking believe this. I can't."

"It's not that big a deal. It was years ago." He hated being on the defensive. He'd paid the price for his stupid choices, oh, so many times, but he'd moved on. "It's part of my past. My employer knows about it, and he doesn't care. It has nothing to do with my ability to look after you."

Lola threw her arms out to her sides. "Oh, it has *everything* to do with your ability to look after me." She sucked in a breath, then blew it out. "You judged me, you fucker. You lectured me. You wouldn't let me have sex because you said the men I chose were creepy, or dangerous, and you... And you..."

"That guy was scary," he said, pointing down the hall. "He probably has a thousand diseases."

"You're no better than him," she yelled. "You were a porn star. You probably have a thousand diseases too!"

"I have zero diseases, Lola. I've been out of the business for over a decade."

"Oh, you quit the business. Good for you, you freaking slime ball." She waved a finger in his face. "You acted like you were so much better than me."

"Why? Because I counseled you? Because I told you to lay off the partying and drugs? I was doing my job, which has nothing to do with—"

"You were being a hypocrite. You're worse than that dumbass gigolo. You fucked on film. Anyone can see you right now, on the Internet. You made fucking *porn*."

Ransom's stomach clenched at her condemning words. Yes, he was worse than the gigolo. He'd made hundreds of films from the age of nineteen to twenty-five, drunk on money and pussy and all the cocaine he could shove up his nose. And yes, you could see all the porn you ever wanted with a simple search for *Rico Rockhard*. Or, in France, *Le Grand Eclair*.

"Don't dare look on the Internet," he said. "Don't even think about searching for those videos."

"You can't stop me." She was in tears. He understood her anger, but he didn't understand the sadness. Had she felt *that* judged by him? As judged as he felt now?

He knew he couldn't stop her from finding his films. He couldn't supervise everything she looked at every minute of every day. She had a laptop, a phone, a tablet, a second laptop she used for her music. He couldn't stop her from watching them, but he wanted to. He'd made ugly, violent films in an ugly, violent business, fucked women like objects, used drugs to make his dick last longer, the same way the girls had used all kinds of fucked up pharmaceuticals to get through the shoots. "Don't watch them, Lola." His voice caught. Her expression was pitiless. "They're awful. All of them are awful."

"Oh yeah? I bet they still turn me on." The glittering tears in her eyes turned harder, into ice blue diamonds. "I need sex. I need release. What am I supposed to do? You won't let me get it anywhere else."

So it was sex, then, or his videos. He shook his head. *Don't do this. Don't force me. Don't blackmail me. Don't make me give in, when I've tried so hard to resist you.*

"No," he said. "Don't even... No."

"Yes. Fuck you. I'm getting off tonight, one way or another." She lifted her chin. "I can't wait to see your pornos, to see your big, fat, tattooed cock. I knew all along you had a porn cock, or you wouldn't act like such an asshole. I'm going to download every one of your films and jack off to them over and over *and over.*"

He wanted to kill her. He wanted to lose himself inside her. He wanted to erase everything bad he'd ever done, but he couldn't. He could only do another terrible thing.

Furious lust replaced horror and humiliation, and filled his porn-sized, lightning-tattooed cock. If she wanted sex from him, she'd get it. He ripped her mesh shirt up over her head, then shrugged out of his jacket and threw it on the floor. "You'll regret this," he murmured against her neck as he grasped her breasts. She moaned and tugged at his buttons, too frantic to pry them open.

Jesus, her skin was so soft, her body so perfect. She was perfect, but he was terrible, and he was going to end up hurting her. "Out of everything," he snarled in her ear, "this is the stupidest fucking thing you've ever done."

8.
SEX

Lola shuddered as Ransom squeezed her breasts, then pinched her nipples. Her hands traveled up to his collar to yank loose his tie. He felt so hard. So big. So strong.

So angry.

But she needed this. She'd wanted this for so long, dreamed of him taking her just like this, in the furious heat of passion. His teeth raked over her ear. Hot breath condensed on her skin.

Lightning.

All this time, her stern and inflexible bodyguard had been an ex-porn actor with a lightning bolt tattooed on his cock. Under that suit, under that tie, under the lectures and warnings, Mr. I Don't Believe in Empty Sex had a *grand éclair* and a sordid past. He thrust his tongue in her mouth, rough and hot, and while it unbalanced her, it didn't surprise her. Somehow her body had known this other person lurked inside him. She'd known there was a reason she ached so hard for him. As his kiss deepened, turned commanding and raw, she knew he'd ached for her too.

He released her, leaving her to shiver from the intensity of his assault. She watched as he strode across the room and went through her luggage, through the pocket where she stored a variety of condoms. She could have backed out now that he was away from her. She should have backed out and said, *never mind, forget it*, and he would have left her alone, but she didn't. She just waited and longed for him until he returned with a gold-wrapped rubber. He threw it on the side table, next to all the normal, everyday things they kept there. Her magazines, his phone charger, his eye drops, her water bottle. Electrolyte water.

He turned and glared at her. "We shouldn't do this."

She held her ground. If she had to, she'd threaten him again with the videos, even though they both knew she was going to watch them either way.

Instead, she told him her honest feelings. "If you don't fuck me, I'm going to die."

"Jesus fucking Christ."

That was all he said, and then he was undressing, tie on the floor, buttons flicked open, shirt and undershirt discarded, dress pants unbuttoned and unzipped.

Oh my God. *My God.* His naked body. The muscles. The chest hair. His...lightning bolt.

Oh.

My.

God.

His huge, erect cock pointed to the sky, and the lightning bolt—the very *long* lightning bolt—pointed there too. She stood enraptured as he finished undressing, then he crossed to her with an impatient look on his face. That was when she realized she was still dressed, except for the top he'd pulled off her. He shoved down her skirt, and ripped off her panties with a caveman grunt that made her pussy throb.

He was naked, right in front of her, and she was naked too. His physicality was a force. His touch grew insistent as his cock poked between them, ridiculously fat and hard and porn-y. *A porn star. Ransom.*

Oh my God.

His hands were all over her, stroking, pinching, pulling her closer. He squeezed her ass and yanked her against his thick shaft. She felt overwhelmed by this animalistic side of her bodyguard, so different from the carefully straitlaced person he pretended to be.

There were so many things she wanted to say. *I've wanted this for so long. You smell amazing. You're even rougher than I imagined. Kiss me again, please.* But she couldn't say any of them because she was so shocked to finally be in his arms. His hands moved up her back and twisted in her hair, guiding her head back so her neck was bared to his kiss. She gave a whimper of pleasure as her sensitized nipples dragged across his chest, across his caveman pelt of hair.

"Oh my God," she whispered. Those were the only words she could call forth as his fingers pressed against her scalp, causing pleasure and pain. Her other lovers were so tentative, so servile, so grateful just to find themselves in Lady Paradise's bed. None of them ever possessed her like this, with glorious hunger and forcefulness.

He shoved a knee between her legs and she was wet, so wet. His hand slid down her back and over her ass, and then down to grope her from behind. There was no delicacy in it, no attempt to give her pleasure, only firm fingers searching and penetrating through the flood of her arousal.

"You want me?" He rubbed his cock against her front. "You want this?"

"Yes." The word came out on a sob. She was already halfway to orgasm, just from the way he manhandled her. "Yes, please."

It had been too long for her. It had been forever. She'd never been this turned on, this overtaken. He nudged her toward the bed and pushed her back on the rumpled sheets. Her bed, not his. She didn't care. She'd sleep in the wet spot. She'd sleep in a thousand wet spots just to enjoy this thrilling experience.

He came down over her, his knees spreading her legs, his cock arching up between them. He reached for the condom and rolled it on like a pro.

Because he was a pro. He'd been a pro. She had to remember that before she totally lost her heart to him.

She'd thought he was just a hardass, a stick in the mud bodyguard, but oh no, he was so much more. He moved his hips so his cock nestled between her pussy lips, but he didn't enter her. She craved him, ached for him, but he only teased her with a long, slow slide over her jangling slit.

Oh God, her clit screamed at the fleeting contact. It was fucking on fire, swollen and super sensitized, and now taunted by his massive tool.

"More," she said. "Please. I want you inside me."

"Do you?" He gazed down at her, utterly controlled when she had zero control. She made a sound like she was dying, but it only made him smile.

"Please, Ransom."

He put a finger over her lips as he teased her again, slick, hard flesh against her pulsing button. What would he feel like inside her? She arched up her hips, reaching for him. He pressed her back, not giving up an iota of control.

"Be still a moment," he said. "I want to look at you."

She lay under him, panting, splayed open for his slick, sliding torment. He did more than look. He ran a hand up her stomach, over her torso and between her breasts. He squeezed her boobs and then slid his fingertips to her nipples. She thought he might pinch them again, but when she tried to turn away, he made her turn back, and then he pinched them even harder than before. It hurt like crazy, but also felt so damn good her mouth fell open. When she tried to writhe away from the overwhelming sensation, he held her hips and forced her to submit. She couldn't take this much longer.

She looked up at him and said, for the twentieth time, "Please, I need sex."

"I know, baby. You're gonna get it."

He was like a god, all his strength and muscles on display, and his control so much more dignified than hers. He held her still and positioned his cock against her entrance. Her pussy blazed like an oven. She was so hot, so wet, so gone. Even wet as she was, she had to brace for the shocking stretch of Ransom's cock invading her walls. He leaned on one arm, pressing her down with the other as he eased inside her body inch by inch.

"Yeah? Is that what you needed?"

She couldn't answer him. She couldn't. She felt too transported to manage words. He captured her half-open lips in another questing kiss as he drove the rest of the way inside her, until she felt too full to move. He stopped then, and held her gaze.

This is a man, she thought. Not a gigolo. Not a groupie. Not an ass kisser. His eyes said, *I'm inside you. Deal with it.*

She squeezed on his girth and he made a soft growl that resonated all the way up to her heart. "I want to fuck you forever," she said, because those were the first words that came to mind.

He didn't laugh, or answer her, only started giving her exactly what she needed. Oh, she'd needed this for so long, ever since he'd told her *I'm here to protect you. As long as you're with me, you're going to be safe.* He made her feel safe, but he made her feel other things too, like happy, and normal, and oh God, so horny.

His body felt so strong sliding over hers. His arms surrounded her like a cage as he drove in with masterful control, filling her to the hilt. He smelled delicious, like sweat and soap and expensive cologne.

He's twice your age, Lola. You're twenty. He's almost forty.

But she was glad he was almost forty, because twenty-year-old boys didn't fuck like this. Every time he surged into her, he lit up some spot that made her body shake with building pleasure. "How are you doing that?" she asked, but it came out a bunch of scrambled syllables, like *oh* and *fuck* and *yes*. He smothered her babbling with a kiss. The man kissed like he fucked, with no-holds-barred possession. He moved a hand beneath her, cupping her ass and angling her so he could thrust even deeper.

God, he just grabbed her and moved her wherever he wanted her. She was losing her mind at the novelty of it. He was taking her somewhere she'd never been, where sex and connection made magic. She'd felt connected to him for a while now, because they'd spent so much time together. She'd played her songs for him. She'd told him things she usually kept a secret, like how worn down and confused she felt sometimes.

But she hadn't realized she could ever be *this* connected to him.

"Beautiful. God, you're so fucking beautiful," he whispered as he held her and fucked her, and turned her inside out with his porn star virility. Rico Rockhard, huh? He was rock hard, all right, and rock solid. He was her rock, and she clung to him as her arousal grew to a fever pitch.

"Oh my God, oh my God, fuck, fuck, please don't stop." The words spilled out in frantic need, and he was there for her, stroking her back, gripping her ass, riding her to an ecstasy more intense than any pharmaceutical high she'd ever experienced. When she finally climaxed, she lost all control. Everything clenched and shuddered, and she cried, "I can't. I can't."

"You can. I've got you."

And he did. His hands were huge and strong, powerful enough to hold her together as her body broke to pieces in fulfillment. He tensed above her, driving deep in a hot, hard cadence, and let out his own long groan of release.

Lola lay still, basking in every sensory detail. His scent, his breath, his heaviness, the sated sounds he made, the quiet murmurs, the feel of his lips moving over her skin. His hair was soft and warm beneath her fingers. His neck felt tense as he moved to kiss her lips. She didn't want him to pull away.

But eventually, he had to pull away. He did it slowly, taking care with the condom so he could protect her in this way as he did every other way.

"Hold on," he said. "I'll be right back."

As soon as he left her, Lola felt lost. A little worried. She couldn't decipher his expression as he left the bed and went into the bathroom. She heard the water run and shut off, and then he returned just as he'd promised, gathering her in his arms.

She had to say something about what had just happened. She had to explain how she'd slept with a hundred men in some quest for validation, but had never known true connection until now. She could have written a thousand songs about the way he'd just made her feel, but when she met his eyes, she couldn't say anything. A minute ticked by, and another.

Reality came crashing back, unwelcome memories, her yelling, her emotional blackmail, his angry words. *You'll regret this.*

She didn't regret what they'd just done. She was afraid of it.

"Are you okay?" he asked, and she couldn't tell anything from his tone. He might be happy. He might be furious. He might feel nothing at all.

She turned against his shoulder and let him pull her closer. "Yes, I'm fine. I feel...wow. Really wonderful."

He made a soft sound, perhaps a laugh. "You finally got laid."

She didn't want to joke about it. This had felt like so much more than "getting laid." It wasn't about bedding her hot bodyguard. It was about what he'd done to her heart. It was about the way he'd surged inside her and connected with her more deeply than men she'd fucked dozens of times in the past.

"I think...maybe..." She squeezed her eyes shut. Good God, was she going to cry? "I need some time to process what just happened. I mean, it was... It was amazing."

He pressed a kiss to her forehead. "It was amazing."

"But I just... I think I need some time before I say any more about it."

"I think we both need some time."

Her fingers tightened on his arm as he shifted. "But I don't want you to leave me," she said. "Please, will you sleep next to me tonight?"

"Of course."

She needed *time to process?* Ha. What was there to process? She never, ever chose to fall asleep next to her sex partners. She'd always sent them home and pushed them from her thoughts as quickly as possible. Now she couldn't even gather her thoughts.

There was only one thought: she'd rather die than move away from the comfort of his arms.

* * * * *

Ransom sat by the window and watched Lola sleep. His tie felt tight. His throat felt tighter. He'd finished packing an hour ago, while she slept like a baby. Incredible sex would do that to you.

She looked so innocent in sleep. She always had, but now it unsettled him, because he'd been inside her, everywhere, and she still looked so *innocent*.

But she wasn't, and neither was he, and now he had to tender his resignation and walk away from this assignment because he was weak, and because she knew now that he wasn't respectable or responsible under his tailored suits and ties. He'd crossed a line no bodyguard should ever cross.

Even if he hadn't lost control last night, he would have had to leave. She knew about his first career now, and she'd use that knowledge against him if he stayed. Their professional relationship was over, and so this assignment was over, even if they'd shared something earth-shattering. The first fuck was rough and sloppy. The second fuck was languid, an exploration of licking, sucking, biting, and teasing that escalated to a sensual wrestling match.

Which led to the third fuck, a rampant raunchfest that carried them through to dawn. He'd ended up in his client's ass, because she loved anal, and he loved anal, and because neither of them had managed to find a boundary they wouldn't cross. He'd spanked her, he'd called her a horny little cunt, and even wrapped his fingers around her neck to hear her moan.

He couldn't believe it now, in the light of day. He wasn't one to do those kinds of things, or rather, the women he dated weren't the type to allow them. The last time he'd fucked a woman like that, cameras had been rolling.

That was the real reason he had to go. He'd fought long and hard to reshape his sexual proclivities, to wean himself from the raw, objectifying fuckfests he performed on camera. He was not Rico Rockhard, that lurid character. He would not let porn and sex define him, and if he stayed here, that was what would happen.

Because they'd never stop having crazy porno sex.

Even now, his cock rose uncomfortably against his restrictive pants. She'd been everything he'd imagined in bed, and so much more. So uninhibited, so wild. They hadn't needed fetish toys or floggers or any of that shit, because their bodies had turned electric together, two live wires crossed, setting off showers of blinding sparks. Looking back, it was amazing they hadn't set the bed on fire.

His phone bleated, a message from his boss. *Got your request. Don't have anyone immediately available to replace you. Can you wait two days?*

Ransom rubbed his eyes. He hadn't confessed what he'd done, out of respect for Lola's privacy. If he'd told Liam those four words—I slept with her—there would have been someone here already to take his place, and he would be out of a job. *You deserve to be out of a job*, his conscience whispered.

By the time he looked up, Lola was stirring. Damn phone. He usually remembered to silence it while she was sleeping, but his brain wasn't firing on all cylinders. She blinked at him, perhaps experiencing the same parade of memories he'd suffered as he watched her sleep.

She made a soft sound and pulled the covers over her eyes. A moment later, she peeked out at him. "Why are you so dressed?" she asked.

"It's almost three in the afternoon."

"Come back to bed." She stretched, reaching out for him. He felt actual, physical pain that he couldn't respond.

"I can't." He tried not to think about how lovely and naked she was, and how much he ached to fuck her now, in broad daylight, with the sun playing over her skin.

She fell back against the pillows. "I thought today was a free day. We don't leave for Italy until tomorrow."

"I can't go to Italy with you. Lola..." His jaw clenched against the words. "I have to resign."

Her seductive gaze melted into confusion. "Why, what happened?"

"You've already forgotten?"

"No, I..." She clutched the sheets closer to her chest. "Because of what we did? That means you have to resign?"

"Yes. I behaved unprofessionally. I'm here to do a job, and now I can't do that job."

"Because we fucked?"

He let out a slow sigh. "That's part of it. It's also that...you know about my past."

"Who cares? So what? You were homeless or something, and you had to do porn to survive. It happens."

"That's not what happened." He stood and went to the window, and looked out at the Paris skyline. "There was no desperation, no exploitation. I chose to do porn. I thought I was hot shit, fucking for money. I thought I was too good to go to college and get a nine to five job like everyone else in my family. I swanned around those sets like I was king of the world. And once you're in..."

Once you were in the porn business, they did everything in their power to keep you in the business, to deaden you to the fucked up shit you were doing.

For the rest of his life, he'd have a lightning bolt tattooed on his dick.

"Okay. You chose to do porn," said Lola. "Whatever. You were young and stupid. I don't care."

"I care." He turned back to her. "I've already tendered my resignation. They'll send someone new in a couple of days."

"I don't want someone new. I want you." She knelt on the bed, her features tense with anger. "Why does the porn thing matter?"

"It mattered to you yesterday. You got pretty angry about it, remember?"

"Yeah, but—"

"It matters because you've lost respect for me, and because I slept with you when I shouldn't have. End of story. I can't continue to function as your bodyguard after..." God, after all the filthy things they'd done. If she hadn't known about the porn, he could have stayed in control of their relationship. He could have put her to bed last night with a lecture on promiscuity instead of burying himself inside her three times. *Three* times.

"I don't want you to go," she said. "The sex is nothing. It's harmless."

"Meaningless," he retorted bitterly.

"So? I don't care."

"I care," he said for the second time. He glanced at his watch. "You need to get up. You have an interview downstairs in an hour."

"What does it matter if we have sex or not? Why does any of this matter?"

"Exactly." He crossed to her and took her arms, and wished he could shake some sense into her. "You don't care because you're an impulsive, short-sighted juvenile. I was too, twenty years ago. I made my first film when I was your age, and I didn't fucking care."

She subsided in his grasp, gazing into his eyes. He didn't want to let her go. What was it about her that made him act this way?

"This shit matters," he said through his teeth. "What we did last night matters. I was hired to give you some boundaries, to keep you on the straight and narrow. What leverage will I have now? Every time I tell you not to do something, you're going to throw my past in my face. '*What right do you have to judge me? You used to make porn.*'"

She didn't say anything, because they both knew he was right.

"I can't do my job anymore," he said, letting go of her and turning away. "So I'm leaving as soon as they can find a replacement. In the meantime, no more sex. Put some clothes on, for God's sake."

He'd expected her to whine and complain about his decision, but he hadn't expected her to barrel into him from behind. He almost fell into the window, then turned around to see all five, naked feet of her quivering with rage.

"How dare you?" she said. "How dare you talk to me this way? How dare you dismiss me after everything that happened last night? You enjoyed it as much as I did. I remember you enjoying it quite a bit."

"Yes, I enjoyed it. I never said I didn't."

"Then don't tell me to put my clothes on." She gave him another hard shove. "Hold me. Be nice to me. Don't act like last night was another of Lola's crazy, misbehaving stunts, because that would make you a massive asshole. Last night..." She burst into tears. "God, Ransom. Last night."

Damn. She was right. He was being an asshole and she was such a sensitive soul. He took her in his arms, even though it slayed him to hold her. He clasped her against him so tightly that he could feel her shivering anger and grief. To be twenty years old again, and feel everything so strongly. When had that part of him died? By twenty-three? Twenty-four?

He thought, for Lola, it would never die. She was the free spirit who'd always feel things strongly, who'd shove her heart in people's faces whether they wanted it or not. Maybe that's why he'd been drawn to her even as she defied and annoyed him. Now she was sobbing against his shoulder, pushing at his suit jacket so he'd take it off.

"Please don't go," she begged, opening her hands against his chest. "I don't want you to go."

"I can't work with you anymore." He had to be the sane one. If he let himself feel as strongly as she felt, they'd melt down together, or combust like the fire they'd created last night. She was so close to him, so hot, so sad, so full of all the emotions he was afraid to show.

"Lola, please," he said, stroking her hair. "This is crazy. You and me...it's crazy. You know it is."

"No." She shoved away from him, renewed fury shining beneath her tears. "I won't let you leave. I won't let you kick me to the curb like some fucking piece of dog shit." Her voice rose in savage conviction. "If you don't stay with me, I'll—I'll ruin you, Ransom. I'll call the police. I'll tell them that you forced me to have sex with you last night. I'll tell them you raped me."

He pulled her back, and this time he did shake her. "No more threats, Lola. Don't you fucking dare."

"And when you go to jail I'll get some other bodyguard who doesn't care about me," she continued, fighting his grip. "And he'll let me start using drugs again, and I'll use every drug I can get my hands on without testing any of them. I'll sleep around with every gross guy I can find. I'll fuck everyone, and it'll be all your fault."

"You were a nympho long before I showed up," he snapped over her tirade. "It's just about the sex for you, isn't it? That's why you want me to stay."

"Of course that's why I want you to stay, you fucking asshole."

They stared at each other, breathless, wild-eyed combatants. There was a knock at the door, and Iain's abrasive voice. "Lola? Are you up? Answer my fucking texts."

"I'm up," she yelled. "Go away."

"We have to leave soon for the interview."

This time Ransom yelled along with Lola. "Go away!"

Ransom turned back to her and studied her in the sunlight. He wished he could express the true depth of his regret at leaving, but all she'd hear was that he wanted to stay. He had to be firm, aloof. "I'm sorry, kid. I know it sucks to have to get used to a new bodyguard, but what happened between us can't be undone."

"You want me." Shit, she was groping him through his pants, finding the hard evidence she needed to keep arguing. "I know you want me. Even now."

"No," he said, pushing her hands away.

"Please."

No. He wasn't falling down that rabbit hole again. He wished he could fuck her a thousand more times, because she was so gorgeous, so responsive, but he couldn't. He was never going to fuck her again. If he fucked her again, he was lost. Outside the hotel room, Iain banged on the door.

"Lola? Lola!"

"Just stay," she pleaded. "Call your boss and say you've changed your mind. At least finish the tour!"

Once again, he told her no.

"Fuck you, then," she shouted, lashing out at him in her pain. "Leave if you want. Go make more films, you heartless asshole porn star. I don't fucking care."

"You do care. We both care." He backed away from her flailing anger, then caught her hands to make her still. "But this is exactly why I have to leave. You see? I'm not okay with you calling me a porn star every time you get angry. I'm also not your sex slave. You can't grope me and drag me to your bed—"

"The way you did to me last night?"

"Last night was your fault," he said, wagging a finger in her face. "Because you threatened to watch my films. You manipulated me."

She brought her knee up between his legs and almost connected. "That's not the reason you slept with me. That is not why!"

Iain knocked harder. "What's going on in there?"

"Go away," she yelled.

"Is Ransom in there?"

Ransom muttered an expletive under his breath, let go of Lola, and went to crack the door. "I'll have her ready to go downstairs by four o'clock," he said to the scowling manager. "Now please, just...go the fuck away." He shut the door in his face. Lola had fled into the bathroom. He heard the shower running over the sound of her pathetic sobs.

"Lola." He tapped at the door, then tried the lock. "Lola, let me in."

"No." The door shuddered from a kick. "If you want to leave, then leave. Fuck you to hell, you fucking asshole. I don't even want to see your fucking face."

"Lola." He could hear her crying on the other side, hear the pain and agony he'd caused her. He'd known he would hurt her, but he hadn't known it would be this bad. He hadn't known it would feel like taking a slice out of his own heart. "Lola, please. Don't be angry. I'm trying to do the right thing."

She'd never believe it, but he was doing this for her, to protect her. If she was like this after one night of sexual connection, how would she be by the end of the tour? Her sobs wrenched at his soul as he stood with his ear against the barrier between them. *Lola, I'm sorry.* He was too old for her, too married to his job. She was traveling the world, living in the spotlight. They didn't have a future. He was supposed to be protecting her, for fuck's sake, not sleeping with her. It all boiled down to that.

He sat on the edge of her bed until he heard the water turn off. At some point, the crying had stopped, because all he heard now was silence. The lock clicked and the door swung open. She stood in a towel, red-eyed and pink-haired. So emotional. So devastated.

When he opened his arms to her, she leaned her head against his shoulder and drew a shuddery breath. "I don't want you to go," she whispered. "Please..."

"Lola. You're making this so hard."

She clung to him. "You can't leave. I need you."

Fuck. Fuck the world. Fuck his life. What had he done to deserve this?

But he knew what he'd done. Three times. Three monumental fucks. He silently berated himself as she huddled in his arms. What had he been thinking, to sleep with her? And how could he fix this?

"Lola," he groaned. "Baby, I have to leave. I can't keep working on this assignment now that I've had you. We crossed a line we're not allowed to cross. If my boss knew—"

"He won't find out. I swear I won't tell anyone. I mean, this is so stupid. If I'd known you'd quit as soon as we had sex..."

"Did you think you could have a bodyguard and fuck buddy rolled into one? It doesn't work that way."

"But it's *us*," she said, stamping her foot. "We have something above and beyond your freaking job. Last night..." She gazed at him, tearful and distraught. "You can't just abandon me. Please stay. *Please stay.*"

He cared too much now. He'd cared too much from the beginning. He needed to run, and run away fast, but how the fuck was he supposed to do that with Lola sobbing in his arms?

He sighed, knowing he couldn't leave her, not after these emotional fireworks. He tightened his arms around her, hating the way she weakened him and made him do stupid things.

"If I stay, there can't be any more sex," he said. "No flirting, no temptation. That's the only way it could work."

She buried her face in his chest. "No sex ever?"

"Not for the rest of the tour. No more diva shit either," he said against her tousled pink hair. "No more screaming and drama. No throwing my past in my face. You have to promise."

"I promise. Just please...stay." She lifted her head to look at him. "I'll be good. I'll behave. I swear I won't do anything to annoy you."

He put as much stock in her promises as he put in his horrible self-control, but the way she cried, and the way she clung to him...

When she finally left with Iain to do the interview, Ransom paced the hotel room a dozen times, then sat at the desk and texted Liam.

On second thought, I'll finish the tour. It's only a few more weeks.

9.
NO FEELINGS. JUST BEATS.

Lola stared at Ransom's ass as she jogged along behind him. If not for that gorgeous view, she would have collapsed twenty minutes ago. Her legs hurt. Her feet hurt. Her lungs were burning. Exercise was bullshit and she'd tell him so, if he'd only let her catch her breath.

He glanced back at her. "Doing okay?"

"Fuck you."

He ignored her and continued jogging along the picturesque path. Every so often he looked over his shoulder to check whether she was keeping up. If she tried to stop, he just looped around and made her start running again.

"I need a break," she gasped. "I'm about to have a heart attack."

"You're doing great."

"I'm literally dying."

He stopped with a sigh, and she pulled up too, resting her hands on her knees.

"Come here." He made her straighten up, and held her arm with one hand while he pressed the other to her neck. She vaguely remembered him doing this once before, as her heart raced and burned in her chest. When she met his gaze, she knew he remembered too. He looked away and dropped his hand.

"You're not dying. Your pulse rate is at an optimal level for your age and level of fitness. Cardio, right? Let's go."

"No." She staggered away from him and collapsed on a bench. "You're my bodyguard. You're supposed to be protecting me from death, not urging me toward it."

"You're not going to die from a jog around a park. Let's finish it, we're almost done."

"I'm not going anywhere. You're evil."

He tilted his head, still running in place. "You wanted me to stay."

She looked up at him, squinting against the mid-morning sunlight that outlined his tall, muscular body. Of course he'd throw that in her face, remind her how she'd begged and cried to keep him on this tour.

Why? Why had she done that? He wouldn't give her sex, or even flirt with her. All the physical attraction between them had been redirected into forced exercise and horrific lifestyle changes. He made her drink spinach smoothies and eat broccoli, and go out for morning runs on days she wasn't performing. She'd weathered two days of headaches in Rome because he made her drink water now instead of diet cola.

Now she was running through a park in Milan wearing sweatpants and a tee shirt that were only ever supposed to be used for sleeping.

"Come on," he said. "Up. Let's go. The pain just means it's working."

"That isn't what pain means. I want to go back to the hotel. I want to go to bed."

He pulled her to her feet just as she said she wanted to go to bed, and his hands on her, his insistent force brought back all the memories. They'd gone to bed together once, and she couldn't get over it no matter how hard she tried. He could make her run a thousand miles and drink a thousand spinach smoothies, and she still wouldn't forget the way he'd grasped and caressed her, and shoved inside her until her whole world felt changed.

There was *before sex with Ransom*, and *after sex with Ransom*. Everything before paled in comparison, and everything after...

Well, everything after was frustrating as hell. When she looked at his hands, she thought about the delectable way he'd stroked her clit. When she looked at his mouth, she thought about his passionate kisses. When he stood close to her, the way he was now, she thought about how much she wanted to drag him to a bed, any bed.

"Lady Paradise. *Lady Paradise!*"

Ransom's head whipped around when he heard the voices. "We need to get going. When you don't run, people recognize you."

Lola nodded and waved to the approaching group of teen fans, then followed her bodyguard as he jogged away. "Sorry," she called, pointing at him. "I have to go."

They waved and smiled and didn't run after her. In Rome, a paparazzo had followed them for two blocks on a scooter, taking photos. He sold them and they ended up online, photos of her huffing and puffing, red faced, in her shitty workout gear. "This is your fault," she'd shouted at Ransom, pulling up the offending sites.

His answer to her meltdowns was always, "You wanted me to stay." Worse was the silent threat: *I can still leave.*

She wondered if he suffered as much as she did. Not at running, of course. He jogged along beside her without getting winded, while she felt close to death. No, she wondered if he ever thought about that night they'd spent together, about the heat, the pleasure, the scent of their bodies in the throes of climax. She wondered if he ached for her the way she ached for him.

Doubtful. He only talked to her now if he absolutely had to. He refused to be drawn into any teasing or flirtation, rebuffing her words with a warning glance. He was the ultimate standoffish professional, just as he'd been in the beginning, but way too much had happened since then, and Lola was losing her mind.

Because she didn't just miss the sex. She missed having Ransom as a friend, or at least a semi-friend. For a while he'd been nice to her. Not anymore.

She jogged along the running path, a two-word mantra droning in her head. *Fuck you, fuck you, fuck you.* Never mind that she felt better because of the spinach and water and exercise. Never mind that she had more energy and better concentration than she'd had in years. That energy and concentration was focused on wanting sex, and he wasn't giving it to her, and if she stared at his hot ass for too much longer, she was going to cry.

She sped up and ran beside him instead, trying to keep pace with his much longer stride. He looked over at her with a smile, like this was fun, like they were two pals out running together. Ugh, why did he have to look so gorgeous, even when he was covered in sweat? Several fan sites and tabloids had begun calling attention to her handsome bodyguard. She didn't even want to think about what *she* looked like, chugging along beside him, sweating and out of breath.

The next day was a performance day, thank God, and Ransom let her sleep late before he ordered her a healthy breakfast, complete with a spinach-and-strawberry smoothie in a nauseating shade of green. "Why do you get to drink coffee?" she groused.

"You can drink coffee if you finish that smoothie."

So cold. So professional. She couldn't take it anymore. When she dressed for the show that night, she slutted out in petty rebellion, piling on the eyeliner and bright red lipstick, and wearing her tightest pair of silver sequined shorts. When she was finished she turned in front of the mirror, studying the overall effect. Wow, her ass looked better, didn't it?

No, fuck him. She wasn't going to be grateful for being bullied to better health. She tied on her tiny matching silver bikini top and struggled to cinch the back.

"Ransom," she called. "Can you help me?"

Iain came in the bathroom instead, and retied the string several times while staring at her over her shoulder. "That's fine," she finally said.

He regarded her in the mirror. "New look with your makeup? I like your hair."

She'd slicked it every which way and dotted it with silver star barrettes, a style that looked as wild as her emotions felt. "Whatever," she muttered.

Ransom carried her laptop as Iain hustled her out to the bus, complaining that she was always late. This from the guy who'd played with her bikini strings way longer than necessary. For God's sake, she wasn't trying to attract Iain with her skintight, silver-sequined get up. She was trying to get the attention of the tall, dark shadow in her peripheral vision, the bodyguard who refused to be her lover anymore.

When they got to the bus, she cut in front of Ransom and sashayed up the stairs, even though he normally boarded first to check for stowaways.

"Wait," he said, touching her arm.

She hoped he had noticed her ass before he nudged past her. If he had, he gave no sign of it as he performed the usual security check and then told the driver to head out. Rather than sit near her the way he did before they had sex, he engaged Iain in conversation, an additional cut to her ego.

How could he be so unaffected after the things they'd done together? Why didn't he *want her*?

Well, someone would want her. Once they arrived at the festival grounds outside Milan, she flirted her way through the backstage area, kissing and hugging all the sound techs, and hanging on muscular roadies as Ransom stared at her from five feet away. The Italian security dudes were top notch. She singled out one of them, a rugged, sexy manwhore with a wide smile, and planted herself in front of him, cooing over his long sideburns and beard.

She didn't like sideburns. She hated beards. But she wanted to make Ransom jealous, so she pretended she loved them.

"Are you going to stand guard for me tonight?" she asked the guy, batting her eyes. "Keep the crazies away?"

"Yes, of course." His smile widened. Unlike Ransom, he seemed moved by her tiny bikini top. His eyes dipped down and meandered over the swells of her breasts.

"And what are you up to after the show?" She slid a hand across his chest and tugged at his security badge. "Maximo? My goodness. What a fitting name for a big guy like you."

She could feel Ransom's frown boring into her back. Another Italian security grunt sidled over as she massaged Maximo's shoulders with a suggestive moan of appreciation.

"Wow," she cooed. "Who's your sexy friend?"

She was in the middle of giving the second bouncer the same chest-stroking, ID-checking attention when firm fingers wrapped around her elbow.

"Time for the sound check," said Ransom through gritted teeth.

"I already did the sound check. Hey, I was in the middle of setting up another threesome!"

"You're not funny."

She shied away from him. "I'm not trying to be funny."

He pulled her into a quiet spot behind the lighting console and let her go. "You don't have to whore around to get my attention. I see you."

"Shut up." She felt a blush rise in her cheeks. She tried to leave, but he blocked her with his body.

"Do you think it's going to make me jealous, to see you hang on the stage crew? Do you think I won't be able to resist you because you dress like this?" He raked a gaze over her mostly naked body, lingering on her booty shorts. "Do you think I'll want you more if I see you coming onto someone else?" When she turned her face away, he wrenched it back with firm fingers on her cheeks. She shoved at him.

"Don't screw up my face. I already did my makeup."

"And I already want you as much as anyone can want you. So these games you're playing are pointless."

"Oh, you want me?" Lola repeated his words with biting sarcasm. "You have a really weird way of showing it. You won't talk to me, won't even look at me. Can you blame me for hitting on someone else?"

"Yeah, I can blame you, when you're only doing it to annoy me. Stop it, okay?" He lowered his voice and leaned closer to her ear. "I'm not worth this. I'm not worth you acting out like this."

She wanted to smack his earnest face. She wanted to punch his beautiful mouth, because he refused to kiss her.

"Why do you fucking care?" she snapped. "You're only here for the job, right? The paycheck?"

Iain waved and beckoned her from the stairs. "Hey, Lola!" He looked irritated with Ransom, Ransom looked irritated with her, and she felt irritated by everyone. Now she had to go out in front of all those happy people and do a happy show when she felt like shit.

He touched her arm and she shoved him away, storming toward Iain while giving Ransom the finger over her shoulder. Fuck him. She had a show to do, and slutting out wasn't helping, and flirting with other guys wasn't helping because she only wanted him. Basically nothing was helping, and while she might feel great physically after pumping herself full of fucking spinach, her feelings were screwed up as shit.

No feelings. Just beats.

Lola squared her shoulders and went up the stairs, ignoring Maximo's wave as she passed him. Ugh, those sideburns. So gross. As soon as the crowd could see her, they made a comforting amount of noise. Ransom said he wanted her? Bullshit. If he wanted her, he would take her. No, these beautiful people, these ravers wanted her, and she was going to give them a fucking show.

She checked over the sound console, making sure her tracks were imported and all the components were working. She grabbed the mic and cued up her #1 EDM anthem from the year before. Her kickass single, her screaming crowds, her musical creativity, and her voice shouting through the forty-foot bank of speakers.

"Milan, are you ready to fucking party?"

The crowd roared with approval. Ransom watched her from the place he always watched, at the top of the stairs, but she tuned him out, focusing instead on building the musical wonderland her audience deserved. If Ransom wouldn't appreciate her sequined booty shorts, at least they looked awesome reflecting the lights.

She danced from one track to the next, delivering the seamless mixes and quirky samples she was famous for. Each time she built to a drop, everyone screamed in manic appreciation. She partied along with her listeners, riling them up until they were an undulating mass of fluorescent happiness. When her time was almost up, she hopped on top of the sound console and moved her body to the music, pointing at the ravers. *You're inside me. I'm inside you. We got this.*

Ransom had told her no stage diving. Her contract said no stage diving, but this Milan stage was perfect for it, not too high, with the crowd right up on the barriers. Sometimes you just had to do shit you weren't supposed to do, because you were irritated and angsty, and because you wanted to piss off your bodyguard. As soon as she threw out her arms to signal her intention to the crowd, Ransom came running toward her from the stairs. Too late.

She soared off the sound console and into the audience just as the song pounded to its peak. The crowd caught her, laughing and shrieking. People always asked if stage diving hurt, but it didn't hurt at all, high or sober. The noise hurt, the shouts, the squeals as the spectators found Lady Paradise suddenly among them, but the hands were always careful. No one pinched or punched her, or pulled her hair.

"I love you," she said as they passed her back and forth in a meandering circle. She opened her eyes and saw Ransom standing at the edge of the stage, yelling and gesturing for the crowd to bring her back.

"Fuck him," she said to her fans. "Don't listen to him. We're having fun."

Crowd surfing didn't hurt. It only took you out of the world into another, different world, which was sometimes a really necessary thing.

* * * * *

Ransom stood in front of eighty thousand screaming ravers, waving his arms like a maniac. They ignored him. All eyes were on Lady Paradise, floating upon the palms of her minions. He shouted for them to return her to the stage as a thousand dire scenarios filled his brain. *Broken bones, asphyxiation, trampling, rape, kidnapping, head injury, mob stampede, death...*

He was going to kill her. He was going to fucking slaughter her for this.

He was so wrought up, so livid by the time security waded into the fray that he could barely look at her. They plucked her from her admirers and handed her over the barricades. When she was close enough, he reached down and pulled her into his arms.

"What the fuck?" he shouted over the din of the crowd. "What the everloving fuck is wrong with you?"

She grinned at him. "I can't help it. It's fun."

When he continued to glare, she laughed and wrapped her arms around his shoulders, and kissed him on the lips. The crowd screamed louder, encouraging her to continue. His body reacted, hardening, responding even in front of all these people. Even when he knew it could ruin him.

He tried to peel her off. Cell phones pointed at them from all directions. One of his friends back in L.A. had sent him a link to a social media blog dedicated solely to him, Lady Paradise's bodyguard. They called him Gilberto. There were fan fiction stories about their romance. None of this was okay, and holding her here in front of all these people wasn't going to put that kind of speculation to rest.

"Get the fuck off me," he said. "Finish your fucking set."

Even through the arousal, through her intoxicating closeness, he couldn't rein in his anger, because it was a fury born of fear. He cared for her. He worried for her. In some way, he thought he was falling in love with her, which was the worst thing of all. Was he driving this wildness on her part? Had this been another stunt to get a reaction? She seemed pretty pleased with herself as she picked up the mic and stirred up the audience again.

He stood beside the sound console for the last few minutes of her set. She wasn't going into the audience again, ever, and as soon as they returned to the bus, they were going to have a talk about her attention-getting tactics. When she finished and signed off, Ransom took her arm to lead her downstairs.

She jerked away. "Leave me alone. Don't get in my face. That was a great set and I don't want you bringing me down."

She ran down the stairs ahead of him, only to be corralled by Iain, who looked equally pissed. Ransom watched as the two started bickering in the midst of the backstage chaos.

"Let's take it to the bus," he suggested, talking over them.

"Gladly," Iain said.

The next artist ran up the stairs, more beats, more shrieks, more glowing, flashing fireworks polluting the air. Lola waved to someone and tried to peel away from them. Ransom redirected her with a belligerent "No."

"You two are so fucking joyless." She stalked to the bus.

"And you're so fucking reckless," Iain retorted.

She stomped up the steps after Ransom checked the interior. "It was one fucking stage dive. Are you seriously going to chew me out? Nothing happened."

"Something could have happened. Sit down." Iain gestured toward the sofa.

"No, I don't want to sit down. That sofa is fucking uncomfortable."

Lola was in full diva mode, and it pained Ransom because he'd come to understand that all these histrionics came from a place of sadness. He restrained himself from interfering as she got in Iain's face.

"I asked for a different bus four weeks ago, Iain, a *comfortable fucking bus*. You're my tour manager, so why won't you help me? When are those MadDance fuckers going to get me a different bus?"

"When you start adhering to the terms of your contract." Iain held up a hand as she started making excuses about the stage dive. "It's not just that. Someone recorded that unauthorized set you played in Hamburg. Now they're peddling the video and audio versions online and your label is pissed, not to mention the 'MadDance fuckers.'"

"It's not my fault someone recorded it!"

"You played the set without authorization," said Iain. "You signed a contract that stipulated no extra performances on this tour."

"It wasn't a set." She turned to Ransom. "You were there. Did I play a freaking set? All I did was monkey around in the DJ booth."

He spread his fingers in a helpless gesture. "I haven't read your contract. I don't know, Lola. I don't know what makes it a set."

"Well, I do," Iain broke in, "and I watched the video and listened to the remastered version, which is all over the Lady Paradise chat boards. I'd expect to hear from Vanguard's lawyers shortly. Those record labels don't fuck around. And MadDance is going to be up my ass thanks to this stage dive, which goes against the terms of your goddamn contract!"

She shook her head as the tour manager's voice rose to a shout. "This is bullshit," she shouted back. "I can do what I want, I can play what I want—"

Iain held up a jabbing finger. "That's the thing though. You can't. You've convinced yourself you're some untouchable, irreplaceable genius. Well, guess what? There are thirty or forty DJs who'd be happy to take your place, who spin better than you. I know them. I've worked with them."

"Oh, really? They're better than me? Did you see me out there tonight? Fuck you. You're an asshole."

"Because I'm telling you the truth?" The jabbing finger came perilously close to Lola's nose. Ransom watched, his body poised to spring if Iain touched her in violence. "And you know what else?" said Iain. "Those people are real artists, actual professionals who know how to abide by a contract."

"Real artists?" Lola spluttered in a fury. "What right do you have to talk to me about artistry?"

"I have every right. I'm your manager on this tour, and I'm going to do my job, you spoiled little piece of shit."

"Back the fuck off," she screamed in Iain's face.

"Okay, kids." Ransom stepped between them, holding up his hands. "Why don't you two discuss things later, when tempers have cooled?"

"What is there to discuss?" Veins popped in Iain's neck and forehead as he held out his phone. "In an hour or so, I'm going to start getting messages from my boss about your shenanigans onstage, or rather offstage. This is the third time you've willfully ignored the personal safety codicil of your contract that restricts you from entering the audience."

"Blah blah blah. Those stage dives are how I made my name in this business. That's what people want, that's what they remember."

"It doesn't matter," said Iain, and Ransom had to agree. It was one thing to dive into the crowd at a small venue. At these festivals...

"Ugh, you talk to her," said Iain. "You explain to her. I can't even deal."

"Here's the thing," Ransom said to Lola. "When you jump into the crowd, you don't only endanger yourself. You can't see it from where you are, but everyone in the crowd surges toward you. Kids get shoved against the barriers and it's not safe. Performers belong onstage."

"I know that," she yelled. "I'm on stage, I'm trying to perform, I'm trying to make these rich fucking pricks more money, and what do I get for it? A bunch of idiotic bullshit restrictions."

"Just fucking do your job," Iain yelled back. "And stop giving everyone around you a headache. You're the only one who has to have a special fucking security guy following you around, because you're such an irresponsible cunt."

"Hey," said Ransom in a sharp voice. "Watch your fucking mouth."

Iain turned his jabbing finger toward Ransom now, even though he still spoke to Lola. "Do you know how much this fucking bodyguard costs MadDance? Do you have any idea of the expense? This tour, this bus, your fucking liability insurance, all of it has a price tag."

"And you too," she shot back at her manager. "You have a price tag too, even if you're shitty at your job. It's all about the fucking money. I know that. None of you gives a shit about me, except for your fucking money, so fuck you." She turned to Ransom next. "And fuck you. Fuck all of you. Fuck all of this. At this point I really don't give a fuck. Find someone else to do your goddamned festival tour. I fucking quit."

She stormed back to the bedroom and yanked the door shut, and threw the lock as Iain shouted, "You can't quit. Don't you understand that?"

Ransom held up a hand to silence him. "What's her deal?" Iain seethed. "I mean, seriously, what's wrong with her?"

"Nothing. I think she understands everything," said Ransom. "For better or worse."

10.
PORNO SEX

Back at the hotel, Lola waited to cry until Ransom was in the shower. She'd be damned if she'd cry in front of him, but the tears still had to come out. As she mopped at her eyes, she listened for the sound of the water shutting off. He never took long enough showers, or maybe she just had too many tears.

She only cried now when he was in the shower, or when she was in the shower. She used to cry when he was asleep, but then she realized he wasn't always sleeping when he looked like he was sleeping, because in the mornings, he'd study her with those dark, brooding eyes.

She couldn't think about his eyes, or all the other things she'd come to love about him. It seemed really important not to reveal how much she obsessed over him, so she'd been stuffing everything down, every awkward, lonely feeling. Maybe that's why she'd lost it after the show, and screamed at Ransom and Iain like a maniac.

The water shut off. Lola unwrapped the towel from her hair and used it to wipe her cheeks. She didn't know what had happened tonight, why she was coming apart one downbeat at a time. She'd been fine until Ransom pulled her out of the crowd. The way he'd glared at her...

If you don't want him to glare at you, don't act like an idiot.

That was easier said than done. When he'd pushed her away in front of all those people, like she was something dirty, it had really hurt her feelings. It made her feel dirty, and her hour-long shower hadn't done anything to help her feel clean again. She looked down at her bare legs under her sleep shirt. Now her skin was too dry.

As soon as Ransom came out in his joggers and tee shirt, Lola slipped past him into the bathroom and shut the door. She could still smell the scent of his soap and deodorant in the humid air. She checked her eyes for redness, splashed some water on her face, then dried off and went back into the room with her lotion.

She sat on the edge of the bed and started moisturizing her legs. He'd probably accuse her again of flirting and seduction, but she felt scaly so he could suck it. Once her legs were done she started on her arms, and then the back of her shoulders where she'd stood under the hot water until it burned. No, she could never get clean enough for him, which made no sense, because he was a porn legend who'd made hundreds of films.

She'd searched Rico Rockhard and found dozens of pages of results: photos, clips, entire films freely available on the web. She'd watched some of them. She couldn't help it.

He'd looked the same back then. Maybe a little less muscular, with darker, shorter hair, but his cock looked the same. That lightning bolt. What the fuck? He was a monster in the vids she'd watched. He'd drilled the women, held them down, berated them, subdued them in violent mastery. She could never watch for more than a minute or two, because it was so shocking to see him that way.

It was also an invasion of his privacy. It made her feel shitty and weak to watch them.

But what else did she have?

She looked over toward the desk, where he typed on his laptop. He had to write daily reports for Ironclad, memoirs of her fuckery. Today's report would include her illicit stage dive and the argument with her manager.

"Want some lotion?" she asked.

He looked up at her. Brooding. Always brooding. "No, thank you."

She held the bottle to her nose. "It doesn't smell girly."

He didn't need lotion. She just wanted to talk to him, which he knew. "I don't want any lotion," he said. "I'm typing."

She rubbed a little more on her hands and tossed the bottle across the room, hitting her luggage by chance. He noticed and smiled.

"We're off to Spain tomorrow," he said.

"Mm-hm."

"We'll have to pack."

"That's what people usually do when they leave a hotel." She clamped her lips shut. She didn't want to make this night worse by smarting off to him. He turned away and continued his report. She got out her own laptop and typed "Rico Rockhard" into the search engine. It autofilled because she'd searched him so many times before. God, she had to stop. This wasn't healthy. She sighed and put on her headphones, but before she could open up a video, he said her name.

"Lola?"

She turned to him as he shut his laptop. Had he already finished his report? Did she look guilty? Did he know she was perving his pornos? "Yeah?"

"Do you really want to quit the tour?"

Oh fuck. She'd said that earlier, in her screamfest with Iain. She shrugged and avoided his gaze. "I don't know."

"Do you or don't you? You must know how you feel. This is the second time you've talked about wanting to quit."

She minimized the search results and stared at her keyboard instead. "It's just so much bullshit, you know?"

"Yeah, I know."

He was gearing up to say something else, but she didn't want to hear it. She didn't want to think about how much she wanted to quit the tour, quit the business, take her guitar and move back to Memphis, and play in some small club with people who were her friends. Real friends, not L.A. friends. But she didn't have any real friends anymore. She'd pissed them all off by becoming an L.A. friend: self-occupied, shallow, a diva, just as everyone said.

"Oh well." She shrugged. "Whatever. I hate Iain." That was something they both could understand. "I hate being on tour. I hate—" *Myself. I hate myself for being a scared, fucked up poser, but I love you, Ransom. Not that it matters.*

"I need a distraction." She leaned her head down on her hands. "I need something to take the edge off."

"Maybe you need to quit the tour," he said without missing a beat.

"No. I need to go out."

"You owe me five miles for the stage dive. Want to go for a run?"

"At this hour?" She sat up, hugging herself. "Fuck no. I need to have some fun. I need sex again, if not from you, then someone willing."

He was already shaking his head.

"I do," she protested. "I know you don't want to hear about it, but it's been ages—"

"It's been less than two weeks."

"I need people. I need activity and energy." She got up and started pacing. "I need to forget about tonight because it sucked. I want to party. I need a few stiff drinks and someone to go to bed with me."

He got in her way, holding up his judgey finger. "You think you need those things, but what you really need is sleep. It's been a tough night. Tomorrow's another day."

"Yes, another day just like this one."

He pointed her toward her bed. "Go lie down before you start losing it. We're not going out. It's too late."

"Go lie down? What am I, your dog? This isn't one of your crazy fetish pornos, Rico."

He pinched the bridge of his nose. "I've told you not to bring that up. And there were never any dogs."

"Weren't there? I bet I could find one." She flopped onto the bed and reopened her search results. "Or at least one where you treat a woman like a dog."

She could never rein herself in, even when she knew she was hurting someone. When she knew she was hurting *him*. He watched her with a frown, his hands braced on his hips.

"Yeah, I'm watching your pornos ," she said. "Whatcha gonna do about it?" She started reading off titles, lurid examples of his worst work. "*Bound Anal Slaves*. That sounds lovely. Then there's the ever popular *Choke on My Cock*. Ooh, *Painal Peril, Part Four*. Bitch hung in there for four rounds of painful anal with your lightning bolt, huh? What a trooper."

"Lola, stop it."

"I think I'm going to watch the whole painal series. I'm sick like that."

He made a noise in his throat. "You'll get a computer virus if you click on that shit. Don't. Lola—"

She clicked it anyway, taking out her headphone jack so the sounds of Rico Rockhard's painal stylings filled the room. Crying, begging, and his animalistic grunts and grumbles, so fake, and yet so terribly real.

He moved then, took away her laptop and shut it, and carried it across the room to drop it on the desk. "When are you going to stop tormenting me?" he said, turning to her. His voice vibrated with fury.

"I'll stop when I get sex. I'll stop when you acknowledge what we had together."

"*What we had together?* We shouldn't have been together." A vein throbbed in his forehead. That vein should have checked her, but she was an idiot and it had been a shitty night.

Instead she took off her panties and pulled her nightshirt over her head, and faced him with her arms spread wide. "I want some fucking painal, Rico. Hop to it."

He strode to her and picked up her nightshirt, and shoved it at her. "You wouldn't survive painal with me. You don't have a clue, not a fucking clue."

"You want it too." She batted the nightshirt away and traced his burgeoning erection through his sweatpants. "You always get hard when you're pissed at me, but that's okay. I like it rough and angry. Maybe I should do porn too. *Painal Peril, Part Five*."

She was going too far. She knew it, but the feel of him vibrating against her was delicious all the same. He gave her a hard look that condemned and lusted at once, and then he was gone, rummaging for condoms in her extensive stash. He stripped and sheathed himself with scary focus, then crawled onto the bed and yanked her legs open. His lightning-emblazoned cock reared between them.

"You want porn sex?" His eyes were scary intense, and black as hell. "That's what you want from me?"

He shoved into her pussy, an abrupt, angry thrust. If his force hadn't made her wet already, it would have hurt. It still hurt a little, and she bit her lip as he pounded into her, hardcore-jackhammer style. She'd seen her share of porn, Rico and non-Rico films, and she'd always wondered how the actresses could stand being pummeled so relentlessly for so long. After thirty seconds, she reached to grip his arms.

"Had enough?" he asked through gritted teeth.

She gazed up at his fury, his torment. Fuck, she'd really pushed things too far. "I'm sorry." Her voice shook from his violent thrusts. "I'm sorry I..."

He pulled away, jumped off the bed and stalked to the other side of the room. She went after him, even though she didn't know what to say. She just wrapped her arms around his waist and held him. He was shaking worse than she was.

"I don't believe I did that." He took off the condom and slung it in the trash. "I don't believe I did that to you."

She rested her cheek against his back, willing his trembling to stop. "I wanted it."

"No, I can't believe I—" He sounded so broken, so upset. His hands curled around hers until she had to release him. He turned to her and lifted her face. "Are you okay? I'm sorry. I'm so sorry."

"No, I'm sorry."

He shook his head. "No, you can't be sorry. I hurt you."

He pressed his fingers over his eyes. His jaw was taut to the point of shattering. She tugged his hands away and he gazed down at her with a woebegone stillness.

"I'm sorry," she repeated. "It was my fault. I pushed you until you lost it. I wanted you to lose it."

She hugged him tight, because she knew as soon as she let him go, he would leave for real. He'd walk out the door as fast as he could pack his luggage, whether there was someone to replace him or not. This was the end, unless she could find a way to make it not the end.

"Ransom," she whispered. "I pushed you because I wanted to hurt you, and I wanted to hurt you because I want you that much." She spread her fingers across his back, then drew them down the tense lattice of his muscles. "You know when you want someone so much that it makes you angry?"

Some response sparked within his stillness. "Yes, I know how that feels. But we can't— Lola, I can't—"

"We can." She pressed herself closer against him. "We have to, or we'll hurt each other even more."

* * * * *

Ransom gazed down at her, shaking his head. There had to be some flaw in her reasoning, but he ached for her, he *hurt* for her, and she was right there, nuzzling him and teasing his senses. He'd never gone fully soft, but now his cock surged even straighter, bucking against her hand. A drop of precum escaped, and she traced her fingertip through the slick fluid, swirling it around the head. He started shaking again.

"Lola, you make me into an awful person."

"Good." She took his hand and drew him to the bed. "Because I don't want to be awful alone."

He knew it meant disaster, but he went with her, crawling onto the same bed where he'd just attacked her. He shook his head even as he covered her and stroked his knuckles down her cheek. She was so young, so soft, so raw, so dangerously beguiling. She called to every fiber of his being, and he couldn't figure out why. If he knew, he might be able to fight against it. As it was, he was lost.

He kissed her the way he'd wanted to kiss her for days now, not angrily, but not gently either. He kissed her lips, her nose, her eyes, her forehead, her delicate pink wisps of hair. She clutched him as he explored her with his mouth. "Don't think about before," she whispered. "Forget it happened. Please don't leave me."

"I won't." He kissed down the line of her neck to her breasts, tracing her nipples with his tongue while she made agonized noises.

"It'll be okay," he promised. "Shh. I'll make everything better."

She shivered as his breath blew across her skin. She drove him mad with her responsiveness, the way every touch or breath elicited squirms of bliss. She was definitely going to bliss out over what he planned to do next.

He slid lower, drawing her thighs wide and holding her open with his shoulders. Her fingers twisted in his hair as he parted her pussy lips, baring her swollen clit. Before he even touched his mouth to that sensitive flesh, she began to quake.

"Oh, I can't." She sighed. "I can't even..."

The first swipe of his tongue brought a rough moan. He held her hips as she arched against his mouth.

"I thought you might like that," he said, and then he went to work.

One thing about being an ex-porn star—he knew his way around the female body. He'd learned to eat pussy—on and off screen—with far more skill and appreciation than the average man. *Lick, suck, pinch, titillate...*

He drove his tongue against her clit and then teased up and down her slit. When her voice rose to a wail, he massaged her pussy lips, then focused on her clit again. He teased with the tip of his tongue until she begged for more, then shoved a finger inside her to find her G-spot.

One thing about being an ex-porn star—he knew how to find a G-spot.

The resulting climax was a gorgeous sight to behold. Her body trembled uncontrollably as she bucked against his mouth, gasping out words that made no sense. It didn't matter. He understood. She yanked him up by the hair and he went, chuckling as she mashed her lips to his. She scratched at his arms as he held himself over her. "I want you," she breathed. "I want your cock."

"I bet you do." He palmed his throbbing length, glad for his other porn-star power. He could hold off as long as he had to, to give her everything she wanted. Epic staying power had been a necessity in the porn business. Based on Lola's exorbitant sexual energy, it would be a necessity now.

"You want this?" he taunted, tracing fingers up the jagged lightning bolt on his cock.

"Yes. Please, Ransom..." Her voice trailed off. Was she blushing? "I actually kind of want the painal."

"*Kind of* want it?" He repeated her tentative words, wondering at her bravado. Painal: Anal sex that hurt, preferably in a good way. If she wanted it to hurt, he could hurt her without really hurting her. "Are you sure that's what you want?"

She nodded. Of course she nodded, she was crazy. Why did he forget that all the time, when it was one of the things about her that sucked him in?

"All right." He climbed off the bed and went for a condom, and lube. "Just remember you asked for it."

He rolled on a rubber and made a big deal of skimping on the lubricant while she grinned maniacally from the bed. When he finished, he put on his show face and stalked to her. She pretended to scramble away, but didn't fight very hard when he caught her by one leg and dragged her back. When she tried to turn over, he barked "No" and made her stay on her back. He wanted to see every minute of this, every note of emotion and discomfort.

He spread her legs, hooking them over his arms, and shoved a couple slick fingers between her ass cheeks. He kissed her hard as he toyed with her tiny hole. She groaned against his mouth, and he could sense her pussy growing wetter against his palm. It would have been easier to just thrust into her there, but she didn't like things easy. She liked things exciting.

When it came to sex, so did he.

"Look at me," he commanded. When she did, he held her gaze and stroked his long, thick cock. "This is going in your ass, and it's going to hurt, and there's nothing you can do about it."

"Oh God." She gave him the perfect combination of terror and *oh yum please yes put it in me*. He knew from their earlier encounter that she enjoyed a deep, thorough assfucking. Her passion inflamed his passion, her need inflamed his need, and her gaze revealed an adulation that filled him with carnal power.

She bit her lip as he worked a finger into her anal channel. She clenched around him, then whined as he added a second finger and started stretching her. There was something so deliciously primal about violating that tight, sensitive space. It was dirty and dangerous in a way most women didn't like, but this one liked it.

"How does that feel?" he asked, sliding his fingers in and out of her, preparing her to take his girth. "You want more?"

"Yes, please." She sighed, then remembered that she wasn't supposed to be enjoying this—the whole "painal" thing. She amended her answer to "Ow, you're hurting me."

"Just wait. It's going to get worse before I'm done with you."

He used his stern voice, the one he used when he worked as her bodyguard. This wasn't work anymore. This was play, dangerous, daring play that might fuck up both of them, but he couldn't summon the willpower to stop. He drew out his fingers and positioned the head of his cock against her ass.

"This whole thing's going in your asshole. Every fucking inch."

"No. Please!"

Ah, she was good at this. He pried her legs wider and leaned to kiss her, then hissed as she caught his lower lip between her teeth.

"No biting. I think you need to be taught a lesson."

He pressed into her ass, breaching her tight ring with careful control, but still enough force to keep her in the game. She pushed at his chest and choked out lovely, distressed noises that made him swell harder as he tried to work his way inside her. Someday he'd shove her down on her stomach and fuck her ass doggy style, but right now he needed to see her face.

Someday, Ransom? You're thinking about someday? A future?

"Yes. Yes!" Her passionate cries distracted him from that troubling thought. A groan of pleasure erupted from her throat and resonated through his reeling senses. He might have reminded her that painal was supposed to hurt, but who fucking cared at this point? It felt so goddamn good. Her ass clenched around his cock as he held her down and drove deep. She was his to capture, fuck, hurt. *Holy fuck.*

He started to move in her, faster, harder, and was rewarded with more wails of pretended agony. She tested even his epic staying power. He closed his eyes and tried not to come, tried not to shoot inside her spasming ass before he could fully appreciate the thrill of being inside her.

She threw her arms to the sides as he bottomed out in her, over and over. The more she squirmed, the harder he held her legs so she couldn't pull away.

"Does that feel bad, baby?"

"Yes. Ow." She pouted theatrically. "It feels awful. It hurts."

"You're gonna take it. Do you hear me? You're going to take my fat cock in your ass until you come."

"I can't come," she whimpered. "You're hurting me too much."

"Then you're going to get fucked and fucked until you're raw, and I'm still going to force you to come."

"Oh, please, don't."

Her protests weren't real, but her building excitement was a hundred percent genuine. He wanted this to be everything she wanted and more.

"Come here, baby." He held her closer as he lengthened his strokes. He pulled out slow, then drove in hard, then pulled out slow again as she spread her palms against his hips. After a few minutes of hard drilling, he stroked her clit, just a tease, a touch. She whimpered and arched against his hand.

"Someone's wrought up," he taunted. "Someone claims it hurts, but she's all wet."

"Please... Oh..."

He massaged her clit again, knowing just how to draw her pleasure to a peak. She was wild from their role play, reveling in his sensual force. Just before he thought she might come, he stopped. Her resulting anger was gorgeous. She tried to pull his hand back, and then gave up and touched her clit herself. He tsked and gripped her wrists, yanking them over her head.

"No touching unless I allow it, naughty girl. You leave your hands right here."

That turned her on so much she was almost levitating. She stared up at him, impaled on his cock, desperate to bring herself off, but not allowed to do it. He held her thighs open and rode her, his thick shaft stretching her over and over. Shit, he wasn't going to last much longer.

"You know why I'm hurting your asshole?" he asked through clenched teeth. "You know why you're getting it so rough?"

"Why?" she panted.

"Because you're a dirty girl. You're naughty and you don't behave."

Which was the damn truth, above and beyond this abandoned tumble into depravity. He thumbed her clit again, and rolled his hips so she felt his entire girth with each thrust. Her mouth fell open as her hands clenched into fists above her head.

"I bet you don't even want to come," he said. "You just want me to keep hurting you."

"No, I want to come!"

While his right hand worked her clit to a frenzy, he gave her another punishing kiss. They were on fire, just like the first time, only hotter. She shook under him and gasped against his lips, begging for completion.

"God... Please. Ransom... Oh my God..."

Ten seconds later she erupted, reaching for him against the edict to keep her hands over her head. He caught her in her arms so he could feel every shudder of her orgasm as he suffered through his. It was suffering, truly, because it was so intense and hot, and because this was so wrong. He shoved himself deep inside her, holding her against him. He never wanted to move.

"Jesus Christ. Holy shit." Her peal of laughter rang out over his hard exhale. "You rule, Ransom. You're so fucking good at making me come."

All those words, all that excitement, when Ransom couldn't summon anything but the need to take another breath. Somehow he had to cope with this. He had to cope with the fact that they connected this way in bed.

But it was more than that.

That's what scared him.

He pulled away from her when he started to go soft, and even then he couldn't find the words he needed. Instead he patted the side of her head and kissed her again in all the wonderful places. Eyes, nose, cheekbones, forehead, lips. *I'm falling in love with you. Why are you doing this to me?*

For her part, she gazed up at him in pleased wonder. So much for resisting her. He was fucked.

11.
NOT WORTH IT

After they showered, they ate pizza and drank San Pellegrino on the same bed where Ransom had fucked her. Lola tried not to stare, but he was shirtless and hungry, and everything about him turned her on. He ate pizza like he fucked, all earthy and shit, with lots of gusto.

Jesus, Lola, you have to stay in control.

She knew she was acting like an infatuated kid, turning stupid over a much older man, but no matter how hard she tried, she couldn't control it. She couldn't be the cool, mythical Lady Paradise around him. When she was with other men, she didn't give a shit about them, so she always had the upper hand. With Ransom, she felt on the verge of falling apart.

"Want another piece?" He offered her the box.

"No thanks."

"It's good pizza." He sank his teeth into another slice with a wicked grin that made her insides turn to mush. Since when was stuffing your face with pizza sexy? Ransom made it seem that way. She went for her guitar and brought it back to the bed, hoping it might provide some outlet for her roiling emotions. His grin widened as he watched her tune it, plucking at the strings.

"And now you're going to sing. Could this night be any more perfect?"

His warm words made a blush spread over her cheeks. It *had* turned into a perfect night. Too perfect, which scared her. When would he withdraw from her again? Would she survive it? She gave an abrupt, dissonant strum and met his gaze.

"I'm going to sing about you," she said.

"Oh, fuck."

"Uh huh. So get ready. I've been writing this in my spare time."

Her spare time: those few and precious moments not eaten up by her manager's demands, her musical tinkering, public relations crap, the endless stream of demos cooling in her Dropbox, and the inordinate amount of time she spent obsessing over Ransom. She strummed again, a chord as present and powerful as her bodyguard-lover, and began to sing some lyrics she'd written over the previous few days.

"*It's been so many years of blue sky rain/ so many years of pink hair pain...*" He smiled at that, which gave her the courage to continue. When had she gotten so shy in front of him? She strummed another chord. "*So many years of losing myself in clouds/ when the sun never came.*"

Pain and *came* didn't quite rhyme, but whatever. Sometimes beats didn't match up exactly either. Imperfect art was still art. Messed up feelings were still feelings. He was the sun in her song, and he knew it. He was the sun in all her songs these days, which was fucked up, because she'd started out hating him so much.

He watched as she strummed out a few more lines, exposing herself to him in a way she didn't expose herself in front of the festival ravers. In the end, she wimped out and omitted the angsty middle verses, and went straight to the end.

"*You say I'm a kid, but maybe I'm grown up enough to see...*" Her voice held the note as her fingers searched for the last chord. "*That sometimes what you didn't want/ is exactly what you need.*"

She put down her guitar and made a face at him to cover her tumultuous feelings. "*See* and *need* don't rhyme. There's an extra d."

A faint smile. A twinkle in his eyes. "Yeah, but you love extra d."

She laughed as he leaned to kiss her, one of his hands resting on her leg. He tasted like pizza and lemon Pellegrino, and smelled like clean, warm bodyguard fresh out of the shower.

"I do love extra d," she admitted when they pulled apart. "Especially your extra d, which is extra thick and extra hard."

"You're extra dirty."

"Not as dirty as you." It was easier to talk about sex than the other things she'd come to feel for him. She hugged her knees to her chest, feeling stripped by his closeness and steady regard. "Thank you for tonight. It was...memorable."

"I try to be memorable."

He'd just be a memory one day. All their carnal hookups would be a fleeting collection of memories, a few magical weeks in time. She couldn't bear to think of that right now. He sobered. He must have been thinking about it too.

"This thing we're doing..." He cupped her face. "This is so against the rules, kid. They're going to fire me over this. All those years working my way to the top of my field..."

"They'll never know." She put her hand over his. "I promise I'll never tell anyone. I swear."

"Whether you tell or not, it happened."

Her expression hardened to match his. "Are you going to be all honorable and make some big, guilty confession to your boss?"

"I try to be honorable."

She put her guitar back in its case. "Don't be honorable over me," she said. "I'm a twenty-year-old raver with pink hair. I'm not worth it."

"Don't say you're not worth it." He moved the pizza box to the other bed and gathered her in his arms. "I want to tell you something." His voice deepened with feigned dramatic resonance. "I want to tell you something about life."

"Ooh, life." She mocked so she wouldn't start bawling. Why did she go weepy every time he held her?

Because she didn't have any other love in her life.

Wait. Fuck.

Love?

You love him, Lola. Just tell him. Admit it.

Five miserable years of partying and posturing and fucking guys she didn't even like, when she could have been with a man like this. An honorable, tender, intelligent man who cared enough to teach her about life.

He cradled her against his chest and rested his chin on her temple. "I know I'm going to sound all parental and uptight when I say this—"

"Which is how you always sound, so whatever."

"So, whatever. My wise advice is that you're worth exactly what you believe you're worth. Do you understand what I mean?" He repeated it again, like she might not have heard the first time. "You're worth exactly what you believe you're worth. Not just monetarily, but emotionally. If you let people belittle and use you—"

That made her sit up in irritation. "You think I let people use me? I don't. I use them."

"I know you do. It's a powerful defensive weapon. But it's still a defense." He tilted her face up to his, and she knew she looked defensive as hell. "Underneath your Lady Paradise persona, I know you're unhappy. You're afraid the next album, the next festival, the next hair color won't be good enough."

"Fuck you," she muttered. "You don't know anything."

He pulled her close again, stroking fingers into her nape so goosebumps rose on her skin. "It doesn't matter. I wasn't even talking about you. I was talking about me. My past. My regrets. In my last career, I let people manipulate me into being less than I was." His slow sigh ruffled her hair. "You're worth exactly what you believe you're worth, Lola. That's the only advice I feel qualified to give."

His quiet voice made her heart ache. When she said *Fuck you*, she really meant *I love you*. He probably understood that. She curled her fingers around his muscled arm.

"How long did you do the porn stuff?"

"Too long." He sighed again. "I did five hundred and sixty-three shoots, which turned into God knows how many movies. I fucked hundreds of women on camera, made friends with a lot of them, watched them succumb one after the other to depression, drugs, and shitty relationships."

She sat up to look at him, but he wasn't there. His tortured gaze was trapped somewhere in the past.

"So many of them hated themselves. That's what got to me in the end. At first, I convinced myself it was okay to trash those women on film, hurt them, hold them down and degrade them, because it was all just business. A performance. But by the end..."

She slid her fingers down to hold his hand. "What happened? I mean, what happened to make you decide you'd had enough?"

He gave a soft, sad laugh. "My conscience happened. I had a friend, a beautiful woman I worked with during the final two years. We grew close because we had a lot in common: big, crazy families, L.A. upbringing, a growing aversion to the business. But once you're in porn, it's hard to get out. The money's good, the lifestyle's flexible, and the producers always pressure you for one more shoot. Rayna wanted to get out but she didn't know what else to do. She didn't think she was good enough..."

His voice trailed off. *You're worth exactly what you believe you're worth.*

"She got into drugs to cope with the lifestyle," he said, continuing his story. "She drank herself to sleep every night, or took pain pills to come down from whatever stimulant she'd taken. We used to have long, emotional talks, but that side of her disappeared until she was only a shell of her former self. I pleaded with her to rehab, to get out, but she was so sunken in despair and self-hate by that point..."

"And you were too." She could hear it in his tone. "What happened to her?"

He shook his head, staring down at their hands. Lola didn't press for clarification. She could imagine the rest. She could imagine his helpless guilt as he watched his friend throw away her life. She could imagine him quitting porn and starting a new career, a career where he could be the protector instead of the assailant. Where he could prevent people from harming themselves through addictions and destructive behaviors, rather than be complicit in their spiral.

She laced her fingers through his. "What happened to her wasn't your fault."

"Oh, I was part of the problem." A muscle ticked in his jaw. "The things I did to her on film, to all those women, day after day, year after year... That's why I can't stand the idea of you watching, or anyone watching. I can't stand that I made films for so long. When I turned to drugs to perform, and alcohol to sleep at night, I already knew how that story ended."

Lola stared at him. Uptight, upright Ransom using drugs and alcohol? She couldn't imagine it. The idea of him high or drunk, outside his iron edifice of control, terrified her.

"So instead, I decided to change my life," he said. "I decided I was worth more than fucking for money. I got clean, shaped up, and applied for an entry-level position at Ironclad. I was honest with my boss about my past. I told him I wanted to make amends, that I wanted to help people. I worked my way up through the ranks, proving myself client by client. Now here I am." The faraway look went away, and her stern bodyguard was back, restating his brisk advice. "You decide what you're worth, Lola. No one else will do it for you. If it was up to those assholes I worked for, I'd still be pumping out porn flicks today."

"Literally pumping them out," she said mournfully. "I'm sorry I watched some of them. I promise I never will again."

"They're bullshit. They're not sexy. They're..."

Again, he didn't finish, and Lola understood why. Some things were too awful to describe. Instead she pulled his face to hers and kissed him, a long, slow kiss to take on his sadness and make it one more thing they shared. When she pulled away, he gazed down at her, a frown marring his handsome features.

"Be careful." He smoothed his fingers over her cheeks. "Don't get too attached to me. There are better things in store for you than an ex-porn star on the bad end of thirty."

She brushed his warnings away, along with his fingers. "I don't care how old you are, or that you used to do porn."

"You missed the important part of that sentence. There are better things in store for you."

She almost scoffed and said she'd never find anything better, that there was nothing in store for her because she was a fucking mess. But then she remembered *You're worth exactly what you believe you're worth*, and she kept the words inside and kissed him again.

"I like being with you," she said when they parted.

"I like being with you too, but there's no way forward for us. I'm too old and you're too crazy." He grimaced as she straddled him. She could feel his cock rising to life, even after their weighty conversation. "I don't want to hurt you," he said, holding her hips when she tried to grind on him.

"I want you to hurt me. I want you to use me like a filthy gym sock."

"No. I care too much to do that to you. And you should care too."

"But I don't." She kissed along the line of his jaw, and licked his delicious, square chin. "So what's wrong with me?"

He gave a helpless laugh. "What's wrong with you? Besides your nymphomaniacal tendencies?" He pretended to look her over, amusement and reproach alternating in his gaze. "Well, you have pink hair, which I guess is fixable. You can be a little headstrong at times, and difficult to get along with."

She gave him a dubious look, since he possessed both the latter qualities. He relented and let her snuggle her hips against his cock.

"Maybe nothing's wrong with you," he said. "Maybe you just need to grow up. Although I'm pushing forty and I still feel fucked up a lot of the time."

"You hide it well."

"With other people, maybe. Not you. You make me forget that I'm supposed to act like a responsible and professional person."

"Responsible and professional is boring," she whispered against his ear, then closed her teeth on his earlobe.

He groaned. "Wait. Hold on. A condom..."

They scrambled to undress, and Ransom rolled on a rubber as she lay back on the bed. "Do you mind if I don't stick it in your ass this time?" he teased. "For once?"

"You can stick it wherever you want," she said, and he eased into her pussy with a stretching, delicious heat and warmth. He was so big and powerful, so intent in his possession.

"Yes," she said, clinging to his shoulders. "Yes, please, please, please..."

"This has to be the last time." His unwelcome words came out on a gasp. "I mean it, Lola."

"But it feels so good."

"Exactly. It feels too good." He stopped inside her, gazing down at her as she swiveled her hips. "You could ruin my life in so many ways."

"Mm. Ruin me," she begged.

He made a rough sound and fucked her harder. His abs moved over her skin, his huge body pressing her to the bed. Her legs flailed and her back arched as he hit that spot, that spot, *that spot...*

"Oh my God. Please, yes. Please more."

"Lola..." His voice shook. His body possessed hers with carnal ferocity, even as he gazed down at her in resignation.

"I'm worth it, aren't I?" she whispered, pulling him closer.

"Jesus, yes." At last, he seemed to surrender. "God fucking help me. You're worth the world."

* * * * *

Ransom spread his fingers in the plush purple carpet and started on his second set of push-ups. Road vibration tickled his fingertips as they made the long trip from northern Italy to Spain. After a couple festivals in Spain, they'd fly to the United Kingdom and Scandinavia to finish the tour. They were heading into the second and final month, which was probably for the best, not that he wanted to say goodbye to her.

The thing was, if he didn't say goodbye to her soon, he was going to start believing they had a future together, and that was a dangerous idea to entertain.

He cocked his head and listened, but he couldn't hear anything but travel noise as he began his third set of push-ups. Travel noise was good. Yelling was bad. The Lady Paradise tour bus had become a very tense place since Iain and Lola's most recent argument. The thunder outside seemed to underline Lola's stormy working relationship with the tour manager. At least someone else was the bad guy in her life now.

When his arms burned, Ransom left off with the push-ups and sat on the couch to check his emails. He was already getting notices from Ironclad about possible future assignments. Dissolute actress up for an Oscar, difficult-to-control boy bander heading out on tour, even a corporate bigwig who needed to be escorted around Bangkok so he didn't get himself into trouble. Wow, the owner of *that* corporation had a thing for underage prostitutes?

He thought he'd take the assignment with the actress, because it would get him back to L.A.

Yes, and Lola lives in L.A.

Ugh. More push-ups. He needed more push-ups. He hit the floor and banged out another dozen, then looked up and saw Lola watching him from her door.

"Hi," she said.

"Hi." He did another couple push-ups, then paused with his arms extended. "Everything okay?"

"Everything's fine, Mr. Olympia." She passed an avid look over his arms and shoulders, that impish, appreciative look that always hardened him to stone. Rain pattered on the bus's roof, filling the silence between them. "Don't want to interrupt your exercise," she said after a moment. "Proceed."

He sat back on his heels as she disappeared into her room. He could do a thousand push-ups and it still wouldn't chase the kid out of his mind. She *was* just a kid. He had to keep reminding himself of that. Young adults didn't mature until their mid-20s, and hell, he'd been a mess well into his late-20s. She had so much growing up to do.

He watched and waited on his knees. She'd left her bedroom door open. Was that an invitation? He'd told her no more sex, but she surely understood that as long as she offered herself to him, he wouldn't be able to resist. A moment later he heard her guitar, and sweet, muted singing, broken up by occasional mutters and repetitions of a musical phrase.

He lay back on the floor and stared at the bus's ceiling. *Breathe in, breathe out.* Maybe meditation could heal him of this affliction, this willful and damaging descent into madness. She was a client, and he wasn't allowed to sleep with her.

But her voice was so clear, so melodic. She was a siren calling him, and he couldn't stay away even though he knew he'd end up dashed on the rocks, or unemployed, at the very least. He sat up with a sigh and went to her bedroom door. He could hear Iain in the other room, snapping at someone on the phone.

"Keep playing," he told Lola when she looked up at him.

She played, but she didn't sing. Now and again she hummed a bar or two. He wanted to push her back and mount her, because she was so rumpled and beautiful. Her small hands were spiders skittering over the guitar strings, and her hair stuck out in unruly tufts. He could see the blonde growing out now, the hint of true color under the fuchsia. She bit her lip and looked up again as her ditty twanged to a close.

"That's a good tune. Better than a lot of the shit that's out there. It's like..." He thought a moment. "Kind of like a chill Alanis Morrissette."

"Who's Alanis Morissette? Someone from the seventies?"

He facepalmed and shook his head. "I forgot you were a fetus. Never mind. So how many of these songs have you written? You must have enough for an album by now."

"No one buys albums anymore." A blush reddened her pale cheeks. "And this music, it's not..."

"Not what?"

"Not going to come to anything." She put her guitar in the case and sprawled back on her pillows. "People don't want that from me. They want EDM music, electronic shit they can dance to."

"Just put a beat under it."

She laughed and crossed her legs, which were even paler than her face, despite their constant exposure to the elements. Even now, on the bus, she wore booty shorts. "Listen to you. Just put a beat under it. I'm proud of you, Ransom. You're learning how things work."

"I'm serious. You could turn that into one of those songs you play during the sets."

"Maybe. But I don't want to." She crossed her arms over her chest, so everything looked crossed and defensive. Ransom would never get used to her puzzling mood swings. The women he gravitated toward were low key, self-assured. Rocks. Since he left porn, he'd only been with women who were rocks, because he thought that kind of woman would save him. But here he was, tumbling head over heels for Lola, who was as changeable as the moon.

"What's the matter?" he asked. "What did I say?"

"This music is *my* music. I don't want anyone else to hear it. Why are you listening at my door?"

"Because you left the door open. I don't really have a choice whether to hear you or not, and anyway, I like when you play your little songs."

"My little songs?" She stared daggers at him.

"What?" He threw out his arms. "Why are you getting touchy? I complimented you."

"I told you, no one wants that shit. They want the electronic stuff."

Slow, Ransom. You're so slooow sometimes. Lola loved playing her folksy, angsty songs, but the money was in EDM music. Her fame was reliant on sound consoles and throbbing beats.

But her heart was tied up in lilting guitar strings.

"Are you sure no one wants it?" he asked. "Have you ever played it for anyone?"

"I've played it for you."

"And I liked it. Who else have you played it for?"

She gazed at him, her lips in a tight line.

He crawled onto the bed and kissed her, kicking the door shut at the same time. He wasn't going to sleep with her, but she looked so vulnerable and conflicted, and so goddamn kissable. "Only me?" he whispered when they parted. "You've only played your songs for me?"

"I used to play them for my father. We used to write songs together. Now I feel like my songs aren't good enough."

"I think they're good enough. I think they're great. You should put them out in the world."

"I can't, because of that whole contract thing Iain is always yelling about." She squirmed from under him and turned away as she latched her guitar case. "I'm locked in with my label, and they're not interested in my vocal stylings."

"How do you know? Have you asked?"

"I just know. And the EDM is easier. There are no words, no emotions. Just..." She waved a hand. "Adrenaline. The songs I write on my guitar are my feelings, and it's too scary to put that side of me out there for everyone to look at, and possibly ridicule. I mean, they might hate them and make fun of them."

He pulled her back into his arms. "I have news for you. Tons of people make fun of rave music. There are people who make fun of country music. There are people who make fun of opera, but you know what, some people fucking go nuts over opera."

"My songs have too much of me, though. Doing a rave set is a skill. It's almost mathematical. It's definitely not based on my sad little feelings."

"And your guitar music is? Then I like your sad little feelings."

He wanted to see her smile. She did smile, and then she tucked her head under his chin. "It's a long way to Barcelona. I wonder what we could do to pass the time."

"We talked about this. Please don't make me defile you any further."

"I want you to." She pressed closer and ran her hands over his hardening shaft. Damn thing betrayed him every time. "It's a stormy night, yeah? Perfect for *lightning*, Ransom. If you don't want to do it dirty, we can do it soft and sweet."

He groaned as she teased the head of his cock through his pants. "You don't know the meaning of soft and sweet."

"Yes I do. I mean, I've never had sex that way, but I bet it's pretty nice."

He let her take his cock out, then she was the one pushing him back, crawling over him.

"God, no," he said, not because he was a prude and didn't want a blowjob. He just didn't know if he could survive a blowjob from her. One more thing to fantasize about, one more thing to miss when he had to leave her.

"Lola, don't..." he began, but he lost the rest of the words as she opened her mouth over his bare cock. All he could produce was a long, guttural groan.

Shit, she was fucking amazing at this. Enthusiasm counted in blowjobs, and she had enthusiasm in spades. The responsible bodyguard wanted to lecture her about condoms, but he knew he was clean, and he didn't want her lips and tongue to stop. She traced up the zig-zagging lightning bolt, then licked around the head with soft hums of pleasure. A moment later, she took him deep, right into her throat.

He groaned again, louder this time, and buried his fingers in her hair. He tried to be civilized, tried not to grab her face and jab even deeper into her throat the way he wanted to. *Lola, please. You're killing me.* He forced his fingers to uncurl, and surrendered himself to the pleasures of this epic blowjob, given by a pink-haired vixen in this goddamn tour bus somewhere between Italy and Spain. When would he have another chance...?

Never. He knew he'd never have anything this fucked up and conflicted and gorgeous again. He'd never get work as a bodyguard again either, but he didn't care, because she was nuzzling against his shaft, teasing him with magical strokes of her tongue.

"I know I'm horrible at this," she said, pulling back a few minutes later.

"No. Not. God. Jesus." It was all he could do to force out single words. "You're amazing, babe, but you'd better stop if you want to get some too." He pulled her up and shoved his tongue in her mouth, tasting her excitement and intensity as he peeled off her clothes. "Look at what you're making me do now," he said as they parted. "I said no more sex."

"I'm sorry, daddy."

He put a hand over her mouth. Damn her, making him feel old and horny at the same time. "No daddy bullshit, you little pervert." He accompanied these stern words with a couple wild spanks on her ass. "I guess you need to be taught a lesson. Again."

"Teach me," she crooned against his fingers. "Or spank me. Either one."

He turned her over and arranged her on all fours. *Fuck.* "Where are the condoms?"

She pointed toward a chest of drawers beside the bed. He ripped open the closest drawer and found what he needed. "No, don't move," he said when she turned toward him. He gave her a couple more spanks before he remembered the bus's thin walls and Iain in the opposite room. Instead, Ransom grasped her hips and thrust deep into her pussy. Her moan was almost as loud as the spanking.

"Yes, give me the lightning bolt, Ransom. Give it to me hard."

"You want it hard?" he teased, stroking a hand up her back as he lazily withdrew. "I think I'd rather do it soft and sweet."

She collapsed on her stomach in a fit of frustration. He yanked her back into position and spanked her again. "Ass up. All fours. I said not to move."

His naughty little sex goddess was on fire, trembling with anticipation. He covered her with his body, held her and surged into her from behind, banging her so hard she emitted a little *umph* every time he drove inside.

"You like this, baby? You like getting drilled?"

"You're so big," she moaned. "You feel so big. You're so deep inside me."

She made him feel big and destructive, and tender, and excited, and emotional, far more emotional than he'd ever felt with anyone else. He was so hooked on her, so fucking addicted to her. When she looked at him over her shoulder, desire jolted through his body. His balls ached from pleasure, and his cock throbbed from her tightness and warmth. So hot, so wet, so soft. So sweet.

Fuck. Fuck. Fuck, he was fucked.

He reached beneath her to pinch her breasts, to arouse her even more so her hips would keep up their frenzied, delectable motion. "Yes, baby. That's my girl. I know you like this. I know you need it."

He lengthened his strokes and trailed his fingers down to her pussy. He knew how to make her come, how to pound her and possess her, and manipulate her clit until her whole body shuddered to completion. But first, he'd tease her, just to hear her moans and groans. Ransom didn't care if Iain heard them.

"You're so bad," he said, to egg her on. "You're such a dirty, naughty girl."

He made her come three times, so he could watch her toss her head back in ecstasy and feel her pussy clamp around his cock. She shared so much sexual energy, and that energy healed him in some way, because it allowed him to be wild and porn-y and not feel guilty about it. When they finally came together at the end, there was nothing in his orgasm but pleasure and bliss. He huddled against her, his nose pressed to her nape so he could breathe in her scent.

This has to be the last time. He opened his mouth to say it, then shut it again. It was hours to Barcelona. They were going to fuck again, that was just basic math, even if it would lead to their ruin.

She smelled like heaven. He kissed along her hairline, and when she shivered and whispered his name, he forgot everything else.

12.
TIDAL WAVE

By the time they arrived in Barcelona, the festival grounds were an epic mud field. Thanks to the rain, the heavy trucks and buses that brought the equipment and performers had pummeled the grass to a slimy, squelching mess.

Lola told herself it didn't matter. People would still show up and dance, because these festivals went on, rain or shine. The ground backstage was covered in straw to soak up the mud and moisture, but her shoes were ruined. So were Ransom's, not that he complained. He had gone from being the primary irritant in her life to a cherished source of sanity. And, well, her only source of sex.

And Iain knew it, judgey bastard. Since he'd overheard their noisy tour bus hookup, he knew they were fucking and he didn't like it. He'd argued with Ransom in the hotel lobby, then barked at her on the way up in the elevator, "I won't report your stud to his boss, but I hope you two are using protection."

"Fucking awkward," she'd snapped back. "Mind your fucking business."

She couldn't wait for the tour to be over, so she could say goodbye to the dour, grouchy manager, but then she'd have to say goodbye to Ransom too.

Ugh, she couldn't think about that. She needed to get in the right headspace to do her set, and she refused to use drugs to get there, so she had to use her own powers of intention. Ransom had taught her about that in the past few weeks, about self-discipline and mind over matter. So much better than almost dying. He'd made her life better in so many ways.

Okay, headspace. Adrenaline. Positive visualization. She jumped in place, elevating her heart rate and bringing a flush to her skin. She thought through the intricacies of her set, what songs she'd play, the drops she'd create, the happiness she'd provide to the kids who were coming to this party to take a little break from life. Ransom hovered nearby, turning away gawkers and crew people who might disturb her. Finally, it was her time to head onstage.

Ransom gave her a fist bump. "Kill it," he murmured.

"Like you with my pussy," she murmured back.

It was fun being his naughty girl. It was fun being a highly paid, famous DJ who dropped beats for a living, so she took the stage in high spirits, eager to do her best show yet. She wouldn't let the drizzle and mud get her down. She walked across the platform to the sound console. One of the tech guys pressed a microphone into her hand and she shouted a greeting to the crowd.

"*Hola*, you dirty motherfuckers." She laughed as she took in her audience. The irrepressible Spanish ravers were making the most of the mud. Most of them were covered in it, painted like cavemen. The mud layers didn't manage to blot out the neon glow sticks, necklaces, earrings, hats, pacifiers, and other luminescent accoutrements that elevated this gathering from concert to rave.

She waved her arms as she started the first track. The entire crowd jumped in unison to the driving beat as she shouted the rest of her introduction. "I'm Lady Paradise, and we're gonna get even dirtier together. How about that?"

At their enthusiastic scream, she cued up a second track and prepared to mix it with the first, creating a seedy, sexy beat that sent the audience into ecstasies. The mud, the neon, the craziness, it was all so silly, but it was fun. After the rest and the rain—and the sex—Lola felt ready for anything. She played a couple popular tracks from her last album, then started experimenting. Harder beats, sultry drops. When she danced, the crowd danced with her. When she screamed into the microphone, they howled back and danced harder.

One of the security guys at the front of the stage looked back at her and gestured with a grimace. Was he telling her to tone it down? This was a rave festival—it was supposed to be loud and frenetic, and everyone had come out in the rain, so she was going to give them a show. The sound was shit tonight, but she could make up for it with good mixes.

She leaned over the console and started a slow build to a drop. The lights flickered and the crowd went wild, losing their fucking minds. They thought it was a strobe effect, but no, there was a problem with the floodlights, probably because of the weather.

As long as Lola had sound, everything was all right. She jumped up on the console, clutching the mic and moving her arms to the music. The crowd shouted as the mix thumped to a fever peak. She bent down to crank up the bass, waving her ass at the audience as the drop arrived on a nerve-throbbing down beat.

"Holy shit, that's hot," she screamed.

She turned to face the audience. The whole crowd was moving in one body, back and forth, like a human tide. The security guys were shouting to each other, pointing out at the kids.

Then the lights went out, all the lights. The music kept pounding, a waterfall of sonic bliss, but the field went black, lit only by neon and moonlight. Shrieks rose over the beats, and shouts intensified from the front of the stage. Lola jerked as someone grabbed her leg. It was Ransom, gesturing for her to jump down from the console.

"The lights," she said.

"I know."

She went around to check the sound board, which was illuminated by faint light from a battery. She heard something pop behind the stage. An electrical breaker? Shit, that's all they needed, a fucking fire.

But it was too wet and muddy for anything to burn. She looked over at the shadow of Ransom's face, then out at the black shrieking sea of the audience. She leaned to cue up another track, because that was show business. You kept playing, no matter what happened.

Then her beats were gone too, turned off. No juice. "Shit. This rain! My set is fucked."

She went to the front of the stage and Ransom came too, squinting out at the audience. A man rushed toward her in the dark, then another. One was from the audience, covered in mud. The other was with the tour. Ransom got in their way, so they screamed at him instead, one in English, one in Spanish. After a minute, he took out his ear plugs and moved closer, and they screamed again.

"There's a situation," she heard. "Tell them to stop moving, to stop pushing."

The men turned to her. The tour official pointed at the microphone. "Tell them to step back," he yelled over the roars and screams of the audience. "People are being trampled. They'll listen to you. Tell them to step back."

Oh, no. The screams that had sounded like excitement now took on a horrifying trill. She stood on the sound console with Ransom's help, and waved one arm as she yelled through the mic. "Listen, people. You have to step back."

Nothing. No sound. She looked out at the audience in dismay. In the moonlight, in the mud, people had gone feral. They were pushing and shoving, trapped by an undulating mass of human aggression. "Stop," she cried. "Step back. People are crushed up here. Give them some space!"

Ransom reached up. "Give me the microphone."

He took it and yelled in Spanish, a rough, authoritative bark not unlike the one he'd used with her a few times. As he exhorted the crowd, the lights came back on, flashing at first, then glaring steadily in the dark. The speakers came back online too, blasting his voice. At last the frantic crowd paused to listen. She motioned for them to back up as Ransom repeated the directions.

Finally, instead of moving side to side, people moved backward. More tour officials and security guards crowded onstage, gesturing for the audience to step back, to step back. A gap formed along the front barriers, toward the middle where Lola and Ransom stood. It was like the lip of a volcano, with ravers standing on the edge, looking in.

All along the gap was mud and...holy fucking shit. People. Motionless, glowing kids sprawled on the ground, some of their limbs twisted at unnatural angles. Lola stared with her hand over her mouth. They looked like they'd been beaten, or felled by some bomb. Security continued to gesture, *back up, back up, back up*. Lola couldn't look away from the sprawl of bodies. Ransom handed the microphone to someone and reached for her.

"There are people down there," she sobbed. She meant *there*, in that horrific seam of destruction in front of the stage. "They need help. They're hurt."

He didn't answer, just hurried her down the stairs and through the melee of activity backstage as the squeal of emergency sirens pierced the air.

"Ransom. Ransom!" She kept calling his name even though he had her by the hand. "What happened? What happened to those people?"

"They fell." His voice was tight. "They slipped in the mud when everyone was..."

His voice trailed off but her mind finished the thought. *They slipped in the mud when everyone was dancing.* She'd been the one playing the music, waving her arms and yelling at everyone to move their asses.

"I should have stopped." The words choked in her throat. "I should have stopped before—"

He halted and turned to her. They huddled in the corner of the backstage area as security personnel and EMTs pushed by. He took her by the shoulders and made her look at him. "This wasn't your fault. Do you understand me? It wasn't you. It was the lights. The sound problems. The rain. The lights went out and people got disoriented."

"I saw them pushing back and forth. People were stampeding. I should have stopped."

"The mud made people slip," he said. "It was the rain."

"It was the music."

"No."

"I didn't know there were people under there." Horror and panic twisted inside her, stealing her breath. "I didn't know they were getting trampled."

"No, you didn't know. It wasn't your fault."

The first stretcher passed behind them. Lola buried her face against his chest. She couldn't imagine what it felt like for those kids to die down there in the mud. They were probably screaming for help, but they wouldn't have been heard over the music.

Her music. She was the one who'd played it. "I was making them crazy. I did it," she said as another stretcher rolled by.

"No."

"I should have stopped playing."

"Damn it, Lola."

A sharp voice interrupted them, speaking in English and then Spanish. "Clear this area now. Everyone must leave. *Rápido*."

Ransom picked her up, braced her against his chest, and made his way through the crowd. She heard crying and shrieks, and frantic chatter. A woman shouted, "They're dead. Oh my God, they're dead." The confused hysteria in that voice echoed her emotions. How could this happen? How was this horror possible? These festivals were supposed to be an escape, a joy, a place to let go of your worries.

She kept thinking of those poor kids screaming, and no one being able to hear.

* * * * *

The police boarded the tour bus within an hour, a pair of poker-faced officers working on the accident report.

"This is not Miss Reynolds' fault," said Iain, shaking a finger between the two men. "Tell them," he said to Ransom. "Explain in Spanish. The field was too muddy, too crowded. The lights went out and caused a panic. MadDance leased this festival site from Danzamia, S.A. If they want to know who's accountable for this, it's Danzamia. They should have cancelled the show."

Ransom spoke to the officers in Spanish as Lola huddled beside him in her damp, muddy clothes. Due to the police vehicles, fire trucks, and ambulances, they'd been unable to leave the festival site for the hotel. Lola wondered if her next stop would be jail.

Iain broke into Ransom's explanation with another torrent of belligerent English. "Danzamia didn't cancel because they wanted MadDance's money. This is about greed overwhelming common sense."

Ransom held up a hand and Iain fell silent. For once, Lola was glad her manager was so argumentative. She didn't want to go to jail, because she'd never meant for anyone to get hurt. She'd played music and told everyone to dance because she'd assumed they would be safe. She hadn't thought about the mud making things slippery, or the fact that they'd set up the festival stage at the bottom of a slope. In good weather, it would have been ideal. In the rain...

Fourteen people dead. Fourteen. Dozens more had been injured, some seriously. She kept repeating it in her mind, because she couldn't wrap her brain around it. Fourteen people had lost their lives during her set. For fourteen people, her performance had been the last thing they were to experience in life.

She made a soft, grieving sound, and Ransom touched her knee to steady her. She felt on the verge of disintegration. The officers gave her a hard look and stood, and said something to Ransom in Spanish. He nodded and walked them to the door. As soon as they left, Iain pelted him with questions.

"Well? What did they say? Are there going to be charges?"

"Not for Lola." He returned to sit beside her on the couch. "If there's negligence, it falls to the venue and organizers. Even then, I don't know if you can say they're to blame for the audience's behavior. It's going to be a huge legal mess, but Lola was only performing as required by her contract. She can't be held accountable for crowd control."

"It was my set," she said. "I told them to get excited, I told them to danc—"

"Stop it." His stern voice silenced her. "You did the same thing tonight that you do every night you perform. The difference is that the field was slippery and the electrical problems made the crowd panic. It was nothing you did. It just happened. In the end, it's no one's fault."

"But people died. So many people died while I stood up there playing stupid music."

"It was an accident."

More tears came, more aching pain in her chest. She'd cried so long and so hard, but it couldn't change anything. It couldn't take that limp, lifeless pile of bodies away. It couldn't erase the stretchers and sirens from her memory.

"It's not your fault." He rubbed her back. "Do you understand me? *It's not your fault.* The officers said we're free to leave once the emergency vehicles clear out."

"And that's the end," said Iain.

Lola wiped her eyes. "The end of what?"

"The end of the tour," the manager repeated, throwing out his arms. "That's it. Kaput. They're not going to put on any more shows after this. They're out of business. People died."

Ransom once again held up his hand to silence Iain. "You don't have to tell her people died. She was there."

"Yes, she was there," said Iain. "And I'm going to lose my job, and you're going to lose your job, but Lady Paradise will be just fine on the other end of this."

"Maybe you should go somewhere else and calm the fuck down," suggested Ransom.

"Gladly. I'm sick of this tour bus and this goddamn festival shit."

"He's such an asshole," said Ransom as soon as Iain stormed off. "Good riddance."

But Lola hadn't even been thinking about Iain. Her mind was stuck on the tour being cancelled. "Do you think he's right? That's it? We're not going to the U.K.?"

"I don't think so, baby."

His voice was gentle. Regretful. *Oh, no, Ransom...* It wasn't just death and sadness. This would mean their parting too.

"I think I'm going to go lay down," she said. "I can't... I have to..."

"Yes, go rest." He ran a hand down her arm. "Try to sleep, if you can. I'll wake you when we get to the hotel."

She could already sense him drawing away from her. Everything was ruined. Everything was shit. People had died tonight because of her. This was the least she deserved, to lose her source of strength and protection.

She was almost to her little cell of a room when she had an awful thought. She turned to him.

"You won't leave tonight, will you? You won't leave without saying goodbye?"

"Of course not. Don't worry about that now."

Don't worry about it *now*, but he'd be leaving soon. His resigned expression told her everything. She wasn't ready. She'd never be ready.

But that didn't matter, because fourteen people had died, and it was at least partially her fault.

13.
LOVE AND TRAGEDY

There was no big meeting, no legal reckoning outside the overwrought media coverage, just an abbreviated email from Mr. Asshole at MadDance. Ransom wasn't even copied on it; it was forwarded to him by Liam Wilder.

Festival associates:

The remainder of the European tour has been cancelled. Hotel and personnel allowances will be paid until the end of this week. We thank you for your participation and regret any inconvenience caused by this cancellation.

No mention of the fourteen people who'd died in a muddy field north of Barcelona, or the two who'd died in the hospital afterward, or the numerous injured, many of whom were still fighting to survive their injuries. No mention of the mental anguish of those who'd witnessed the tragedy, like the exhausted twenty year old sleeping in the other room.

Ransom let her sleep while he worked out the next steps with Ironclad. Lola was still under their protection, so they'd flown her on a private jet to London, to an Ironclad safe house where she could wait out the worst of the news cycle frenzy. The media clamored for interviews with her, interviews she couldn't bear to give. U.S. promoters tried to line up stateside shows, but Lady Paradise remained hidden as the world watched the footage of her staring down at the carnage with her hand pressed over her mouth.

Rave culture and EDM was suddenly under the global spotlight, and the big news stations did top-of-the-hour stories about the drugs, the partying, the relentless music. He watched them on his phone while Lola slept. Many of the reports accused her of inciting the crowd, showing outdated fan footage as evidence, clips of her twerking atop her sound console or diving into the audience. They conveniently left out the weather issues and sound problems, and condemned the "dangerous" EDM scene, focusing on Lady Paradise because she was the most ratings-worthy scapegoat. Even though reporters painted her as a villain, the community stood behind her, and the tragedy spiked a perverse boost in her sales.

When she was stronger, when the worst of the fallout was over, he would escort her home to L.A. Once she was settled in, he'd have to say goodbye and let some other bodyguard take over. She didn't need his specialized protection anymore, didn't need someone to rein in her partying ways. She was a different person now, more thoughtful, more cautious and self-aware.

He'd helped with that. He'd reformed her, put her in touch with her inner strength, and he ought to have been proud. But he wasn't proud. He'd broken the cardinal rule of protection and gotten sexually involved with his client. Not just once, in a moment of weakness, but many times. He'd succumbed to her youth and vitality, and preyed on her loneliness. She was twenty, a kid, and he was a dirty old lecher. An ex porn star. Sad.

The doorbell rang. He'd known his boss would show up once they were in London, but now that he was here, Ransom felt unprepared.

"The media's found you," he said as soon as Ransom opened the door. "There are reporters outside. How's the client?"

"Tired. Sleeping."

Liam looked around the unassuming, hyper-secure flat, then turned back to him. Ransom tried to keep his expression neutral beneath his boss's regard.

"Sleeping or sedated?" Liam asked.

"She won't take sedatives. She's very anti-drug now, even though she could probably use some. She's devastated by what happened. She blames herself."

Liam shook his head as he sat on the couch. "That's bullshit. I don't know what they were thinking, packing those kids onto that hill in the mud and rain."

"It wasn't a hill." He took a seat in the armchair across from him. "More like a slope. But they were crazy before the show even started, throwing mud all over each other. When the lights went out, they lost their shit."

"Did you see it happen? Did you see the kids go down?"

"No one saw it happen. Even the security guys didn't know." He swallowed hard. "No one knew. The crowd was surging back and forth and no one realized there were kids underneath. Or if they realized it, they couldn't do anything about it."

"I saw the footage of you yelling at the crowd."

"By then it was too late. By then..." He suppressed a shudder, remembering the twisted bodies revealed when everyone stepped back. "By then, so many of them had already died."

"Now the tour's over." Liam put his hands on his knees and sighed. "I may have an option for you to work with the client a while longer. We put in a contract bid with her label in L.A., since they pay for security when she's stateside. I haven't heard back yet, but..."

Ransom wanted to pounce on the opportunity. He wanted to stay with her.

But he knew he couldn't. They'd continue sleeping together, and he couldn't guard her properly if his heart was involved. "I don't know," he said, because that made more sense than *please, no*.

Liam studied him a moment. "It's been a tough tour, and an awful week. Maybe you need a break? A leave of absence?"

"No, I..." He'd just spend a leave of absence following her around. "I'll be fine. I'd just prefer a different assignment. Some time away from the ear plugs and raver kids."

"The raver kids love you. There are fan blogs about you, you know."

Oh, yes. The Gilberto and Lady Paradise bloggers, who posted and captioned photos of them together, and even wrote bawdy stories about their sexual adventures. Thank God none of them had discovered his porn background, but it was only a matter of time. He looked his boss in the eyes and said the sentence he'd practiced beforehand. "I think it's best if I take a new assignment once she's back in L.A."

His lips twisted as he said it, because it was the exact opposite of what he wanted. Liam's brow creased and his mouth turned down in a frown.

"I see." He looked back at his phone. One of his fingers tapped the side. "Perhaps I should have removed you from the situation after she overdosed."

The situation. Ransom's mind stuck on those words. Lola wasn't a situation. She was a person, a scared kid who was full of moxie and feelings. He loved her. He would always love her, no matter how inappropriate it was. But he couldn't say that. Instead he squared his shoulders and shuttered his aching heart. "She's an...emotionally taxing client," he said. "She'll need a bodyguard with his head on straight."

"What do you mean, 'emotionally taxing'?"

"She's just..." He wanted to explain her complexity, her vulnerability, but how to do that without veering outside professional bounds? "As famous as she is, there's this conflicted person inside her. Not Lady Paradise, but a person who's lost both her parents, who makes impulsive choices, who's struggling to grow up, to grow beyond all the fame and immaturity."

Liam made a sound. "About the immaturity: she's twenty years old."

"She plays the guitar when no one else is around, and pours out these songs that could break your heart—"

"Your heart, Ransom?"

The man's voice stopped him cold. It was a warning. Say any more, and he would have to investigate the nature of their relationship, and shit would come out that Ransom could never explain. An uncomfortably long silence stretched between them. He didn't dare open his mouth.

"Speaking of immaturity," Liam finally said, "how do you think she's doing as far as her drug issues? Will she still need a minder?"

Ransom thought about that, his heart sinking in his chest. Would she remain stable once he said goodbye to her in L.A.? Or would she fall back into her crazy party girl habits? The overdose had scared her straight for a while, but when she was back with her posse, she might forget what he'd taught her. She might even act out in order to reclaim his attention.

This sucked. Holy hell, this entire thing sucked. He'd thought, by the end of the tour, he'd be able to say goodbye. He'd thought she'd be bored of him by then, but the tour had ended too quickly.

"I don't know if she'll need a minder. That might be something to discuss with her label."

"I think it makes more sense to discuss it with you." Liam leaned back, tapping his knees with a questioning expression. "You spent the most time with her. What do you think?"

"I think she needs someone young to look after her. Someone flexible and energetic. Someone patient. She might go off the deep end again, but I don't think I'm the best person to deal with it."

"Why?"

Had he worried about Liam opening an investigation? This was the investigation. His boss's close regard didn't waver, and he didn't dare look away. He felt like he was on the opposite side of an interrogation table. He shifted in his chair and cleared his throat.

"The thing is, she's just a kid. Like you said, twenty years old. It was hard for me to relate to her in a...in a professional way."

He met Liam's searching gaze. He'd told him the goddamn truth, as much as it was a lie. After a moment, Liam scratched his neck.

"She was a pain, huh? Too much of a handful for you? You're getting old, my man."

Ransom smiled and said the expected line. "Way too old."

"The bloggers are going to be sad."

"Maybe the next bodyguard will be more photogenic."

Liam chuckled and the danger seemed to pass, even though he still felt on the defensive.

"I have a job in Vegas," his boss said, looking back at his phone. "Sixty year old soul singer who hits the pills and booze too hard. You could start as early as next weekend. You sure you don't need some time off?"

"No."

Liam nodded. "We can take care of Lola from here on out."

"I'll see her back to L.A. I promised I'd take her home."

"I'm sure she'll appreciate that. And once she's in L.A., we'll get another bodyguard on the case." Liam smiled. "Someone younger and more photogenic."

"Someone more blogworthy," joked Ransom, even though it was hard as fuck to banter when his heart was cracking in his chest.

A knock interrupted their conversation, along with a strident male voice. "Lady Paradise? I'm a reporter with National News Network. Could you answer a few questions?" Another knock, and a second male voice. "Lady Paradise?"

Liam raised an eyebrow. "I'll assemble a team to hold the perimeter and keep them out of your face. When Lola's ready to go home, let me know." He stood and straightened his tie as the reporter knocked again.

"Lady Paradise? *Lady Paradise?*"

The banging and yelling must have woken Lola. She appeared in the living room doorway in her wrinkled robe, with a grievous case of bedhead. She frowned at Liam, as if the tall, suited man might be the interloping reporter.

"This is my boss," Ransom clarified.

"Liam Wilder, Ironclad CEO. I came to see if I could help with anything." He approached her with his hand outstretched, as if he did business with pink-haired DJs all the time. "Don't mind the reporters. I'll take care of them on my way out."

"Good luck with that."

He paused, holding her hand between his. "I know you've had a disheartening week, but I don't want you to worry about anything. All of this will die down. Everything will be okay."

Liam had a way of speaking that reassured people even in the most fraught circumstances. He could see his magic working on Lola. Her shoulders relaxed and she almost smiled. Almost.

The reporters pounded on the door again and Liam excused himself to deal with them. A few sharp words, a few legal threats, and they were gone. Liam was great at his job, but Ransom felt like a failure. He'd slept with a client, and now he was going to leave her. It was wrong and terrible, but he had no other choice.

"It's going to be okay." He took her in his arms and stroked her hair. "Liam's right, things will get better. This won't last forever."

"I know." She clung to him, still groggy with sleep. But no sedatives, no drugs. That had been her choice. If he had to leave her, at least he knew he'd changed her for the better.

Small solace, when both of them would be alone.

* * * * *

By the time they left London and flew over the ocean, Lola had finally begun to emerge from her numb haze.

So many people had died. The staff at Ironclad's Barcelona office helped her send cards and money to their families expressing her grief. A third of them had been returned with furious replies. She forced Ransom to translate those replies for her, even though the words hurt. They accused her of riling up the crowd with some evil, murderous purpose. She knew she hadn't done that. She'd only been riling them up to help them have fun.

I didn't mean to hurt anyone. I never meant to hurt anyone. Ransom woke her one night and told her she'd been crying those words in her sleep. She believed it, because her sleep had gone to shit, and the fact that people had lost their lives during her set weighed heavily on her heart. The EDM movement was supposed to be about freedom and happiness, not drugs and death. At some point she'd have to explain that to the media, give interviews and tell her side of the story, but she didn't have the energy right now. She didn't even want to play her guitar.

But she'd brought it home for when she felt better. It was packed, along with everything else, in the hold of Ironclad's private jet. On the way through the airport the media had ambushed her, because it was hard to blend in with pink hair. Teams of reporters had trailed her and shouted questions about her guilt, her regret, her future plans.

Ransom had shielded her and turned them away so she didn't have to deal with it. He'd used his bodyguard voice and his stern expression and told them to leave her alone. Lola had gotten a little teary because she would have been lost without him.

She *would* be lost without him, very soon. He had told her, kindly and gently, that he'd accepted an assignment in Las Vegas, guarding some drugged up soul singer. She understood why he had to move on. He had a career, he had to keep working. He couldn't stay with her just because she'd been stupid enough to fall in love with him.

She let out a sigh and he looked over at her. "Okay, kid?"

She nodded. His hand moved closer to hers on the center armrest, but he didn't take it. Since the tragedy in Barcelona, he'd been all bodyguard. He called her *kid* and acted as if they'd never been lovers, as if they'd never found ecstasy in each other's arms.

She was pretty sure she wasn't going to have any other lovers for a while. She'd learned a lot of things on this ill-fated tour, and one was that she didn't need to be so free with her body. She could be choosier about her partners. Sex could be special and emotional, and maybe she'd hold out for that. She'd also learned that life was short, that tragedy could strike down anyone, even kids younger than her. She needed to reassess everything.

"I'm going to be different." She said it out loud, because she needed someone else to hear it and acknowledge it. She wanted that person to be Ransom.

"What's that?" He looked over at her in the harsh cabin light.

"I'm going to be different from now on."

He waited for her to elaborate, but she wasn't sure she wanted to elaborate, because she wasn't sure she could put her feelings into words. He never pressed her when she felt thoughtful or conflicted. She appreciated that about him, the way he let her work through things. He knew when to be quiet. No one else in her life did.

"I mean that maybe...I know myself better now than I used to. I understand that I can be who I want to be, not the person everyone expects me to be. The person everyone pressures me to be."

He nodded after a moment. "You should strive to be yourself. The best version of yourself."

"Yes, the best version. That's what I mean. I wasn't thinking about that before. I was just...being. Reacting. Trying to make people love me."

A corner of his mouth tilted up. "People will always love you."

"But they should love me for me. And I should love myself...for me."

His approving nod warmed her. She wanted to take his hand but she didn't want it to be awkward.

"I think you're on the right track," he said.

She thought so too, and he'd been a big part of getting her there. *The Love and Tragedy Tour.* Next time she went on a club tour, that's what she'd call it. She'd honor this turning point in her life, and in doing so, honor the people who had died.

She'd honor the people who had convinced her she needed to live a better life.

14.
SEX AND SADNESS

Ransom braced for another media ambush when they got to Lola's residence, but the sidewalk outside her gate was empty. After two weeks, the story was dying out. A Spanish court had handed down a judgment, fines levied against Danzamia and MadDance for negligent business practices, but the deaths themselves had been ruled an accident, and Lola wasn't named in any of the litigation. There was no longer a reason for reporters to congregate outside her door.

It was a relief to be left alone, to have some privacy. It made all of this easier, this long, wretched goodbye.

Lola's place was nothing like he'd imagined. He'd expected something more pink, more pop-star, a cavernous chrome and glass confection overlooking the sea. Instead, she had a solid wood bunker in Hollywood Hills. Wood paneling, wood tables, wood beams, wood bookcases full of CDs and audio equipment. You could almost imagine yourself in an old Memphis club.

He left his luggage and suit jacket by the door and helped her carry her electronics downstairs to her music studio, then roll her suitcases down the hall to her sunlit bedroom. The room where she slept looked homey, especially to someone like him, who never took the time to make any place feel like home. Bright red curtains, a sage and crimson quilt on a raised bed, and piles of pillows, many of them in the shape of one-eyed creatures or tufted monsters. Cute. Twisted, but childlike. *You little monster*, he thought. *You've brought me to your bedroom, and you know I'm weak.*

Since Barcelona, he hadn't touched her except to hug and comfort her, or draw her from a nightmare. Now, looking at the sun shining across the bed, he wanted to lay her down and comfort her in earnest, and make all her troubles disappear.

I'm going to be different from now on, she'd said, and he was in full support of that, so instead he turned toward the door.

"Show me the rest of your place, Lola."

She indulged him, showing him the two guest suites, the expansive kitchen, the living room with a huge floral couch and more wacky pillows, and then her recording studio in the basement.

That was when she came alive. They sat in front of her massive work console, lounging in black ergonomic chairs while she pointed out her four high-line laptops, her rack of expensive headphones, her mixing tables and hi-def monitors. A disco ball dangled over their heads. "This is where I make the magic," she said.

"Do you record all your music here?"

"I didn't at first, but now I can. All this equipment is production quality. There's even a booth for recording vocals." She pointed to a door in the corner.

"Could you record your guitar songs down here?" Her guitar was propped over in the corner. When he was gone, he'd miss hearing her play it. "Maybe you can record a few of your songs for me. Send them to Vegas."

They hadn't talked about whether they'd stay in touch, but he hoped they would. He'd like to remain her friend so he could keep tabs on her, just in case her life started spiraling out of control again once he was out of it.

She shrugged. "I told you, no one's interested in my folksy bullshit."

"You're interested in it. You said you were going to start being who you wanted to be, not who everyone else wanted you to be."

"Still, I can't do whatever I want and damn the consequences." She ran a hand through her hair. It looked especially disheveled today. "I have to give people what they want, or I can't pay my bills."

Ransom understood all that from his porn years, about giving people what they wanted to keep the money flowing. But he'd also learned a thing or two about being true to yourself.

"Anyway," he said, "if you ever feel like recording your 'folksy bullshit,' send me a copy. I can't stand your electronic songs, but I love your voice."

She laughed. "You're so judgey, Ransom. Where will I be without your judgment in my life?"

He didn't know. He was afraid to think about it. His chest ached with unspoken emotion as the silence strung out between them.

"Play me one more song," he said, just to fill the oppressive emptiness.

She hesitated a moment, looking down at her lap, then said, "I can't."

"Why not?"

"Because I don't want to spend my last moments with you playing the fucking guitar."

"I like when you play the guitar." But it was hopeless. His arms opened and she crawled into his lap. She pressed her face against his cheek and traced fingers over his stubble.

"Don't try to seduce me," he whispered.

"Don't tell me what to do," she said with perfect Lola sass, and then she lifted her face and kissed him. God, he'd miss her so much. He'd miss the way she always took what she wanted without caring about the consequences. Right now, she wanted him, and he didn't have the power to deny her this last hookup. As their kiss intensified, he ran his hands up under her shirt, over the lithe, powerful body he'd come to crave.

"Let's go upstairs," he said.

"No, here. I want to remember you here when I'm working. I want to remember us together."

He'd never had sex in an office chair, not even during his porn days. The reclining back worked well for the girl-on-top position. He kissed and groped her as she worked open his shirt and undid his fly. They had to pause a moment while she went for a condom. By the time she returned, his shirt and pants were on the ground, and she was gloriously naked. She knelt between his legs to roll on the rubber, prepping him to fuck her like some imperious queen.

Lady Paradise. That's what she was in these moments. Raw, courageous, open to anything, greedy for everything.

"Come here." He pulled her into his lap. "I'm going to fucking ruin you."

She straddled him, but when he would have thrust inside her roughly, she prevented him. "Not this time," she said. "Soft and sweet."

Soft and sweet. Jesus Christ. He gazed at her, lost in lustful misery. If she wanted it soft and sweet, that's what he'd give her—something emotionally moving to remember him by.

Not that either of them could ever forget.

He moved into her slowly, impaling her inch by inch. Her tight wetness challenged his control. He wanted to fuck her hard, bounce her up and down on his lap, but he kept himself in check and went at her pace. Her deep blue eyes held his in a connection that went deeper than physical mechanics. As she rode his cock, he stroked her soft skin, marveling at the taut, responsive muscles underneath. She was so strong from all her dancing.

As for him—his strength was hers to exploit as she wished. She ran her hands over his muscles, massaging, squeezing, controlling the depth and speed of his thrusts with her hips. She made sounds more beautiful than any music, even her guitar music.

His shaft felt alive with the slow, sensual pleasure of their joining. This "soft and sweet" thing wasn't half bad. He felt subjugated and yet powerful, holding true paradise in his arms. "I want you," he said over and over, in low growls or whispers against her skin. "I want you." Because he wanted her forever, not just for this moment in time.

Lola ignored the steel chair arms digging into her calves and concentrated on the feeling of his warm hands roving over her skin. She couldn't get close enough to him, no matter how hard she tried. His cock stretched her in long, heavenly strokes, pushing her open, making her feel like he was a part of her. But that was nothing compared to the depth of his gaze.

When she neared the last few quivering steps to climax, she took a moment to study his beloved face. Strong brows, dark eyes, the ever present five o'clock shadow, the tentative smile. Why didn't he ever smile full out? He was such a serious person.

"Smile for me," she said. "A real smile."

"Every smile I give you is a real smile." He moved his hips so his cock rubbed over some ecstasy nerve inside her. She gasped and he smiled, a real smile. He squeezed her breasts and rubbed over the spot again, making her breath shudder and her legs tremble. Their bodies arched together, so different in size and strength but so necessary to each other. Her pussy felt heavy, ready to explode. She ground her clit against his pubic bone, grasping him close, forgetting inhibition. "Oh, God, please..."

He groaned in answer, teasing her nipples until her hips bucked. "I know, baby," he told her. "You're going to get what you want."

Not everything I want. But she'd take what she could get. She held onto him and watched his face, his lips, the intelligent intensity in his eyes, all the things she'd have to learn to live without. *I want you. I want you. I want you.*

"I'm coming." She clenched around his cock, grateful for his arms holding her on the chair as her body went wild. The orgasm shook her, wave after wave of pulsing completion. His grasp on her tightened and he growled in her ear as he rode out his own climax. God, she loved his forcefulness, even though this was supposed to be soft and sweet.

When he finished and went limp, she melted against him, skin to skin. Eventually she drifted back to reality, to the dark metal and glass of her home studio. This chair would forevermore be her favorite chair. She told him so and he chuckled so his chest moved against hers. It felt so perfect to be close like this.

"I don't want you to leave," she said. "Not yet."

"I won't. Not yet." His voice sounded thick. With sex? With sadness?

"But I can't stay too long."

"How about dinner? And maybe...I don't know..." She gave him a flirty look from under her lashes. "Some assfucking later, that's not so soft and sweet?"

She could feel his response to that suggestion in his cock. "You're such a bad girl, Lola. So naughty."

She buried her face in the crook of his neck, pressing into his delicious warmth. "You make me feel naughty. It's all on you."

He laughed and she lifted her head to see his smile. His real smile. She drank it in like a drug, still buzzing from the orgasm.

"I'll stay for dinner," he promised. "As for the rest..." He shook a finger at her, the stern-faced bodyguard again. "We'll see."

* * * * *

Lola woke to sun in her eyes, and the feeling of home. Her bed, her room, her sun. She did a slow stretch. Every part of her ached, but in the best way possible. Ransom never let a little thing like sleep get in the way of sex. After dinner, he'd given her an assfucking to remember, and then taken her twice more in the darkness of night. Raw, sleepy sex, close, urgent, and beautifully erotic. She couldn't sleep afterward. She'd clung to him, alternately drowsing and crying until he'd pushed inside her again.

Ransom.

She sat up and looked around. He'd straightened his side of the bed as if he'd never slept there. She felt a queasy moment of panic, but she knew he wouldn't leave without saying goodbye. She went into the bathroom to brush her teeth and get dressed. She frowned at her messy pink hair in the mirror.

Pink hair? Maybe it was time to grow up. Maybe if she acted more grown up, Ransom wouldn't make such a big deal about their age difference. Plenty of people found love, people who were twenty, thirty, even forty years apart, although the last was kind of icky. Seventeen years was nothing.

Not really.

Well.

Don't cry again, Lola. You've already cried enough.

She squared her shoulders, ran her fingers through the worst of her tangles, and went downstairs. She found Ransom at the kitchen counter with a cup of coffee. He was in his suit, ready to go.

"Want some coffee?" he asked.

She shook her head, and then thought she should have said yes, because he might have waited longer to say goodbye. She could see goodbye written all over him, in his posture, in his expression, in the way he put down his cup.

She sighed. "I don't want you to go."

"I know, but you can't hold me here. You're not strong enough. I'd eventually escape."

"I'm not joking. Tell me again why we won't work. Why we can't work. If we love each other—"

"You're too young to know what love is."

His words shut her down. *Goodbye, goodbye, goodbye.* There was no getting around it.

"I don't care about the age thing," she said. "You know I don't care. I wouldn't care if you were fifty. Sixty."

"I will be fifty and sixty, way before you. You need someone young, with decades of remaining virility."

She went to him and snuggled against his body. "I need *you*, Ransom. If you're leaving me because you have to work, if it's about money—"

"Lola."

"No, listen, I have plenty of money for us both. You wouldn't have to work. You could just travel with me, and keep me safe and happy." She slid her hands down to grab his delectable ass. "And sexually satisfied," she added in sultry invitation. "It would be perfect."

He frowned at her. "To be your kept man?"

"Yes, exactly."

His frown deepened into a grimace. "I'm done fucking for money, baby. I can't."

"That's not how it would be. I wouldn't be paying you for sex. We'd be in love. Don't you love me?" She huddled against him, trying to make him respond. He had to understand that he couldn't leave. She couldn't bear to live without him. "I love you, Ransom. I need you."

He made her draw back and meet his gaze even though she didn't want to. "You're too young to know what love is," he said a second time, in his stern bodyguard voice.

She pushed away from him. "Fuck you. You're a fucking asshole. Why won't you even consider it? Would it be so awful to stay with me? You care about me."

"Yes, I care about you."

"You like me. You love me, I know you do! You said last night that you needed me. So stay. Just stay with me," she pleaded.

"And what? Live as your cabana boy in your big, gated house?"

"No, we'd be in a relationship. I love you. I need you in my life."

"You want me to quit Ironclad and be in a relationship with you? So all the tabloids can dig up shit about how I used to be a porn star?"

"That won't happen."

"I made a ton of fucking films," he said. "It'll come out. That gigolo in Paris recognized me. Someone's going to recognize me eventually, and what then? Headline news: *Lady Paradise's Lover Has Secret Triple-X Past.*"

"It doesn't matter! Everyone has a sex tape now. Who cares? Did you even hear the part where I said I loved you? Do you think I would care what anyone said about your past?"

He stood from the barstool and banged his fist against his chest. "I care. I don't want to be that aging porn star riding the young ingénue's coattails. I don't want all that shit coming back."

"I don't care what you want." She stamped her foot, out of control with passion and sadness. "I want what *I* want."

"Yes, because you're a stubborn, impulsive kid who doesn't think things through, and you should stay that way as long as you can. Being a grown up sucks, but one of us has to do it." He seemed to deflate, to blow himself out. The kitchen fell silent, his last words echoing off the walls.

He held out a hand to her. It was steady, while she was trembling all over. "Come here and kiss me," he said.

"No, because it'll be a goodbye kiss. I don't want that."

He lowered his hand and she swallowed, fighting tears.

"What do I have to do to make you stay? Please, Ransom..."

He shook his head, and the tears finally came. She stumbled toward him as he opened his arms and gathered her close. "I'm sorry," he murmured against her ear. "I'm sorry, I'm sorry, I'm sorry. One day you'll understand why I'm doing this to you."

"I won't." She ground her face against his chest, against his damn red tie. "I'll never understand."

"You will, and then I hope you'll forgive me. You deserve someone young and fun, like you. I'm a grouchy old bodyguard. I'm always traveling."

"I'm always traveling too. We could make it work."

He drew away from her, and grabbed a tissue from the box on the counter to dab away her tears. "How about this? Let's stay in touch. Let's be friends who care about each other, who talk every once in a while."

She took the tissue from him in irritation. Friends? Long distance friends who talked every once in a while? Long distance meant she couldn't have his arms around her whenever she wanted. It meant she couldn't have his kisses and his rough lovemaking, and his stern faces, and his stubble.

"That's not what I want," she said.

He ignored her, taking a card from his wallet and writing on the back. "This is my email address, okay? It's my work account, I check it every day. Write me whenever you feel lonely, and I promise I'll write back."

She glanced at the card, not taking it. "I'm not going to write you emails. Why would I? I don't think you care about me at all."

He finally dropped the card on the counter. "I'll write to you then."

Another long silence, tense with misery. She reverted to the diva, because the diva couldn't be hurt as much as the real girl. "All I ever liked about you was the sex. Can we do sexting?" she asked.

"No."

Neither the diva nor the real girl could withstand his steady, forbearing gaze. "I didn't mean that about the sex," she said, tearing up again.

"I know. Come here and kiss me. I mean it."

He held out his hand, and she knew it would be the last time, the last offer. The last kiss. She went to him even though she dreaded it, and offered her mouth to be ravaged by his own agony and regret. He said she'd understand one day. She hoped that was true, because she was so angry right now. She let him have her anger, along with all the pain.

By the time they drew apart, her lips felt bruised. Her heart felt bruised. "Don't say goodbye. Please don't say goodbye."

"Okay, I won't." He walked past her toward the door, where his suitcase and overnight bag leaned against each other. "The car will be here in five minutes. I'll wait outside."

"No." She wrung her hands. "You don't have to wait outside."

"Help me carry something?"

She took the overnight bag while he hauled out the larger suitcase. They went down her sidewalk to the iron gate, while he filled her in on businesslike, official things.

"Ironclad negotiated with your record label to do your security, for gigs and promotional purposes. You also have a pretty generous allowance for personal security hours, so use them. Liam's already sent your file to a handful of local agents on staff." He looked at her as he propped his luggage against the gatepost. "Are you listening to me?"

She wasn't really. She felt too sad. "Another bodyguard?" she asked.

"Yes, there's a team that works with L.A. celebrities. All the agents are good. There'll be one or two on call for you at any time, should you want to go out. Ironclad will coordinate everything."

He opened the gate as a black sedan pulled up to the curb, and carried out his bags. She looked at him through the iron bars. "I'm never going out again."

He gave her a tired smile. She'd never seen him look that tired, not until this moment. "If you don't want to go out, then record one of those songs for me. Or write me an email. I'll watch for it."

She didn't reply, just gritted her teeth together so she wouldn't cry in front of the driver. She'd had plenty of bodyguards before, and would have more in the future. You weren't supposed to cry over them. She promised herself she'd never cry over one again.

"So..." she said, once the driver slammed the trunk shut.

"So," he said, touching her fingers through the bars. "Be good."

He pulled the gate all the way shut so the latch clicked. She was safe inside, and he was leaving. He waved and folded his tall frame into the passenger seat. The door closed and she couldn't see him anymore, because the windows were shaded. Was he looking at her? Did he still look tired? Did he look sad?

If he loved her, why was he going away?

She'd never understand this, no matter how old she got, no matter what he said to the contrary. Not in a million years. She let go of the gate and ran into the house, and up to her bedroom. She threw herself into the pillows. She could still smell a hint of his masculine cologne.

She threw the pillows off the bed, hating him for being an idiot. Then she collected them up again, buried her face in the scent of his memory, and cried for everything she'd just lost.

15.
DEAR LOLA

Ransom Gutierrez
(r.j.gutierrez@ironmail.com)
April 26 2:48 AM

Dear Lola,

I wonder how you've been. A week already, and I haven't heard from you. I hope that means you're busy doing creative and fulfilling things. Las Vegas is fun. Bright and loud, but we all knew that.
Drop me a note sometime if you have a minute. Just hit reply.

Ransom

* * * * *

Ransom Gutierrez
(r.j.gutierrez@ironmail.com)
May 3 12:30 AM

Dear Lola,

It's been too long, kid. Would love to hear from you.

I know you were unhappy about the way we parted, and I understand why. I've said it already but I'll say it again: I'm sorry. I made a mess of things, which is exactly what I wasn't hired to do. I shouldn't have become involved with you in the first place, so everything that happened between us was my fault.

I should stop bothering you, for all the reasons stated above, but I worry about you and how you're doing post-tour. Hope you're well.

Ransom

* * * * *

Ransom Gutierrez
(r.j.gutierrez@ironmail.com)
May 7 1:12 AM

Dear Lola,

Sorry for my last email. It was lame and whiny. I'm not sorry we became involved, because you brought a great deal of happiness to my life. I'm only sorry that I haven't heard from you, and that you're (presumably) still angry about our parting. I hate that I hurt you. All of that's the bitter truth, the facts. My other excuses are just whining so I won't subject you to them anymore.

But I'd still love to hear from you. Written any good songs lately? The incessant drumbeat kind, or the twanging guitar kind? Have you done any more gigs? My current client performs almost every night, but much tamer shows. Less neon, more feather boas.

I won't write again, unless you write to me.

Ransom

Lola M. Reynolds
(lolaebola@tmail.com)
May 21 10:32 AM

Ransom,

I haven't really felt like writing to you. I kind of still hate you, but I miss you too.
Things here are okay. I played a small venue last night, the first show since Barcelona. I thought I'd be more nervous but once I was up there, everything got easier. My bodyguard stood on the side of the stage, like you used to. He's very chill. His name is Caleb and we're NOT sleeping together. I know that will make you proud.

Lola

* * * * *

Ransom Gutierrez
(r.j.gutierrez@ironmail.com)
May 22 3:52 PM

Dear Lola,

I am indeed proud to learn you're not sleeping with Caleb. Is it your willpower keeping you apart, or his?
Just kidding. I know you've grown past your bodyguard-seducing stage. I still remember what you talked about on the plane, about being different. Hope you're staying true to yourself. Are you working with any other bodyguards? Maybe I know them.
I'm glad to hear your first gig back went well. I knew it would. I try to keep up with you in the news, not in a stalker way, but because I always enjoyed watching you perform. I know, I know, I hated the music, but you were so energetic. Are you still energetic? Getting enough sleep?

Taking care of your health? My soul singer could take a few lessons from you. I can't gossip about clients but she's a hot mess. I'll leave it at that.

Are you still playing your guitar and writing songs? I'm waiting for my track.

Ransom

* * * * *

Lola M. Reynolds
(lolaebola@tmail.com)
May 26 12:01 PM

Ransom,

The only bodyguard I ever tried to seduce is you. Just sayin. And the other bodyguards are William and Aaron, but it's usually Caleb, since he lives closest to Hollywood Hills. William's okay, kind of bug-eyed, like there's danger around every corner. Aaron is built like a bulldozer and wears light blue suits. My friends call him Great Blue Aaron. Get it? Like Great Blue Heron?

I've started going out again to parties and nightclubs, but I behave myself. No drugs. I get panicky now in big crowds. When I see people getting wound up during dance sets, I run for the outskirts because I don't want to get caught up in it, or if I'm playing the set, I feel like I have to dial things down. It kind of sucks. I can't believe I used to jump into the audience and crowd-surf. Why did you let me do that? Haha.

I still miss you. I'm still angry you left. I guess I'll get over it. What does the 'J' stand for in your name? Just curious.

I haven't recorded any guitar songs yet.

Lola

Ransom Gutierrez
(r.j.gutierrez@ironmail.com)
May 29 2:03 AM

Dear Lola,

The J in my name stands for Javier. And I know Aaron, he's exactly as you describe. The other two are new to me. As long as they're keeping you safe...

I'm happy to hear you're being careful. I'm sorry about the nervousness. I expect you'll feel a little anxious about rowdy audiences for the rest of your life. Did you see that MadDance and Danzamia are suing each other? The whole situation is sad. I hope you, at least, are happy. Write again soon.

Ransom

* * * * *

Ransom Gutierrez
(r.j.gutierrez@ironmail.com)
June 5 1:45 AM

Dear Lola,

Haven't heard from you in a while. Hope everything's good in L.A.
I miss you, kiddo.
Write again soon.

Ransom

Lola M. Reynolds
(lolaebola@tmail.com)
June 21 3:37 PM

Hi Ransom,

Sorry I haven't written in so long. The thing is, I got really busy. NOT fucking my bodyguard, I promise. What happened was that I finally did what you suggested and recorded some of my songs, and played them for some friends. They liked them!

Then I thought, hey, maybe I can do both. Maybe I can put out some techno tracks and then some folksier albums. I've been writing a lot of emo shit. I know, big surprise, but I think the songs sound okay.

So THEN I re-recorded and remastered them and uploaded a few to a secure site. I'm going to see if I can put together some kind of album concept and pitch it to the folks at my label, you know, like "The Other Side of Paradise." My agent says I'm crazy but I'm going to try.

And I know you asked me so many times for some recordings so here you go. Maybe you can listen and let me know what you think. Here's the link: Lola's Emo Shit

Lola

* * * * *

Ransom Gutierrez
(r.j.gutierrez@ironmail.com)
June 22 10:47 AM

Dear Lola,

Your songs are amazing. The world needs them. Don't listen to your agent, just follow your heart.

And upload more music for me. Three songs aren't enough.

Ransom

P.S. Happy birthday. You can legally drink now. But don't.

* * * * *

Lola M. Reynolds
(lolaebola@tmail.com)
June 25 1:07 PM

Hi Ransom,

I have more songs recorded, just haven't uploaded yet. Do you really like them? Thanks for the birthday wishes. I haven't been drinking, because I've been too obsessed with songwriting. It's so different from organizing beats! It's like opening up the other side of my soul. I still like the first side, but this side needs air too sometimes. Does that make any sense?
And you know, I think my pop would have loved this music. He loved anything with feeling in it. God, I'm so excited about these songs. I have an appointment with the brass at Vanguard this Monday at noon, just to sound things out.
So WISH ME LUCK.

Lola

* * * * *

Ransom Gutierrez
(r.j.gutierrez@ironmail.com)
June 25 1:47 PM

Dear Lola,
GOOD LUCK. You're going to kill it.
I have my fingers crossed for you.

Ransom

Ransom almost missed the red-eye flight to L.A., then his cab got caught in traffic, so he showed up ten minutes late to the Vanguard offices. At least he was able to sign into the lobby with his Ironclad credentials. He looked around but he didn't see Lola or her pink hair. Damn it. She must already be in the meeting.

He blew out a breath and collapsed into a cluster of chairs by the reception desk. With any luck, he'd catch her on the way out. He had no doubt her meeting would be successful. He'd listened to her demo songs a hundred times by now, marveling at the way her clear voice blended with the layered guitar tracks. Little smarty pants with her laptops and mixing table. She was an accomplished music producer at the tender age of twenty.

No, twenty-one.

But twenty-one was still too young. He had to remember that. He looked down at the small ivory bag he'd brought, her birthday present. *Why are you here, Ransom?*

She's still too fucking young.

He silenced the chiding voice in his head. He'd practiced great restraint to this point. No nightly phone calls. No sexting, even if he thought about sex with her at least a dozen times a day. No hops over to L.A. to see her, not until now, but he had to come because this was a big day. He understood how much this meant to her, because he'd been on the bus with her as she strummed away on her guitar, seeking deeper feelings and deeper truths, and sometimes just making up ditties about his penis.

It was good. He wanted her to be happy. He'd gotten her a delicate silver wrist cuff with two words engraved on it: *Love Yourself.*

He looked up from the bag and noticed that the man sitting across from him was wearing Ironclad credentials. He noticed Ransom's badge at the same time. They acknowledged one another, then leaned to shake hands.

"Hi. Ransom Gutierrez."

"Oh. You're Lola's last bodyguard." A muted grin cracked his taciturn regard. "The famous Gilberto."

Ransom grimaced. "Yeah, that's me. I came to wish her luck."

He gestured toward the elevator. "She's already upstairs. I'm Caleb Winchell."

"Nice to meet you."

Ransom pushed down feelings of cranky inadequacy. How old was this kid? Twenty-two? Twenty-three? Even so, he was tall and capably built, with a cool Texas drawl. If Lola hadn't tried to seduce this golden-haired wonder five dozen times already, the world made no sense. He studied Caleb Winchell, wondering if he had carnal knowledge of Lola. The idea made him want to punch the man in the face.

He was losing his mind. What right did he have to do that? He was the one who'd removed himself from Lola's life.

And Caleb looked like a world-class bodyguard, despite his youthful pretty-boy appearance. Serious, professional, composed in a way Ransom wasn't. For fuck's sake, he'd flown here on a whim from Las Vegas, barely giving Ironclad time to find his soul singer a backup agent for tonight.

"How is Lola? Was she nervous when she went in?"

"Nervous, but determined. You know how she gets."

Yes, I know how she gets. Do you know how she gets?

Maybe he should just ask Caleb if he was sleeping with Lola. No, he probably wasn't, and if Ransom didn't get his possessive emotions under control, Caleb might put two and two together and figure out why the bodyguard from her European tour had turned up at Vanguard's headquarters even though their professional connection was long since over.

"I guess I'll wait here until she comes out." Ransom settled back in his chair and attempted to act casual. "You don't mind?"

"Why would I mind?" Caleb nodded at the gift bag. "You brought her something?"

"It's a birthday present."

"Oh." One pretty-boy eyebrow crept up. "When was her birthday?"

"A few days ago. She turned twenty-one."

"I didn't know that."

Well, now you know. They both looked at their watches. Ransom wanted to ask how old Caleb was, but it would just make him feel bitter and pathetic. Instead he sorted through messages on his phone and thought, *she's here. She's right in this building with me.*

It's going to be great to see her again.

* * * * *

Lola sat outside a conference room on the third floor, on a beige upholstered bench. When people walked by, they looked at her guitar and smiled. What the fuck was that about? She wished they'd mind their own business. She didn't know any of these people. Her last deal had been made by her agent. All she'd done was show up at her lawyer's office to sign papers.

She had a meeting today with Kym Mecklin, vice-president, and Michael Gore, talent supervisor. What was a "talent supervisor"? The person who wrangled the monkeys? And what was with his last name? *Gore* made her think of horror movies, or that field in Barcelona...

Pull yourself together, Lola. It's time to be professional. It's time to grow up.

She let out a breath just as the door swung open. An older redheaded woman and a young, heavyset man with dark hair looked out at her.

"Lola!" they both cried at once.

Lola stood up and juggled her guitar to shake their hands. It was hard to match their level of fake enthusiasm. When they went into the conference room, Kym sat behind the table while Michael sat in front of it. They gestured her to a chair that faced both of them. Kym studied Lola, her face screwed up in a question.

"Something's changed about you, hon. What is it? Did you get surgery? Your nose?"

Lola touched her light blonde locks, which were growing longer. "No, I didn't have my nose done. Maybe...I used to have pink hair."

"That's it," said Michael, snapping his fingers. "Pink hair, and now she's blonde. It looks very nice on you. Very fresh. Who's your colorist?"

"Uh, no one. The pink was just a wash. I'm a natural blonde."

"Amazing," said Kym, clapping her hands. "From pink to blonde. Spectacular. Sit down. Oh, you brought your guitar! What do you have to share with us today? Something new?"

"Well, I called and talked to someone here about it..."

Michael raised his hand. "That was me. You said you were doing some songwriting. Now, what did you mean? Electronic songs with vocals?"

"No, it's not electronic music. And I think I talked to a woman."

Kym and Michael stared at each other, puzzled. "Meredith? Hillary?" They argued back and forth for a moment about whom she might have talked to. Lola stopped listening and leaned down to open her guitar case. She just needed to start playing. Once they heard what she'd been writing, they'd understand what it was. Music from her heart, organic rather than electronic.

"So, I've been working on some songs that are more...organic," she said, when they stopped bickering.

"Organic?" said Kym. "Like a concept album? Those are hot. I can't wait to hear what you have for us. Is there a demo recording? A file? Did she send a file?"

Michael turned to his laptop and started clicking the mousepad.

"There's no file," said Lola. "I mean, I have a few demo tracks uploaded to a personal site—"

Kym waved a hand. "Okay, we can give those a listen later. Play us your favorite, right now. Let's hear what you have for us."

"Okay." Lola's fingers hovered over the first chord of a song inspired by Ransom. She hoped she could get through it without crying. "This one's called 'Worth the World.' It's about... Well, it's complicated. But I think a lot of people could relate to it."

Kym and Michael gave her nothing, no comment. Okay. Lola squared her shoulders and strummed the intro. Her father's guitar sounded beautiful no matter where she played it, and her voice definitely benefited from the frosted glass walls. She couldn't look at them while she performed. This song was too personal. If she ever did acoustic shows, she'd have to learn to face the audience, feelings and all. How had her father done it?

By owning the way he felt.

Bolstered by that thought, Lola gave freer rein to her emotions, and even managed to look up a time or two. Whenever she did, Kym and Michael stared back at her. They seemed to be concentrating really hard. She hoped that was a good sign. When she finished the last line, she put her fingers over the strings to silence the lingering tones.

Kym said nothing. Michael said, "Well."

Well what? Well, that was great? Well, that sucked ass? Lola rushed to speak before he said anything else. "I know it's different than my usual sound. I thought that might be a plus. You know, two completely different sides of the same performer."

Kym laced her fingers together and leaned her chin on them. "Yes. It's just...very different. Your usual sound is much more energetic. A hundred times more energetic."

"I have a few that are more upbeat," she said, launching into "Five O'clock Shadow," which also happened to be based on Ransom. In fact, the reason she'd only uploaded three songs for him to listen to was because the rest of the songs were so obviously about him. But before she could get to the bridge, Kym held up a hand.

"I'm going to stop you right there, hon." She exchanged a glance with Michael. "That was...interesting. Bluegrass is hot in certain markets. Certain very small markets."

"It's not bluegrass," said Lola, hugging her guitar. "It's folksy female vocal stuff."

"Folksy lyrics with bluegrass music," suggested Michael. "Whatever. If it's hard to categorize, it's even harder to sell."

"But I already have an audience," said Lola. "I can sell to them."

"You have an electronic dance music audience," Kym pointed out. "They're not buying a lot of bluegrass."

"It's not bluegrass!" Okay, so they didn't like it, but they didn't have to keep calling it bluegrass. It wasn't the least bit country. It was clean and clear and full of pure emotion, like the blues her pop used to play, only not so downbeat.

"A lot of artists step outside the box," she said, determined to keep pleading her case. "Like...like when Bowie did that Christmas duet with Bing Crosby."

"Okay, some kind of holiday collaboration with another artist." Michael nodded. "We can work with that. You could cut a classic holiday track with Beyoncé or Bono, or Eminem. We could put it out in November and it'd definitely chart."

"I don't want to do a holiday single," said Lola. "I want to do some guitar and vocals music. I've made Vanguard a lot of money with my last two EDM albums. I've been touring, gaining momentum—"

"And we don't want to lose that momentum," said Kym. "Your fans expect a certain sound from you. If you don't give them what they expect..." She shook her head. "You don't want to know what happens."

"I could record these songs on a different imprint then, under a different name."

"No, Lola, listen to me." Kym leaned forward on the table. "It makes no sense for us to support a side project that's going to take time away from your Lady Paradise persona. That's what makes us money. That's what we'll support. Go back to your studio and finish your next record. Forget the bluegrass crap. No one wants that from you. Trust me on this."

"It's not bluegrass," she said for the third time, but it didn't matter. The answer was no.

"You call this label 'Vanguard,'" Lola said as she got to her feet. "Do you even know what 'vanguard' means? It means being on the forefront of new movements and ideas."

"Honey, there's not going to be a bluegrass movement anytime soon," said Michael. "But I love how you own it. Your songs are sweet, they just aren't..."

"They aren't what your listeners are looking for. At all." Kym's strident summation had Lola stalking for the door. "But we can't wait to hear what you've been working on for next year's EDM release."

"Yeah, sure," said Lola over her shoulder. "It'll be great."

Michael ran over to hold the door for her, and then stood in the way so she had to struggle to fit her guitar through. Before she could escape, he took her arm and gave her an awkward air kiss. "Take care, sweetheart. See you soon."

She wanted to whack him with her guitar, but it might get damaged and her father had bought it for her. Instead she walked down the hall and stepped onto the elevator. Of course her songs were crap. They were overly emotional, self-indulgent, female anthem shit, and if Ransom had pretended to like them, it was only because he liked her.

Ransom. She needed him right now, damn it. She'd give anything to run to his arms right now. How far away was Vegas? Maybe she could take the bus.

But Ransom didn't want her around, because she was too young and stupid. He'd made that perfectly clear, and she needed to put away her acoustic dreams too, and get back to business. She had a huge gig in Sacramento in less than two weeks. She needed to get her shit together.

She lifted her chin as the elevator doors opened to the lobby. Caleb would ask her how the meeting had gone, and she'd have to say something without crying. She'd have to pretend she didn't care.

But it wasn't Caleb she saw as she walked out of the elevator. It was Ransom, her earlier longings made real. Had he always been so beautiful, or had she missed him that much? She walked toward him as if in a dream, then dropped her guitar and ran into his arms. She started crying before they even closed around her. She buried her face against his comforting presence and all her tears poured out.

* * * * *

When Lola crossed to him from the elevator, there were three things Ransom noticed.

One, she was blonde now, a light, pale blonde that made her look even more innocent.

Two, she didn't look toward Caleb, didn't so much as spare the man a glance. She came straight to him.

Three, he was still deeply in love with her. He'd thought those feelings might fade away when he had some distance. They hadn't.

When she came into his arms, the love he felt was so shocking, so overwhelming, that for a moment he couldn't speak. He couldn't say *hello*, or *what's wrong*, or *I missed you*, or *it feels so incredible to hold you again*. He could only bury his fingers in her non-pink hair and try to survive holding her body against his.

In a fleeting moment of awareness, he saw Caleb sit down and look away. Ransom wondered how long they'd been standing there, how long she'd been sobbing against his chest. He tried to remember if he'd pressed a kiss—or more than one kiss—against her soft hair as he embraced her.

"Shh," he said, trying to calm her. "What's the matter? What did they say?"

"They hated me. They hated my music," she sobbed.

"What? I can't believe that."

"It's true!"

"Well, they're idiots."

Caleb brought over a tissue and faded again into the background. Good kid.

"Calm down a minute." He wiped at her tears. "Tell me what happened."

"They kept calling it b-bluegrass." She took the tissue from him and used it to blow her nose. "They said I should do a holiday collaboration with...with *Eminem*."

Ransom sighed. "They have no hearts. No souls. They're music execs, you know? Hey, Lola Mae, look at me."

She did. Her deep blue eyes were tainted a miserable red. He wanted to go upstairs and slaughter whoever had made her cry like this.

"What they say doesn't matter." She shook her head but he put a finger under her chin. "It doesn't matter. They're greedy, they want you to do whatever makes them the most money. They didn't even try to understand your musical vision, did they?"

She shook her head. "They didn't understand. They hardly listened."

"But you understand, and I understand. And other people will understand. Don't give up because a few knuckleheads didn't like it."

She pushed away from him in frustration. "Those knuckleheads control my career. What am I supposed to do now? Upload my songs to some dumbass music sharing site?"

"Yes."

"You're stupid." She sniffled into the crumpled tissue, then looked back up at him. "What are you even doing here?"

"I brought you a birthday present." He presented the ivory gift bag, a bit crushed now from their embrace.

She stared at it. "You came all the way from Vegas to bring me a birthday present?"

"And to help celebrate your success."

She started rooting through the tissue paper. "Well, there's nothing to celebrate. There's seriously no fucking point." She took out the bracelet and he turned it over to show her the inscription.

"*Love Yourself*," she read. She stared at the words while he studied her new, longer hair. So blonde. So different. But so much the same. "Love yourself?" she repeated in an even angstier tone. "That's ironic, coming from you."

His eyes narrowed. He was aware of Caleb sitting a few feet away, but he still asked, "What's that supposed to mean?"

"I think you know what it means. You didn't love me enough to stay with me, so what's the point of this shitty gift?"

A minute ago she'd been clinging to him. Now she was glaring, her lips mashed in a line.

"The point is..." *What is the point, Ransom? Why are you here?* "It's a gift. It doesn't have to have a point."

But that was a shit answer, an evasive answer. "Do you really want to talk about this now?" he asked, glancing toward Caleb.

"I want to know why you brought this to me." She waved the bracelet in his face. "I think you bought the wrong one. Couldn't you find one that said *Get Lost, Kid*?"

"Lola—"

"Or *You're Not Enough For Me*?"

"You know that's not why—"

"Do you think they even make bracelets like that? Because that would've been the perfect way to express your feelings."

"Wow. Are you done?" He suppressed the urge to shake her, especially with her new, young bodyguard watching from a few feet away. "I brought you a gift because I thought you might like it. I came here to support you. You might try saying thank you."

"You might try not giving people *Love Yourself* bracelets when you've treated them like trash."

"I never treated you like trash."

"You threw away what we had," she said. "You left me."

"I did that for your benefit. I left you because we'd never work. It didn't have to do with loving you, or not loving you." Every word out of his mouth made him sound more like an asshole, and she was already wrought up from her disastrous meeting. Her expression darkened with every syllable he uttered. "You're twenty years old," he said through his teeth.

"Twenty-one, remember? You brought me a fucking birthday gift." She waved the bag in front of his face, then shoved the bracelet back down into the tissue paper. "Whatever. I don't want anything from you, especially something that tells me to love myself when I feel like a crappy, rejected piece of shit." She thrust the bag back into his hands. "Take this to Vegas and give it to your fucked up soul singer. I have to go."

Caleb materialized beside her and picked up her guitar case. As they walked away, Lola turned and snatched the bag back from his fingers. "No, you know what, I'm keeping this. Yes, I can love myself. I think I'm the only one who does."

"Lola—" he began, but she gave him the finger and stalked toward the door. Caleb followed with a brief, mystified glance back in his direction.

Lola 2.0. Less pink, but moody as ever.

Ransom 2.0. Willing to admit he deserved her outrage, because he'd made the wrong fucking choice.

16.
WORTH THE WORLD

Lola composed twelve different emails to Ransom that evening, and deleted all of them. Then she almost called him, but she couldn't. She wouldn't. It had been so difficult to see him, so difficult to feel his warmth and strength and remember what she was missing. She'd almost gotten over him, and now she felt broken in pieces again.

At least this time, she'd done the leaving. She'd been the one to turn her back and walk away, and she hoped he felt as shitty as she'd felt when he abandoned her.

No, she didn't hope that. Ugh.

Once she got over her red-hot anger, she remembered why he left, and why he would have left her again, even if they'd gone out to dinner or something for old times' sake. She understood he couldn't get over their age difference, and that he worried about his porno past besmirching her brand or some such bullshit.

He was also worried about losing his job, even though she could have supported him. She hadn't envisioned a cabana boy situation, but she could see how he'd imagine things that way. He had a lot of pride, and major issues around sex and money. She understood all that, but it didn't make the outcome any easier to bear.

She missed his face, his direct gaze, his muscular arms. She missed his half smiles and the way he offered support when she felt blue. She missed having someone around who accepted her for who she was, but still encouraged her to be better. To be happier.

She looked down at the bracelet he'd given her. It fit perfectly on her wrist. It was so pretty and shiny and polished, and the engraving was nice. *Love Yourself.* It was what he'd taught her to do, to love herself more. It was a thoughtful present. She shouldn't have freaked out on him. For days afterward, she stewed about what had happened, until she thought she had to find some way to make things right.

But when she tried to apologize and explain her feelings in an email, she said too much, and then she'd delete all the emotional stuff until the email was so bare there was no use in sending it. Then she'd do an Internet search for Rico Rockhard just to look at him, and then she'd feel guilty, because she knew how heartbreaking his porn years had been. Then she'd feel frustrated and depressed because she'd rejected him when he was trying to be kind to her.

Then she'd compose another email and start the cycle all over again.

Dear Ransom,
I need you to come back to me.

Dear Ransom,
I'm different now. I've changed. I'm more mature.

Dear Ransom,
Sometimes I have nightmares about Barcelona, and you're not here.

Dear Ransom,
No one has ever kissed me like you.
What does that MEAN?

She spent hours on her guitar trying to work through her feelings. The songs wrote themselves, songs about loss and longing and hard muscles and deep gazes and sexual fireworks.

She wondered if he was seeing someone else by now. You couldn't walk six feet in Vegas without bumping into a bimbo, and looking the way

Ransom looked, he might have slept with four dozen women. She imagined him banging them in elevators, or drilling them against walls while their fake boobs bounced and they cried *Ooh, ooh, ooh...* Seriously, all he had to do was snap his fingers.

But he wasn't the finger-snapping type, and she knew she only imagined those scenes because she'd watched too many of his films. He'd told her more than once that he didn't like empty sex. He was a caring person who preferred for sex to mean something.

And...he'd had sex with her, so she must have meant something to him. He'd never fucked her in an elevator or up against a wall. He'd *felt something for her*, even if he'd left afterward out of some misplaced sense of honor. The staying-away was the issue, the obstacle. She had to figure out how to get him to reconsider that choice. If he'd give their love a chance, just for a while, he'd see that she didn't care about their age difference, or his porno past.

He'd see that she wasn't a wild, idiot kid anymore, but an emotional woman who wanted to love him.

Maybe if she could get him to come to the festival in Sacramento, she could make some grand gesture to explain how much she needed him, how much she missed him. She could play one of those guitar songs he loved, one of the ones she'd written about him. She'd share it with all the thousands of people in the audience, but especially him. She'd invite him to stand beside her at the sound console so she could gaze right into his eyes when she introduced the song.

The whole scene rolled out in her mind like a movie. He'd smile. He'd give in. He'd kiss her. As for the audience, ravers were an easygoing crew. She could play one folksy song, and they wouldn't mind. Hell, she'd put a beat under it, the way Ransom suggested, and turn it into a totally new sound. The crowd would love it. Would he come to Sacramento if she asked? Even after their altercation?

She'd write an email. He preferred emails, and she'd for sure cry if he rejected her over the phone. She'd share her feelings and leave the rest up to him. She had to hurry, because the Sacramento EDM Fest was just a couple of days away.

Lola M. Reynolds
(lolaebola@tmail.com)
July 6 11:15 AM

Dear Ransom,

I hope you're doing great in Vegas. I'm writing belatedly to thank you for your gift, and to thank you for coming to L.A. last week. I'm sorry I flipped out and stormed off. Even though I changed a lot after Barcelona, my inner diva still flares up sometimes, and I behave like a jackass. I don't have any excuses.

But I regret it now, because I would have liked to spend more time with you. I miss seeing you. I know you're busy but I'm doing this huge set on Friday at the Sacramento EDM Festival (flyer attached.) I know you LOVE EDM MUSIC more than anything in the world. Ha. Maybe not. But please, if you can, come to Sacramento. I'll make sure you're on the list to get backstage. Maybe you can stand by the stairs the way you used to. And maybe, if you felt like it, we could get some coffee afterward...

She wrote more, then deleted more, then simply signed it with her name and pressed Send. God, she hoped the email made sense. She hoped she wasn't being ridiculous or childish.

She really, really hoped he showed up.

* * * * *

Ransom didn't quit Ironclad because Caleb ratted him out to the management. On the contrary, there hadn't been any blowback from his meeting with Lola in the Vanguard lobby, even though Caleb had seen enough to ask some serious questions.

No, Ransom quit Ironclad because Lola never gave him enough lead time to be where he needed to be. She'd invited him to come see her show and he wasn't going to disappoint her, even if she seemed to have no concept of necessary travel time between Sacramento and Las Vegas.

The bodyguarding was just a job. He could get another one. He could take five years off and not run out of money. Would five years be enough to get Lola out of his system? Would she mature enough in five years to realize she'd be better off with some younger guy?

Maybe. Maybe not. Of more pressing urgency: How was he going to get to fucking Sacramento in time for her festival set? He'd told her he would be there, but once again, the universe conspired against him. Cancelled flight. Lost luggage. He'd had to set up a new rental car account now that he wasn't working for Ironclad, and he never realized it took more documentation than applying for his fucking driver's license in the first place.

By the time he worked out the rental car shit, located the festival site, and paid twenty dollars for parking a good half-mile from the actual festival grounds, Lola's set was already underway. He knew her songs by now, knew every one of them down to the number of beats per minute. He stopped, banged his fists together, and looked back at the car in the far, far distance. His ear plugs. Damn it.

He wasn't going back now.

As he trudged toward the entrance kiosks, kids sent him sideways glances. It hadn't occurred to him until now that a designer suit might raise suspicion at a raver event. If only he had a neon necklace or something. If only he hadn't worn the Ferragamo shoes.

The festival officials, a bunch of hipster college kids drunk on power, asked him three times if he had any drugs or weapons on him.

"I'm supposed to be on the backstage list for Lola—Lady Paradise," Ransom explained. "She invited me here. I worked in Europe as her security guard."

Another "official" sauntered over. He was about Lola's age, with a ring in his nose and a long, braided goatee. "You got some security credentials on you?" he asked.

Out of habit, Ransom reached for his waist, where he usually clipped his badge. No longer there. Fuck. "I don't work in security anymore," he said.

The hipster crew exchanged glances. "Can you call someone?" Ransom asked, pointing at the head guy's two-way radio. "I've been traveling since five AM to get here. She's going to be pissed if I miss her set."

That wasn't a lie. Lola had a temper when she didn't get her way, and Ransom's own temper was surging just like Lola's beats and drops. To his relief, the kids agreed it was a good idea to call the backstage manager. The backstage manager responded after the world's longest five minute silence and confirmed that yes, Ransom was on the backstage access list. Thank God.

Ransom moved through the turnstile only to be stopped by the braided goatee kid with the walkie-talkie. "Uh, sir, one-day passes cost seventy-five dollars."

"Are you fucking kidding me?" Ransom chewed the inside of his lip as he reached for his wallet, subduing the urge to rip the kid's goatee out by the roots. He handed over his credit card and waited for them to swipe it. He then submitted to the indignity of having a skull-printed paper band affixed beside his Mont Blanc wristwatch by a girl with rainbow-painted lips.

"Can I go in now?" he asked through his teeth.

"Have fun," said the main kid, who was damn lucky to still have his goatee.

Ransom shook off his anger and wove through the clusters of ravers dancing at the edge of the main festival field. Apparently they thought he was dressed in a suit to announce himself as a dealer, since several kids asked him, "What have you got?"

"Love," he snapped back each time.

They nodded or flashed peace signs at that answer. These kids understood love, or at least thought they did. All of this was love and life and beats, and neon and glitter, and drugs they'd regret taking when they were older.

But his love was deeper, tempered by age and experience, and the knowledge that he'd let go of a soul mate, however different Lola might be. He looked up at the stage, at her tiny silhouette, her arms waving, her light hair bobbing to the music as she leaned over the sound console. He remembered another time, just a few months ago, when he'd followed Greg's bald head through a similar crowd. He hadn't had ear plugs then either.

That evening, he'd looked up at Lola and thought she was just a crazy, dumb kid.

Now, he understood her emotional complexity. He understood how her worst choices mostly came from anxiety and fear. He understood how many feelings she stuffed down in order to keep up her Lady Paradise persona. He understood she could be violent as a tornado or playful as a puppy, usually within the same half hour.

He understood that he needed to be with her—if she could forgive him for taking so long to figure that out.

He made his way toward the front, sliding into spaces and muscling through when he needed to use more force. He didn't take much notice of the spirit hoods or glittering bindis now. He didn't mind the reek of patchouli and sweat. He just needed to get through this crowd so he could meet her backstage the way she'd asked. *Yes, please, I want to try again, and not fuck up this time.*

If he didn't show up, she might make one of her snap decisions and cut him out of her life for good. She had security around her that could keep him out as handily as it allowed him in. One word from her, and he'd be a *persona non grata*, with no access.

No access but standing out here among thousands of other people, bathed in her light.

He moved faster, moved closer, pushing past kids who were too high to care. He could tell she was nearing the end of her set. The lights flashed faster, the beats boomed deeper, and she danced harder, waving her microphone. Then everything went silent, and he and one hundred thousand other spectators froze and looked up at her figure atop the console.

"I want to play something for you," she said. "Can I play something for you?"

The crowd came to life again with shouts of agreement. A slow beat thumped every few seconds, as if left behind from the previous wall of sonic noise.

"You can't dance to it," she teased. "So maybe you'll hate it."

Fervent shrieks of denial greeted this warning. A group of girls to his left screamed, "We love you, Lady Paradise."

Her head turned in their direction. He was close enough now to see her eyes, her blonde hair, her beautiful features...and the delicate silver bracelet on her wrist.

He could have yelled that he loved her too. Maybe then she would have turned to him, but she was back in motion, taking her guitar from behind the console. As soon as she sat and began to tune it, a hum spread through the crowd. When a techie carried over a mic stand, the hum rose to a roar.

"Yeah, kids." She adjusted the mic and did a quick *check, check*. "I'm going to sing you a song. Like around a campfire, but more sparkly."

She worked crowds so well. Her audience had gone quiet, but it was a pleased, expectant quiet. All he could see were smiles. Her smiles, their smiles, even the guy who'd brought the mic stand was standing to the side with a smile.

"I'm gonna tell you the truth." She crossed her bare legs and cradled the guitar in her lap. "I played this for my record company and they thought it sucked. But I love it, and I love you." Screams of adulation interrupted her speech. She yelled over the noise to finish her thought. "And I hope you love this, because I wrote it for someone I love. Make some noise if you believe in love."

The screams and shouts of a hundred thousand love-mad ravers assailed his eardrums. Ransom covered his ears against the din, then lowered his hands. He didn't want to miss one note of this. Her silver bracelet caught the light as she began to play.

* * * * *

Lola felt caught between excitement at the audience's reaction, and devastation. She threw a glance at the stairs again, but Ransom wasn't there. He'd written that he was coming, but he hadn't come. Maybe he couldn't come?

Maybe he'd decided not to come.

Either way, she'd made a promise to herself that she'd play this song in Sacramento. She'd promised she'd put it out there to be judged by the greater world, and had even cleared it with festival management so they'd help her set up the microphone and stand. Now she only had to sing it.

The audience got quiet as she strummed the first chords in time with the slow beat she'd programmed ahead of time. *Just put a beat under it.*

I know, Ransom. I know.

She'd decided to sing "Worth the World" because out of all her songs, it showed her heart the most. If Ransom had come, he could have heard the words she was too afraid to say to his face. Maybe he'd still hear them, if the song ever got any legs. She'd uploaded it to all the indie sales platforms a couple days ago, under the name Lola Mae Reynolds.

Doing that had been easy. Anonymous and quick, the push of an upload button. This was way harder, this massive audience and her simple, wistful melody having to stand on its own. She looked out at the sea of faces, curious and mostly accepting of this slow-beat interlude.

Help me, pop. Help me play like you. Help me feel it.

She closed her eyes and sang the first verse along with the sultry, sexy bass accompaniment. Here, now, in front of all these people, the words felt painfully personal, but the one person she wanted to hear them wasn't here. "*You forced me to go/where I didn't think I could survive,*" she sang, thinking of their early days. "*And once I was there/I started remembering I was alive. I didn't notice the cold/or the stares of the passersby/ just tossed my hair from my eyes/ to take in the big sky.*"

The big sky and the big picture. He'd helped her see the bigger picture of her life, and no matter what happened, she'd never forget. That was the next verse, all about changing and needing, and never forgetting. She chanced a look out at the audience. Some of them danced slowly, waving their arms along with the back beat, while others only stood and watched. A few lighters flickered in the air.

It was enough to sustain her to the final chorus. She strummed louder and gave the audience all her frustration and grief. "*You say I'm worth the world, love/but what does that mean?/You're worth way more than the world to me.*" She took a breath and closed her eyes. "*You say I'm worth the world, love/but when are you gonna see?/You're worth way more than the world to me.*"

She drew out the last trill of notes, bringing the song to a close, then reached behind her to kill the electronic beat. By the time she turned back, people were applauding. No, shouting. Screaming. Her heart bloomed like a flower. She felt proud, sad, avenged, stripped naked, and held up by all these friends who meant the best for her.

Then she saw someone in the front row who wasn't clapping or screaming, just staring back at her. Dark suit, red tie. Wise, beautiful eyes.

Ransom. He'd made it after all.

"Oh my God," she said. "Oh my God, oh my God. Ransom."

For a minute she didn't know what to do, then she smiled and did the only thing she could do. She pretended she was going to dive into the audience, into his arms. She had him for a moment—he shook his head sharply—but then he wagged a finger at her and smiled.

She gestured for him to come onstage and join her, and somehow he did. The security guys helped him clamber up over the barriers and jump onto the platform, and then she was in his arms. He took her guitar and held it out of the way, and hugged her close, pressing his forehead to hers.

"Lola Mae. Beautiful girl." His fingers spread on her back, warm and firm. "Sorry I'm late."

"I sang you a song."

"I know. I heard it." His eyes shone from the lights. "It was so good." His fingers twisted in her hair, tugging with a sudden intensity. "I loved your song. I love you. God, I love you so much."

"I love you too. I've missed you." The crowd had gone quiet. She didn't want them to listen to this private moment, but she couldn't seem to let Ransom go. "I've missed you so much." Her eyes welled with tears. "Please don't leave me again."

"I'm not leaving you again, I promise. I've come back, because I never should have left in the first place. I love you, even if I shouldn't. That's just the way it is."

She tilted her face up and he kissed her in front of everyone. *I've come back. I love you, even if I shouldn't.* Lola happened to believe there weren't any *shoulds* or *shouldn'ts* when it came to love, but maybe that was because she was a dumb kid. She melted against his front, grasping his lapels to pull him closer as his mouth moved over hers. His kiss was an apology, a pure, passionate confession, and Lola forgave him for hurting her, because they were both wiser now. All the tension and emptiness of the past few weeks ebbed away as they reconnected.

But a hundred thousand pairs of eyes still watched them. She became aware of pockets of voices in the audience. "Gilberto," they cried. "It's Gilberto, her bodyguard."

She pushed away from Ransom to look over his shoulder at the spectators.

"Is your set over?" he asked. "Maybe you should send them all home."

"Yeah, I should tell them good night." She looked back at him. "But you ought to say hello first."

She turned him around and wrapped an arm around his waist, and held the mic with the other hand. "This is Ransom, everyone. Not Gilberto. But you were right, I love him. I'm so in love with this man."

There were whoops and fist pumps as the crowd bobbed and weaved as far as the eye could see. It wasn't an angry, primal weaving, like in Barcelona, but happy weaving, a dance without music, a dance that came from the heart. Festival fields and beats would always be her life, and these ravers would always be her people, but she could have other things too, like sweet, wistful songs and older, responsible boyfriends.

"Thanks for listening to my heart tonight," she said to their uplifted faces. "I love you. Thanks for giving me a chance."

The mass of people roared their support as she looked over at Ransom. He'd come back. He was staying. She leaned close and spoke in his ear so he could hear her over the crowd, and repeated what she'd just told the audience. "I love you. Thanks for giving me a chance."

17.
DEAL

Ransom guided her backstage, his eyes scanning the crew and bystanders out of habit. He wasn't her bodyguard anymore, but he still wanted to protect her. Her official bodyguard, Caleb, flanked her other side as they made their way to the hired car. Once they found it, Caleb walked around to the far side to give them a moment of privacy.

Ransom gazed down at Lola. Was she returning to L.A. tonight? Was she exhausted? Was she available?

What now?

"I'm staying at a hotel downtown," she said. "Do you... Would you... Do you have to head back to your soul singer?"

"No." His gaze strayed down to her lips. "Someone else is watching my soul singer."

"Well..." She looked deliciously anxious. "Will you... Can you..."

"Yes. I'm coming to your hotel. I'm staying all night. Actually, I'm staying for as long as you'll have me, but we can talk about that later. Right now, I have to find my rental car. I parked..." He gave a rueful laugh. "I parked a long way from here."

"We'll have the driver take you to your rental, then we can drive your rental to the hotel. Is that okay?" She turned to Caleb. "Can we do that?"

He shrugged. "I don't see why not."

She turned back to Ransom and grasped his hands, twining her fingers with his. He was aware of Caleb watching, of people gawking at them from beyond the metal barriers that surrounded the backstage area. He helped her into the car, then climbed in beside her while Caleb settled into the front passenger seat. Ransom felt sympathy for him. How many times had he been an unwilling witness to a client's private, emotional craziness?

They could wait until they were alone to hash through everything, all the concessions and adjustments and avowals they'd doubtless make in order to be with one another. For now, he only held Lola's hand, rubbing her fingers between his. They talked about safe, easy things like his flight from Vegas, and the rental car mess. She gasped when he told her he'd quit his job.

"I would have been fired anyway." He nodded toward Caleb, but hell, thousands of people had seen their onstage kiss tonight. Plenty of cameras had recorded it for posterity; it was probably already posted online. "I don't know if it was any more honorable to quit first."

"There's nothing dishonorable about what happened between us," she insisted in her diva voice. "You didn't do anything wrong."

"I'm not sure my boss would agree with you."

"I'll talk to him then. I'll explain."

He shook his head. "You don't have to. He's not my boss anymore. And it's all right, baby. I had to quit to have more time with you. Isn't that what you wanted?"

She studied him, her pretty blue eyes clouded with gravity. "Yes, but that wasn't what *you* wanted."

"I guess you could say my priorities have changed."

She buried her head against his shoulder. "I hoped that song would convince you."

"I was convinced before the song." He cupped her face and stroked a finger across her cheek. "But the song was beautiful. They'll play it at our wedding, yeah? If you don't figure out in time that I'm too old for you."

"You're not too old." She pulled his face down and pressed her nose to his. "I'm twenty-one now, so we're only sixteen years apart."

"Sixteen and a half," he said as she licked his chin. His cock throbbed, hardening to stone. "But who's counting?"

She found his length in the dark, furtively stroking him. He had to stop her, or he'd lose control of himself and really give Caleb something to be embarrassed about. He'd been in that situation too many times also, watching clients go at each other as if he were only a statue, or a painting on the wall. "Wait," he chided in a whisper. "Wait until we're alone."

"But I want you," she whispered back.

Oh, God. It seemed to take forever to find the rental car. Caleb offered to drive, but Ransom drove instead, so he wouldn't be tempted to assault Lola in the back. Lola sat very still in the passenger seat as he navigated Sacramento's streets, but he was constantly aware of her presence. Her closeness.

He felt like he could breathe again.

All the travel hassle had been worth it, quitting his job, disrupting his life, everything. Now that she sat beside him, he understood how empty his life had been since he left her. He'd been missing a whole part of himself, the part Lola nudged to life with her vibrant energy and emotional depth. He didn't understand why the universe had chosen to pair them as soul mates, he just knew it had happened.

When they got to the hotel, Caleb helped carry Ransom's luggage as the three of them headed upstairs. The young bodyguard said goodnight to Lola with grave professionalism, then shot Ransom a fleeting smile before he disappeared into the adjoining room. Good kid. Not sleeping with her.

"Caleb's closer to your age," he said as they went into her room. He threw his wardrobe bag over a chair. "Better looking too. Why not him?"

She pushed him back against the door as it closed behind them. "Because he's not you," she said. "And I want you."

"You want me, huh?" He kissed her long and hard, burying his fingers in her hair. Blonde, not pink. God, she tasted like sugar. "I've missed you so much, baby. I've been waiting all this time to hold you and make you mine." He pulled her right against him, against the pulsing, agonizing solidity of his shaft. "How do you want it? Soft and sweet?"

"No, nothing soft. Nothing sweet. I want it hardcore."

She pushed off his jacket and yanked at his tie. He took over undressing himself lest she choke him to death in her impatience. He'd teach her the art of restraint someday, the art of delay and seduction and longing.

That day was not today.

When he was naked, she moved her palms across his chest, his pecs, his shoulder, his abs, then down to his granite-hard cock. He grasped her hands and told her to wait.

"I want you now," she whined.

"Be good."

He tugged off her tiny shorts, her miniscule crop top and bra, then grasped her ass and lifted her in his arms. As he carried her toward the bed, he noted the location of windows, closets, doors. Bodyguard stuff, but then his mind was back on her, or more specifically, what he might do to her. They had weeks now, months, years. There was so much to do to her.

He dumped her on the bed and went to his luggage for a condom. After considering a moment, he grabbed a handful, along with a vial of lubricant he deposited on the table beside the bed.

"You brought lube?" she asked.

"Of course. I know you, Lola."

He crawled onto the bed and forced her legs back, and leaned down to trail his tongue up the center of her pussy. She whined and clutched at his shoulders, arching for more. As soon as he tongued her clit, she went wild and flailed beneath him. Jesus, he'd missed this. He grasped her legs tighter and told her to be still.

"But I want you," she moaned in an extremely loud voice. "I want your cock in me."

"Okay, now the whole hotel knows. But listen to me." He wrestled her to stillness and made her meet his gaze. "We're doing this my way. First I get some pussy, and then I'm taking your ass."

"Oh God. Wow."

He nodded at his wide-eyed lover, then sank down again to jam his tongue into her wetness. He took his time, exploring her, nibbling, pinching, teasing her to a fever pitch as he drifted on her scent. When she was close to coming, he stopped. She yanked at his hair but he only laughed and ordered her to turn over.

"Please, let me come," she begged.

"Oh, you will. You'll come the way *I* want."

She made a sound between frustration and excitement. "With your cock in my ass?"

"You know a better way? Now put your face in the fucking pillow, and get that butt in the air."

"Yes sir," she said, melting into submission at his tone. Good God, her tight, round ass was about to make *him* melt into submission. He needed to be inside it as soon as possible, but he wanted to get her a little more worked up first. He massaged a finger over her clit and was rewarded with a lusty cry.

He shushed her. "Caleb's next door, and he doesn't want to hear you getting your ass fucked. Put your face back in the pillow like I said."

She obeyed for the few seconds it took him to put on the condom, which was longer than he expected her to comply. Then she was looking back at him again, riling him up with the hunger in her gaze. He kept one hand pressed over her clit as he used the other to slick up her hole.

"Don't use too much," she said. "I want it to hurt when you push in."

"You fucking flirt." He pinched her clit until her hips bucked. "Face. Pillow. Now."

Lola sucked in a breath at the sight of his huge, hard cock looming behind her. She wanted him so bad. She needed his power, his expertise in this. His protection, even when he made her hurt. Just a little, though. Just enough for it to be a submission, a sacrifice. *I want you. I'm yours.*

He spread his fingers on her back as she prepared to accept his girth. "Tell me if it's too much," he murmured. "If you can't find the words, tell me with sounds."

Then he was pressing into her and she was making all the sounds, every agonized and sex-starved utterance. The head of his cock forced open her ring, causing a dull, rising pain. She reached back to touch his legs and ground herself. She felt objectified and rectal-fied. She felt stretched open and erotically surrendered.

And safe.

He worked her clit, sending shivers of pleasure through her entire body even as his thickness caused intensifying discomfort. She forced herself to relax and open to his invasion, then he was sliding deeper, and her high pitched sounds of agony deepened to sounds of excitement. She turned her head to the side, heaving a gasp.

"Please, please..."

He paused mid thrust. "Please what?" His voice rumbled with strain. "Do you want me to stop?"

"No, no, no, no."

"You want it deeper? Harder?"

"Please."

He made her turn her head back into the pillow and then he gave her what she wanted, a hard, steady ass drilling. His thighs held her trapped, and her wrists were collected in one of his huge, strong hands and held over her head. The other hand flitted over her clit with the precise amount of dexterity needed to drive her crazy.

"You like that, baby?" His rough voice turned her on as much as his cock pounding her from behind. "I own you right now. Your ass is mine."

She was already adrenalized from playing her set, and excited from their reunion. Now the sensations became almost too much. He stroked her clit until her hips jerked, until she was almost there, and then he stopped and tugged at her nipples, setting off completely different explosions of pleasure. Her trapped hands curled into fists as he returned to teasing her clit.

All the while, he drove into her ass, stretching her, and yes, hurting her a little. It felt heavenly when he fucked her pussy, but when he was in her ass, it felt naughtier and more thrilling. It felt dangerous and primal and *oh, fuck, she was going to come*—

He stopped again and pinched her nipples. It felt so, so hot, but she wailed in frustration at her lost orgasm.

"Put your face in the damn pillow," he said. "I'll let you come when I'm ready."

He smacked each of her thighs, a hard, sharp blow, and she wondered how it could feel both so bad and so good. "Don't spank me," she cried, but she really meant *Please spank me oh please spank me some more*, which he totally knew.

He gave her a few more smacks, hard enough to hurt, but not so hard that she forgot he was still in her ass. "Someday I'm going to take a belt to you," he said, and she almost went off then, lost in fantasies of spankings and Ransom and belts.

But she managed to hold on to her control, and she didn't come. She didn't want this ecstasy to end, or maybe she was waiting for his permission to come. In every other sexual relationship she'd had, she'd called the shots from start to finish, but now, with Ransom, all of that went out the window, and it was a beautiful thing.

"Oh, please," she said, not that he could hear her, since she'd finally obeyed him and buried her face in the pillow. Her fingers curled and uncurled as he toyed with her clit again. She tried to pull her hands away from his grasp but it was impossible. She was under his control, trapped under his powerful body, having her ass plundered by his powerful cock.

Later, when they lay in each other's arms, she would touch and caress him, trace his lightning bolt tattoo and take her fill of his gorgeous, golden body, but for now he was in charge. *Nothing soft. Nothing sweet.* She pressed her clit against his fingers, seeking release. Her cries of ecstasy built to a near scream as he found the perfect spot and rubbed it over and over, teasing it just the right amount. Her ass gripped his cock as she bit the pillow. Her whole body trembled with the pleasure of stimulation and the pain of his cock surging deeper, deeper...

"Come now," he said. "Come while I'm deep in your ass. Come, now. Come." With each word, he drove into her with shudderingly firm thrusts. Her mind was too gone to obey, but her body responded, released from restriction. She ground against his fingers and contracted around him, her ass and pussy both pulsing, her whole body suffused by the intensity of her orgasm.

As for Ransom, his fingers closed around her wrists to the point of pain as he bucked against her in a stuttering rhythm. "Yes, God, yes," she heard him utter under his breath. "Oh, God. Yes."

That pretty much summed it up. *Oh, God. Yes. You're meant to be with me. You're meant to be inside me, Ransom, both my body and my heart.*

He finally released her wrists and touched the bracelet he'd given her, the silver cuff she wore all the time now. *Love Yourself.* He leaned down and pressed a kiss to her cheek. His heart thumped against her back, pounding as fast as hers. They were both sweaty from erotic exertion.

"Again?" he whispered against her ear. "After we take a shower?"

That was the thing about dating ex porn stars. They had incredible stamina.

"Yes." She turned to press herself against him. "Again and again and again."

* * * * *

Lola woke to nuzzles and kisses. *Ransom*. His dark hair filled her peripheral vision, along with his customary red tie.

"Why are you dressed?" She tugged at his collar. "I want more."

The look in his eyes said he'd be perfectly willing to give her more. Then he broke the spell by looking at his watch. "No more. Not now. We have to get to the airport. No, don't freak out," he said as she pouted. "I managed to book a ticket on your flight. Caleb's going to use it and let me sit next to you in first class."

"He's a champ." She'd have to arrange some kind of bonus for Caleb when she told Ironclad she didn't need him anymore. She wouldn't need bodyguards very often now that she'd be going out with one.

"Are you really going to stay?" She sighed, snuggling into his warmth. "You said you'd stay as long as I wanted you to."

"That's true. I'll stay as long as you need me."

"That's forever then, because I'll need you forever."

He snorted. "Says the girl who's barely reached adulthood."

She ignored his comment and sat up, trying to think how everything would work. "Will you move into my house? You can have your own room, so you'll have a place to go if I really drive you crazy. There are plenty of rooms. I'll buy any kind of food you want. You won't have to do housework because I have a houseke—"

"Shh. Listen." He pulled her back down into his arms. "I'll stay as long as you need me, wherever you need me. Any more questions?"

"You're really going to stay," she said, and it wasn't a question. She finally believed him. Those eyes never lied. "What changed your mind? Why did you come back?"

"Because I couldn't not come back." He looked down at their intertwined hands. "There are a lot of reasons you and I wouldn't work out, but there are also a lot of reasons we should try. One of those reasons is that..." He paused long enough to press her palm to his lips. "One of those reasons is that I need you. I need your smile and your craziness. I need your mood swings and your beautiful, heartfelt songs."

"And you need my ass."

"That goes without saying." He swept his arms in an arc, designating her entire body, then pulled her close again. "It's all a package. I want it all."

She'd gone a little teary during his recitation. She rested her cheek against his shoulder and cuddled into his chest. "I love everything about you too. When you're not around, I don't know what to do with myself. Now that you're back..." Ugh, she didn't want to cry. She wanted to look to their future together. "Now that you're back, we can figure everything out. We'll manage. I'll—I'll try not to be a dumb kid."

"You were never a dumb kid." He scratched her with his stubble to make her laugh. "I was just a know-it-all bodyguard who didn't understand you. We'll do better after this. Deal?"

She nodded. "Deal."

"Because we've been through a lot together. Maybe we can settle down now and get to know each other, and build a life that's not taking place in European hotel rooms and tour buses."

"And maybe you can use your stern bodyguard skills to keep me steady," she suggested. "You know, when I get a little too wild. Especially in bed." She batted her eyes at him and caressed his cock through his pants.

He clamped a hand around her wrist and shook his head. "No. Pack your bags. Airport. Don't tempt me. You have half an hour until we need to meet Caleb downstairs."

That got her up and out of bed. While she showered, she thought back to the time she'd stared at his soap and shampoo in Hamburg. She'd wondered how the hell she was going to live with the guy. Now she didn't want to live without him.

Now she wouldn't have to live without him. She started singing, because shower stalls were great for acoustics. "*You say I'm worth the world, love/ but when are you gonna see?*" She heard a deeper voice join her on the chorus, chiming in from the other room. "*You're worth way more than the world to me.*"

18.
OUR SONG

When they got to L.A., Ransom took Lola to his place so he could pick up a few things. He wasn't in a rush to move everything to her house, but he imagined he'd do it soon. His apartment was a cheap sublet near the airport, just there for when he blew through the city. It was empty and it didn't feel like home.

When he got to Lola's and threw his things down in the middle of her wood-paneled living room, he felt like he was home. He kicked off his shoes in her foyer, then picked them up to inspect the damage from the festival grounds. "Not sure these can be salvaged."

She frowned at the dust and grass stains. "I'll buy you some new shoes."

He gave her a look. She quickly backtracked.

"Nope, no. Not buying you any new shoes. Not paying for anything. You've got your own money. You're not gonna be my cabana boy."

"Do you even have a cabana?" he asked. "Is this the only house in Hollywood Hills without a pool?"

"I can have a pool put in if you wa—" Again, she bit her lip and backtracked. "Nope. No pool for you. You're not here for my luxury lifestyle. You're here because you love me, and because I love you."

Ransom threw the shoes down and kissed her. No more sex for money or money for sex. No more porn star shame, although...

He drew away from her. "They're going to find out about my past, you know. Do we have a plan?"

Lola turned and went to sit on the couch. At first he thought he'd pissed her off, but then he realized she was thinking it over, twirling a blonde strand of hair and brushing it against her lips.

"Do we really need a plan?" she asked after a moment. "It happened. Why not just own it? Be open about it?"

"How open? Are you comfortable with your fans knowing what my cock looks like?"

She grinned at him. "It's an impressive cock. I mean, the lightning bolt and everything." She beckoned him to sit beside her.

He slouched back on the cushions and rubbed his eyes. "The thing is, I don't want you to have to make excuses for me, or field questions about my dick tattoo during interviews that ought to be about you and your music."

"I'll never get tired of talking about your cock. Believe me."

She thought this was funny. He didn't. He frowned at the floor, wondering why his twenty-year-old self ever thought it was a smart idea to fuck on film. Lola crawled into his lap and lifted his chin, and looked into his eyes. Understanding dawned in her expression.

"You'll feel exposed, won't you?"

"Yeah, a little."

"And it'll be my fault, because I'm the famous one. Shit."

"It doesn't matter," he said. "I have to be with you. If exposure is the price, it's worth it. As long as you don't mind..."

"I do mind. I mind if you're unhappy, or embarrassed." She sat up straighter, her brow wrinkled in thought. "What if we... What if we changed the conversation? Flipped it on its head?"

"What do you mean?"

"I'd have to talk to my PR people, because they know how to do this kind of shit, but we'd flip the topic, you know? If and when your past is uncovered, you could deflect the conversation from Rico Rockhard to the problems you saw in the porn industry. Instead of your lightning bolt, you could talk about your friend who struggled with depression and drug addiction, and your decision to leave the business. You could steer the discussion from your porn past to your search for a healthier, better life. Maybe it will help someone else change their life. You changed my life, right?"

She got out her phone without waiting for him to answer, and started composing an email to her public relations agent. He sat beside her and thought about her words. *You changed my life.* With Lola's scope of influence, he could change other lives too. He could educate at-risk teens and young adults about the predatory aspects of the porn industry. He could enlighten young women who might fall prey to sketchy producers.

You'd approve of that, Rayna, he thought. *If I can help even one person like you...* He looked at Lola, intently composing her email. If she accepted him as an ex porn star, the rest of the world could too.

As she typed, his phone rang. He looked down at the caller. "It's my boss from Ironclad."

She stopped typing and looked at him. "The festival yesterday... We were kissing onstage."

"Yeah, I'm sure he's seen it by now." Ransom managed a courageous smile. "What's he going to do, fire me?" He took the call, greeted his former employer, and spoke before Liam could chew him out.

"I'm sorry about my conduct on the Reynolds job. I'm sorry if my relationship with Lola reflects badly on the company going forward. I enjoyed working with Ironclad—"

"Ransom."

"It was never my intention to do anything that might hurt Lola or jeopardize her safety under my protection—"

"Dude, shut up for a minute. I got your letter of resignation. I'm not happy about it."

Ransom closed his mouth and rubbed his chin. Lola watched him, her fingers around her throat in fake death throes.

"Are you with Lola now?" Liam asked.

"Yes. And I plan to be, for the foreseeable future."

"Yeah, no one could 'foresee' that." The sarcasm was gentle, if blunt. "Listen, I suspected something was going on. I chose to let it ride because I sensed caring, not exploitation. I would have questioned you about your relationship with her eventually, but I wouldn't have fired you. Not if you were in love."

Ransom was quiet for a moment. "I tried not to fall in love." Lola made a face and he gave her a pinch. "But it happened anyway. I meant what I said about Ironclad. You gave me a chance when a lot of other people wouldn't, and I'd never want to do anything to harm the agency's reputation."

"You haven't harmed anything. People love you. The Gilberto blogs are proliferating, and have you seen the music charts since last night?"

"The music charts?"

"Take a look after you hang up. And if you want to stay on at Ironclad, please do. We can find you part time assignments in L.A, subject to your schedule and discretion. God knows there are plenty of protectees in that area who could use your special touch."

So Liam wasn't calling to light into him. He was calling to try to rehire him. "I might take you up on that offer," Ransom said. "But first I'm going to take a few weeks off to..." *Spend time with Lola. Get my shit together. Have far too much sex.* He didn't say any of that, but his boss doubtless got the gist.

"Take all the time you need," he said. "And let us know when you're ready to work. We'll reinstate your credentials."

"Yes, sir. Thanks for your understanding."

"Thanks for being an Ironclad agent. And Ransom..." He chuckled. "Be sure to take your vitamins. You're going to need them to keep up with her."

Ransom grinned at Lola, who leaned closer and mouthed "What did he say?"

"Now go search 'Worth the World,'" said Liam, "and make sure she's sitting next to you when you do."

"Got it. Thanks."

Ransom hung up and turned to Lola, who was bouncing on the couch beside him. "What did he say? Are you in trouble?"

"I'm not in trouble. In fact, I can keep working on jobs around L.A., if you can spare me now and again."

"I can't." She collapsed dramatically on his lap. "I can't spare you."

"Ever?"

"Maybe one or two hours a week you can guard some other celebrity fuck up, but the rest of the time, you need to be guarding me."

He leaned to kiss her, then tickled her until she almost kicked him in the head. "I'm not paying you either," she shrieked. "Except with sex. And guitar songs. No, stop. Stop. Stop tickling me!"

He granted her wish and opened a window on his phone. While she caught her breath, he put her song into a search engine and pulled up the results.

"Holy shit, Lola. Holy fucking shit."

"What?"

She stuck her head in his line of sight as he opened a news story about her impromptu acoustic performance in Sacramento. There was a photo of them embracing, and the headline "*Rave Artist's Torch Song Goes Viral.*"

"That's why I have so many messages," she said. "I thought a spam bot got me."

She went back to her phone and scrolled through her inbox until she got to an email from Kym Mecklin at Vanguard. She laughed out loud. "Oh God, look at this. Kym wants to reconsider her position on the 'bluegrass experiment' I pitched to her." She snorted and flipped the bird at her phone's screen. "Fuck you."

"Fuck you indeed." Ransom pulled up the indie music site where she'd uploaded the song. "You've already sold almost half a million copies. Holy fucking Christ." He started to laugh. Everything Lola touched was magic. She was magic, sitting right beside him on the couch. He swept her into a hug and squeezed her until she squeaked. "Your father would have been proud," he said, and her lips trembled a little.

"Yeah, he would have been happy for me. And he would have liked you a lot. I wish you could have met him."

Ransom looked down at the smiling woman in his arms. "I think I can guess the kind of man he was." Anyone who could raise an emotional ball of creativity like Lola was okay in his book. He looked back at the song's listing, and wondered how much money she'd made in downloads since last night.

Well, it didn't matter. It wasn't about the money. It was about the love.

"How did this happen?" She still stared at the screen, half aghast and half delighted. "God, Ransom. They really love our song."

Our song. He liked the sound of that.

"I guess we all need a good love story to inspire us sometimes." He took away her phone and placed it on the side table beside his, then swung her off the couch and into his arms. "How about you and I head to the bedroom and make a different kind of music? Something that's not going to be heard by half a million people around the world?"

"Something soft and sweet?" She squeezed his shoulders and wrapped her legs around his waist.

"Nothing soft. Nothing sweet," he said in his bodyguard voice.

She smirked at him from under her lashes, a loving gaze and teasing grin, and he knew their song would be enough to sustain them for the rest of their lives.

And if they went through some bad times, well...they knew how to handle that.

They'd just put a beat under it until it worked.

THE END

A Final Note

Thanks for supporting my Ironclad Bodyguards series. It was fun to get back into this world. With *PAWN*, my first bodyguard book, I did a lot of research into competitive chess. With *DIVA*, I waded into the universe of raves and dance music, a six billion dollar industry. A big shout out to J. Phlip, Cassy, Nina Kraviz, and Tokimonsta, four female DJs who are rocking it in a male dominated business. You can see some of their performances on YouTube. Thanks also to Eats Everything and Calvin Harris, who provided the rest of my writing soundtrack for this novel.

I'd like to extend my appreciation to my readers and editors on this book: Lanie S. Flin, Riane Holt, J. Luna Scuro, and my faithful Audrey K. Thanks for making me a better writer.

If you enjoyed this book, I hope you'll spread the word to some naughty friends, or leave a review. Your word of mouth means the world to me, as does your readership. May your silver sequined booty shorts always catch the light.

Coming Soon:
BEARD (Ironclad Bodyguards #3)

Jenna entered a fake marriage ten years ago when she was young and reckless, in hopes it might advance her failing Hollywood career. Ten years later, she can't undo her mistake. Her A-list husband is too famous—and too cowardly—to admit he's in a long-time gay relationship with a fellow actor, and at thirty-four, Jenna's dreams have faded to dust.

Then Caleb Winchell enters her life. The taciturn, Texas-bred bodyguard is as handsome as he is capable, and Jenna's lonely world is rocked. He's a true and honest force in her dishonest existence, standing by her side as she fake smiles her way through the smothering farce of her life. Caleb helps her breathe again, but she can't act on her deepening feelings toward her bodyguard. He's a professional, and he never breaks the rules.

And she's a married woman…even if it's all a sham.

Also Available:
Pawn (Ironclad Bodyguards #1)

High stakes chess competition has always been a man's game—until Grace Ann Frasier topples some of the game's greatest champions and turns the chess world on its ear. Her prowess at the game is matched only by her rivals' desire to defeat her, or, worse, avenge their losses. When an international championship threatens Grace's safety, a bevy of security experts are hired to look after her, but only one is her personal, close-duty bodyguard, courtesy of Ironclad Solutions, Inc.

Sam Knight knows nothing about chess, but he knows Grace is working to achieve something important, and he vows to shelter her from those who mean her harm. When she leans on him for emotional support, attraction battles with professionalism and Sam finds his self-discipline wavering. Soon the complexity of their relationship resembles a chess board, where one questionable move can ruin everything—or win a game that could resonate around the world.

Explore More Worlds with Annabel Joseph (Molly Joseph's kinky alter ego)

The Cirque Masters series

Enter a world where performers' jaw-dropping strength, talent, and creativity is matched only by the decadence of their kinky desires. Cirque du Monde is famous for mounting glittering circus productions, but after the Big Top goes dark, you can find its denizens at *Le Citadel*, a fetish club owned by Cirque CEO Michel Lemaitre—where anything goes. This secret world is ruled by dominance and submission, risk and emotion, and a fearless dedication to carnal pleasure in all its forms. Love in the circus can be as perilous as aerial silks or trapeze, and secrets run deep in this intimate society. Run away to the circus, and soar with the Cirque Masters—a delight for the senses, and for the heart.

The Cirque Masters series is:
#1 *Cirque de Minuit* (Theo's story)
#2 *Bound in Blue* (Jason's story)
#3 *Master's Flame* (Lemaitre's story)

THE ROUGH LOVE SERIES

Have *There's rough sex, and then there's rough love. The challenge is learning the difference...*

Chere's a high-class call girl trapped in a self-destructive spiral, and "W" is the mysterious and sexually voracious client who refuses to tell her his name. Over the span of four years, their tortured relationship unwinds by fits and starts, encompassing fear and loneliness, mistrust, aggression, literal and figurative bondage, and moments of excruciating pain.

But there's also caring and longing, and heartfelt poetry. There are two deeply damaged people straining to connect despite the daunting emotional risks. When he slaps her face or grasps her neck, it's not to hurt, but to hold. His rough passions are a plea, and Chere's the only one so far who's been able to understand...

The Rough Love series is:
#1 *Torment Me*
#2 *Taunt Me*
#3 *Trust Me*

ABOUT THE AUTHOR

Molly Joseph is the "vanilla" counterpart of New York Times and USA Today bestselling BDSM romance author Annabel Joseph. Annabel and Molly both love to explore deep and complicated relationships on the pages of their books, except that Annabel's couples have BDSM dynamics, and Molly's couples don't.

You can learn more about Annabel (and Molly) by visiting annabeljoseph.com, where you can sign up for her newsletter to stay current on upcoming releases. You can also find Annabel/Molly on Facebook (Facebook.com/annabeljosephnovels), and Twitter (@annabeljoseph).

You can write to either Molly or Annabel at Annabeljosephnovels@gmail.com.

Made in the USA
Middletown, DE
18 August 2016